A Killing Fair

Also by Glenn Ickler

A Carnival of Killing

Murder on the St. Croix

To Ray and Rena —
Stick with me on this one.

A Killing Fair

Glenn Ickler

Glenn Ickler

NORTH STAR PRESS OF ST. CLOUD, INC.
St. Cloud, Minnesota

Dedication:
For Kathy, who loves the Minnesota State Fair
more than anybody else I know;
for Dick, who introduced me to Pronto Pups
at the Minnesota State Fair;
and for Paul, whose theater sets the stage
for some of the actors.

Acknowledgements:
My thanks to the *MetroWest Daily News* in Framingham,
Massachusetts, for the bizarre real-life crime stories borrowed on
the days that Mitch Mitchell reports from the police station. As
Mitch keeps saying, "You can't make this stuff up." Thanks also
to forensics expert D.P. Lyle, MD, for advice on toxic substances.

ISBN: 978-0-87839-713-6

First edition: June 2014

Printed in the United States of America

Published by
North Star Press of St. Cloud, Inc.
P.O. Box 451
St. Cloud, MN 56302
northstarpress.com

Chapter One

A Square Meal

NAME SOMETHING EDIBLE, anything remotely edible, and you're likely to find it impaled on a stick at the Minnesota State Fair.

There's the usual ho-hum stuff you can get anywhere on a stick, such as hot dogs and ice cream and caramel apples. But beyond that, the State Fair choices include such delicacies as butterscotch cake on a stick (gooey and crumbly), dill pickles on a stick (both fresh and deep-fried) and Reuben sandwiches on a stick (messy—how do they keep the sauerkraut juice from running down your arm?).

The list goes on and on *ad infinitum* (and *ad nauseam* for some of the more adventurous diners who get on rides that whirl them in circles immediately after sticking it to themselves).

This is why I was surprised—yea, amazed—when Don O'Rourke sent Al and me to the Minnesota State Fair on a hot and humid Wednesday morning in late August to cover the introduction of a new food product on a stick. I simply could not imagine what pliable comestible was left to stab a stick into.

Don O'Rourke is city editor of the *St. Paul Daily Dispatch*. Al is Alan Jeffrey, the paper's best photographer and my best friend. I'm Warren Mitchell, better known as Mitch, and I think of myself as the paper's best reporter, whether anybody else does or not. In order for Don to send us on this assignment, he was either expecting the impaled goody to be very unusual, or he was anticipating an extremely slow news day. It being late August, I suspected the latter.

Both the temperature and the relative humidity had already reached 80 at 9:45 a.m. when we stepped out of the *Daily Dispatch's* air-conditioned Ford Focus onto the sun-baked asphalt in the Giraffe Parking Lot at the Minnesota State Fairgrounds. The unveiling of the new gustatory delight was scheduled for 10:00 a.m. on the Heritage Square stage. We had arranged for a quick preview by Lorrie Gardner, the fair's public relations director.

"What do you suppose this new wonder on a stick is?" Al asked.

"Must be pretty special to rate an introductory dog-and-pony show," I said.

"Maybe they've figured out a way to serve soup on a stick."

"You can stick that idea where the sun don't shine," I said.

It was only a four-minute walk to Heritage Square, but perspiration was dripping from my nose onto my light-brown moustache, and the armpits of my short-sleeved white shirt were soaked by the time we got there. I was glad I'd left my coat and tie draped over my desk chair in the newsroom.

Al had also stripped down for the weather, but a shoulder-slung camera bag left dark wet impressions everywhere it pressed against his light blue shirt. I saw him wiping moisture from his forehead and his dark-brown beard as we walked.

The fair wouldn't open officially until the following day, but the grounds were bustling with vendors, exhibitors, and thrill-ride providers setting up for action.

At Heritage Square, which is an aging music stage located north of the Midway at the western end of the fairgrounds, about fifty people were standing around waiting to watch the introduction of the new stick-impaled wonder. Apparently they'd been drawn to the scene by the sight of people moving on the stage.

Beside the steps leading up to the stage, Lorrie Gardner was facing away from us, talking to a blonde television reporter named Trish Valentine, who always seemed to be reporting live from wherever Al and I were sent. We never complained about the competition because seeing Trish was always a pleasure. She had a heart-shaped face that looked darling on TV and a well-rounded figure that she displayed generously, especially on hot summer days. On this muggy morning, her sleeveless electric-pink blouse was open deep into her cleavage and her snug white skirt with its visible bikini panty line ended above mid-thigh.

Lorrie, a tall, slender brunette, looked patriotic in a red tank top that stopped half way down her back, a pair of blue shorts that barely covered the cheeky territory south of the border and white boots that came to mid-calf. Part of a tramp stamp that looked like the crown of a devil's head peeked out over the top of her shorts. I wondered what her boss, who was a suit-and-tie guy all the way to 100 degrees Fahrenheit, would say about the appropriateness of this ensemble.

Oh, well, not my problem. I was busy enjoying the view.

"Hi, Lorrie. Hi, Trish," I said. Lorrie turned toward us, gave us a come-hither wave with her right hand, and we fell in beside Trish. I scanned the small crowd and saw no other reporters. I wasn't surprised. What could be newsworthy here?

"Hope you guys are ready for an exciting presentation," Lorrie said. "You won't believe your eyes when you see it."

"What is it?" I asked. "A whole roast pig on a stick?"

"Oh, good idea. I'll have to write that one down for next year. With an apple in its mouth. Probably take both hands to hold it. But, no, it's nothing that exotic. Well, it's exotic in its own way. You'll have a great time taking pictures, Al."

Knowing from past interviews that Lorrie could bubble on all morning without answering my question, I asked again, "What is it?"

"Will I need a wide-angle lens," Al asked. This brought a snicker from Trish.

"No, no, nothing like that," Lorrie said. "Although it is a good size chunk of food for presentation on a stick. Probably bigger than any edible item on a stick we're presently offering. Bigger than anything we've ever offered I'll bet."

"I'll put you on a stick if you don't stop babbling and tell us what it is," I said.

"Ooh, you big old nasty man," Lorrie said with a twitch of her hips that indicated where she anticipated the stick might go. "Okay, ready? Here it comes. Ta-dah!"

She whipped three copies of a press release out of a folder she was holding in her left hand and passed them to us. "It's called Square Meal on a Stick."

Sure enough, it was. The illustration on the press release showed a substantial stick with a large cube-shaped block of something brown on the end.

"It's brown," Al said. "What the hell is in it?"

"A square meal," Ellie said. "In the center is a cube of filet mignon so tender it'll melt in your mouth. Around that is a thick layer of mashed potato embedded with small bits of veggie, probably broccoli. The beautiful golden brown you're seeing is from deep-frying the entire cube."

"So you're eating almost raw steak and deep-fried mashed potato skooshed with broccoli," I said. "And you really think people will buy this?"

"People eat rare beef sandwiches and mashed potatoes all the time," she said. "The only difference here is that the mashed potatoes are french-fried, which is another American favorite. Besides, it's the State Fair. People here will buy any crazy thing you put on a stick—but please don't put that in the paper."

"You're right about that," I said. "Who dreamed up this particular crazy thing?"

"A very highly respected St. Paul restaurant owner," Lorrie said. "None other than Vinnie Luciano, owner of King Vinnie's Steakhouse." King Vinnie's had been an institution on St. Paul's lower West Side for thirty-some years. Vinnie Luciano's shtick was to greet his customers wearing a gold crown, which sat above the gray fringe of hair on his balding head, and welcome them as his royal guests. Pictures of Vinnie wearing his crown with all of Minnesota's big-name athletes and big shot politicians decorated the dining room walls. The Lions, the Jaycees and the Rotary Club all met at King Vinnie's, and the annual Minnesota Twins fan appreciation dinner was held there.

"Makes you wonder whether Vinnie's starting to lose it," Al said. "This thing looks as big as my daughter's softball." His daughter was an ace pitcher for her high-school team.

"That's about right," Lorrie said. "Only remember that it's square. It's a square meal being introduced at Heritage Square by Minnesota's best known square dance caller, the one-and-only Scott Hall."

"I can see the headline," I said. "Everything's on the square at the Minnesota State Fair."

"Ooh, I like it," Lorrie said. "Will it make page one?"

"Not for me to say," I said. "You have to bribe somebody else for that."

"Who needs bribin'?" said a loud male voice behind me. I turned and found myself chin to heavy black eyebrows with King Vinnie Luciano, complete with glistening gold crown. At six-foot-one and 190 pounds, I was six inches taller but thirty pounds lighter than Vinnie, who had me on girth by a broad margin. "Who needs bribin'?" he asked again.

"My city editor," I said. "Lorrie wants to see a picture of your ungodly concoction on page one."

"What do you mean ungodly?" Vinnie said. "This is a meal made in heaven."

"I'll leave that to the clergy," I said. "As far as eating that thing, I'd have a hard time getting past saying grace."

"Grace would love it," Vinnie said. "It's delicious. I must have ate thirty of 'em while we were goin' through the test stage."

This triggered my grammarian reflex, and I was starting to say "have *eaten,* not have *ate,*" when Lorrie grabbed Vinnie's arm and aimed him toward the stage.

The square dance caller, Scott Hall, was a tall, slender man in his early forties. His hair was dark brown and so was the neatly trimmed moustache that graced his upper lip. He was already on the stage, a statuesque figure dressed in full red-and-white western square dance regalia, complete with a red bolo tie and a white ten-gallon hat. I don't know how he stayed cool but I didn't see a drop of sweat on his grinning face.

Al hauled out his camera, I pulled a small notebook out of my shirt pocket, Trish Valentine's cameraman appeared from somewhere behind us, and we all stood poised for the great media moment.

Lorrie took the microphone, waved to the minuscule media-moment audience and introduced Scott and Vinnie. Behind the trio at the mike, about a dozen men and women wearing everything from square dance outfits to sun tops and shorts were scattered about the stage like window dressing.

Lorrie explained the importance of the occasion and handed the microphone to Scott Hall, repeating what she'd said to me about a square meal being introduced by a square dance caller on the Heritage Square stage. This drew a polite ripple of laughter.

The caller took the mike, popped off a couple of one-liners with the word square in the punch line, which also drew a polite ripple of laughter, and announced that it was time to introduce the main character—King Vinnie Luciano's fabulous new square meal.

Right on cue, Fairchild, the Minnesota State Fair's official mascot, appeared at the foot of the stairs. Fairchild, a six-foot-tall happy-go-lucky gopher with an oversized plastic head had a perpetual buck-toothed grin painted on its face. He wore a green-and-white striped sport coat, a black bow tie and a green-and-white straw boater. Carrying the Square Meal on a Stick high in the air for all to see, Fairchild bounced up the stairs onto the stage and handed the stick to Scott Hall.

Scott's smile faded to a look of surprise, probably at the size of the package, but he quickly regained his grinning composure. He thanked Fairchild, and Fairchild bowed, bouncing back down the stairs and disappearing through the crowd, which had now grown to maybe a hundred curious souls.

"And now we come to the moment of truth, which is in the eating," Scott Hall said. "It's appropriate for me as a square dance caller to introduce this wonderful square morsel, but it's the creator of this magnificent-looking concoction who should have the honor of taking the first bite." He passed the stick to Vinnie and stepped back to let Vinnie have the microphone.

Vinnie smiled his acceptance and thanked Scott in a thunderous voice. Vinnie raised the stick at arm's length above his head and posed like an obese Statue of Liberty as he shouted, "Here's to square meals and square dancing." He waved the fried cube in circles before taking a substantial bite off the top and bowing, with arms spread, to the crowd.

As Vinnie chewed, the smile left his face. "Tastes kind of bitter," he said in a low voice. A tiny crumb of potato poked out at the corner of his mouth.

Forcing the smile to return, Vinnie took another bite, chewed and swallowed. He frowned. "Might be stale cooking oil," he said. "This ain't right." He shook his head and his eyes opened so wide that the whites were visible all the way around.

Vinnie opened his mouth to suck in some air and grasped his throat with his left hand. His legs wobbled and his knees buckled. He sat down hard on the stage, gasping. "Can't breathe," he said in a whisper. The Square Meal on a Stick fell from his right hand and landed in his lap.

"Oh, god, a heart attack," Al whispered beside me.

Vinnie's body began to jerk and twist. He flopped onto his back and the crown popped off his head and rolled to the edge of the stage. The convulsions grew more violent and went on for a moment before he arched his back, leaving only his heels and head touching the floor of the stage. This launched the Square Meal on a Stick into the air, where it performed a somersault before plopping onto the quivering belly of its stricken inventor.

As we all stared in silence, Vinnie's convulsions continued for maybe another minute before his body went limp and he dropped flat on his back on the floor. Another twitch, then another, then nothing. Vinnie lay motionless with his partially-eaten concoction standing at a forty-five-degree angle on the down slope of the mound above his belt. There wasn't a whisper of sound from the mouths of the onlookers watching this bizarre performance.

Scott Hall was the first to find his tongue. "Is there a doctor in the crowd?" he shouted into the mike. "Please, is there a doctor anywhere around?"

"Here," said a female voice in the back of the crowd. A middle-aged woman with flaming red hair began pushing her way toward the stage as dozens of stunned people started to babble about what they'd just seen.

The doctor climbed the stairs and knelt beside the fallen restaurateur. She stared into Vinnie's open eyes as her hand went to his throat to feel for a pulse.

On the ground around the stage, dozens of cell phones appeared. Some of their owners were taking pictures, others were texting, tweeting and punching in numbers.

I hollered at Lorrie to call 911, and she said she'd already done so. Al was clicking off pictures and the Channel 4 cameraman had moved to the edge of the stage to film the action close up.

The doctor rose to her feet and turned to Scott Hall, who still held the microphone. When she spoke softly to Hall, her voice was carried by the sound system. "This man is dead," she said. "There's nothing I can do."

With that, all hell broke loose in the crowd as some people pushed their way closer to see the body and others pushed away in fear and revulsion. The onlookers onstage began leaping off the edge and the musicians grabbed their instruments and bailed out over the side. I heard a siren in the distance heralding the approach of an ambulance. It would be King Vinnie Luciano's transportation to the morgue.

Chapter Two

Quizzed by the KGB

I GOT PIX OF EVERYTHING," Al said. "From Scott Hall's introduction all the way to the priest from the audience giving Vinnie his last rites."

"Just what I've always wanted to see in the paper," Lorrie Gardner said. "It's a PR person's dream to have a celebrity die in a spectacular manner on camera in the middle of your event."

"It won't hurt the fair attendance," I said. "It might even bring in a few more people. You know—the ghouls who want to see the spot where the body fell."

"Yuk," said Lorrie. "Don't need them."

The three of us were sitting on a park bench not far from the Heritage Square stage. We'd been instructed to wait there until one of the officers investigating Vinnie's sensational demise could question us. Trish Valentine and her cameraman had managed to fade away after shooting the arrival of the police.

Although most Minnesotans think of the State Fairgrounds as being located in St. Paul, it actually lies in the adjoining suburb of Falcon Heights. This meant that the investigation was being led by a Falcon Heights detective, not any of the people I had worked with for years in the St. Paul Police Department. I was wondering if information about this investigation would be more difficult to extricate from a stranger.

Al had e-mailed his pix to the photo editor, but I needed to get to the office and get started writing the story. I was considering making an end run to the car when a tall, straight-backed young woman wearing a dark blue pantsuit jumped off the stage and strode toward us. We all rose and went to meet her.

"Good morning," the woman said. "I'm Detective Barnes of the Falcon Heights PD. I'm leading the investigation of what took place here." I guessed her age at thirty-five and her height at close to six feet. Her steely cold eyes were matched by her military stance as we took turns shaking her hand. We each gave our quick version of Vinnie's final moments and Al showed the detective some photos of the dying man.

"Jesus," Detective Barnes said when she saw the picture of Vinnie's body arched on the floor with only the head and heels touching. "Looks like classic strychnine poisoning to me."

"Those are the classic symptoms of strychnine?" I asked.

"Oh, shit, you're a reporter aren't you?" she said. "Forget it. Nothing I've said here is official."

"I can look up the classic symptoms," I said.

"You're free to do that. I'm not saying another word except that I need to talk to all of you one at a time at the station."

"Can it wait until after I've written my story?" I asked.

"Assuming you can write it in less than four hours," Barnes said. "I want to see you by three o'clock."

"Can do," I said. "Oh, by the way, do you have a first name?"

"I go by my initials," she said. "K.G. Barnes."

I wrote that down. "Nice initials for an investigator," I said. "KGB."

"And don't you forget it," said Detective K.G. Barnes. "Three o'clock. My office. Is there anybody else from the media that I should talk to?"

I tattled on Trish Valentine. KGB wrote down the name, thanked me and went back to the stage where EMTs were, with some difficulty, stuffing Vinnie Luciano's bulky body into a black plastic bag. Al took some shots of the bundle being loaded into the ambulance and we were about to leave when I thought of something important.

"Wait here a minute," I said. "I'll be right back." As I started walking toward my target, a yellow-and-brown booth with a sign that said *Pronto Pups,* I heard Al shout, "Get me one, too."

I had been going to the Minnesota State Fair since I was ten years old and I had never left the fairgrounds without at least one Pronto Pup in my belly. This was the one food on a stick that was special to me. It's a hotdog dipped in a tasty cornmeal batter, deep fried to the precise second of golden perfection in hot fat seasoned by time, and brushed with a golden splash of mustard. It was, for want of a better cliché under the current circumstances, a treat to die for.

My fiancée, Martha Todd, said it's "just a damn corn dog," but she was wrong. A Pronto Pup had a special panache, a flavor and texture all its own, thanks to the consistency of the coating and the experience of the cooking oil. Your bland, every day corn dog was like a sleeping dachshund compared with the wide awake pit-bull taste of a Pronto Pup.

"I couldn't leave the fairgrounds without my Pronto Pup," I said to Lorrie as I returned with a mustard-coated treat in each hand. "I'm just glad they're open for business already."

"How can you eat those after watching a man die right there in front of you?" Lorrie asked.

"It's a religion with him," Al said as he took the Pronto Pup from my left hand. "I just go along with him because I belong to the same church."

"As the fair's PR flack, I'm sure you're aware that Pronto Pups were the first food on a stick ever sold at the Minnesota State Fair," I said to Lorrie. "They opened in 1947, and their signs said 'A Banquet on a Stick.'"

"You've been looking at what I put on our website," she said.

"You're right. I wanted to have some background to use as filler in case today's story was a snoozer."

"I don't think you'll need any padding for this one," Lorrie said. She rose and walked slowly away, head down and shoulders slumping.

"Your turn to buy next time," I said to Al as we started toward the car.

"Have I ever failed to return your generosity?"

"Yes, you've dogged it several times."

"Doggone. I was hoping you weren't such a good watchdog."

*   *   *

I FINISHED MY STORY with time to spare, and was daydreaming about a side trip to the fairgrounds for another Pronto Pup on the way to meeting Detective KGB, when Don O'Rourke appeared beside my desk.

"Great story," he said. "Spectacular pix. And the only people who have them are us and Channel Four."

"Nobody else showed up for the great unveiling of the new delight on a stick," I said.

"Now you know why we cover everything, no matter how meaningless it sounds." He turned and walked back to his desk.

I resumed my Pronto Pup daydreaming. I had just decided to go back to the fairgrounds and make the dream real when my phone rang. "*Daily Dispatch*, Mitchell," I said.

"Homicidebrown," said the familiar voice of Detective Lieutenant Curtis Brown, the St. Paul Police Department's chief homicide investigator. He always blurred his name and identification into a single word.

What the hell? I thought. I've called Brownie a million times but he never calls me. "What can I do for you?" I asked.

"You can tell me what the hell went on at the fairgrounds this morning," he said. "Channel Four has breaking news about Vinnie Luciano choking on one of those goddamn meals on a stick that he supposedly invented, but I can't get any details out of the Falcon Heights PD."

I resisted the temptation to say, "Now you know how I feel when you won't talk." Instead I gave Brownie a quick rundown of the morning's calamity. "And Vinnie didn't choke," I said. "The Falcon Heights investigator blurted out that it was a classic case of strychnine poisoning before she thought about me being a reporter. I looked it up online and she was right. Vinnie's actions—the arched back and all—do fit the classic description of a death by strychnine."

"No wonder they won't talk," Brownie said. "It's a homicide, not an accident. But who the hell would want to poison poor Vinnie?"

"That's what I'm going to be asking," I said. "Do you have any suspects?"

"I've never in my life heard a bad word said about Vinnie. I can't imagine who'd want to kill him."

"Me neither. Any recommendations on who to talk to at the Falcon Heights PD?"

"I don't know," Brownie said. "I talked to a hard-ass detective named Barnes and got a shitload of 'no comment.' I wanted to talk to the chief, a woman named Victoria Tubb, but she wasn't available. I've dealt with her a couple of times, and she's pretty hard-ass, too."

"Great," I said. "So do you have any advice for me?"

"Don't call the chief Vicky. She doesn't like informality."

"In that case it's probably better not to call her Tubby, either."

"I'd stick to 'Chief' if I were you."

"Good advice. Let me know if you hear anything about a suspect."

"You do the same. Have a good day, Mitch." And the line went dead.

*   *   *

AL AND I MET TRISH VALENTINE at the Falcon Heights police station as we were going in and she was coming out. "Have a good time with the KGB woman," Trish said. "She is one tight-assed broad."

"All work and no play is she?" Al asked.

"No sense of humor," Trish said. "What she needs is a night in the sack with some hottie like that square dance caller at Heritage Square."

"Scott Hall?" I said. "You think a roll in the hay with that grinning goombah would loosen up Ms. KGB?"

"Like I said, that grinning goombah is hot," Trish said. "I'll bet he gets plenty of action from the women in his club."

"No way," Al said. "Square dancers don't do the bedroom do-si-do with anybody but their own partners. That's part of being square."

"Boy, have you got a lot to learn," Trish said. "Like I said, have fun with the KGB. And thanks a whole hell of a lot for giving her my name."

"All in the name of good government," I said. "You were reporting live even closer than I was when Vinnie bit the dust. I thought maybe you saw something I didn't."

"Not likely. I closed my eyes when he hit the floor and started to twitch."

Al and I went in and were told to wait in the small lobby while the desk sergeant contacted Detective Barnes. Soon she appeared, pointed at Al and said, "You're first." I was relegated to a hard wooden chair near the door.

A half hour later we swapped seats. My new one was at a battle-scarred wooden table in a very small interrogation room. This chair was also hard and KGB was harder. She sat across from me and snapped off questions like a sniper firing at a moving target. Her gray eyes never left mine and her spine and shoulders never relaxed as a tape recorder on the table preserved our words.

I tried to lighten the mood a couple of times but I couldn't coax a smile or a soft word from her lips. When she indicated that the session was over, I rose and was starting toward the door when KGB's phone rang. I stopped and went back, pretending to be looking for something on the floor, while she took the call.

"What?" she said. "Are you shittin' me? Where? I'll be right there." She snapped off the phone and looked at me with the same grim expression she'd used all during the interrogation. "Drop something did you?"

"Not really," I said. "Just snoopy. Was that something about Vinnie?"

"You might say that," she said. "They just found the kid who plays Fairchild, wearing nothing but undershorts, bound and gagged in a tool shed. He said somebody hit him from behind and tied him up and stole his costume while he was out."

"So the Fairchild who delivered the poisoned square meal was a phony?" I said.

"A phony with a mission," Barnes said. "Whoever was wearing Fairchild's costume is our killer."

"Okay if we follow you to the fairgrounds?"

"It's a free country." She actually smiled when she added, "Just stay one car length back for every ten miles per hour or I'll tag you for following too close."

Chapter Three

Not So Fair

THE TEENAGER WHO PLAYED Fairchild looked too frail for the job. He also looked too tired and too scared to talk about being sapped, stripped and strapped. I could picture Lorrie Gardner smothering him with hugs and worse. Apparently he could, too, because he sat with the back of his chair against a wooden wall with only his face, from the nose up, showing above a gray army blanket held at port arms. Al got a great photo, which we used big on page one.

Detective Barnes asked his name and he said, "Tommy." She inquired as to a last name and he said, "Grayson." She asked his age and he said "eighteen." He didn't look that old to me but she didn't press the issue.

Slowly and painfully Barnes dragged out the details. Tommy was whacked on the head from behind by an unseen and unheard assailant. He awoke in the tool shed with a headache and a lump. His hands and feet were bound and his mouth was stuffed with a bandanna wrapped around a stick. A killer with a dark sense of humor no less.

"What time would you say you were attacked?" Barnes asked.

"I'd just got into my costume, except for putting on my head piece, when I stepped out the door," he said. "Must have been a few minutes after eight."

"Is eight o'clock your starting time?"

"Yes, ma'am. I work from eight to four. Derek Sloane takes over then and works till closing time. He's older and can deal with the drunks . . ."

"Thank you, Tommy," Barnes said. "Did you see your attacker at all?"

"No. He snuck up behind me and hit me before I could move."

"You're sure it was a he?"

"Well, I . . . I guess so. He had to be pretty strong to hit me that hard."

"But you didn't see the person or hear the person speak?"

"No. I suppose it could have been a girl . . . a woman. Like I said, she'd have to be pretty strong."

"Do you think I look strong enough to knock you out and drag you away?"

"You look pretty strong, ma'am," Tommy said.

"Is that a yes?" Barnes asked.

"Uh, I guess so." She glared at him and got an instantaneous, rapid-fire response. "Yes, ma'am. That's definitely a yes."

"Thank you, Tommy. And I take it you saw no one until someone came to the shed looking for equipment this afternoon."

"That's right. I was really glad to see Tiger."

"Who?"

"Tiger. Tiger Wyberelli. From the maintenance crew. We call him Tiger because—"

"Thank you, Tommy. I take it Tiger was the person who opened the door at . . . what time?" she asked.

"Must have been almost four. That's when Tiger starts, four."

"And he always starts by opening the tool shed?"

"Oh, no, ma'am," said Tommy. "He just happened to need some cutters. Normally he might not open the door for a week." He paused for a second and said, "Oh, shit." His complexion, already pale, turned piecrust pasty white. "I could have been here for days before . . ." His voice trailed off as he thought about the possibility.

"Before anybody looked in?" I asked.

"Yeah. Holy shit, I could have—"

Barnes cut him off. "No, you couldn't have. Somebody would have come looking for you when you didn't get home overnight."

"Oh, yeah," he said. "I'm sure somebody would have. Still—"

"Forget it," Barnes said. "Go home and get some rest. I'll talk to you some more tomorrow."

Tommy didn't need a second invitation. He tossed off the blanket, revealing a Hardrock Café T-shirt and baggy khaki shorts, and ran out the door. When he was gone, Barnes turned to me. "Get enough for a story?"

"I've got everything but a comment from the lead investigator," I said.

Barnes frowned. "The lead investigator has no comment beyond the obvious 'we're investigating this vicious attack.'" She whirled and followed Tommy out the door.

"That is one up-tight broad," Al said as he put his camera away.

"If she was strung any tighter she'd hum in the wind," I said. "But that's her problem, not ours."

"I have a feeling it'll be your problem every time you try to get a statement for a story," Al said.

I groaned and turned to Lorrie. "How did Fairchild, or rather the fake Fairchild, get hold of the Square Meal on a Stick?"

"It was delivered by a man from the sales booth. It wasn't open for business yet, but they were supposed to pass out free samples right after the ceremony," she said. "At least I thought he was from the booth."

"Was the square meal made at the booth?"

"Yes. Vinnie had it made up this morning by a cook in the booth. He put it in an insulated container to keep it fresh."

"Did the delivery man hand the container directly to Fairchild?"

"No, he handed it to me," Lorrie said. "I gave it to Fairchild. The fake Fairchild."

"Was there a time when Fairchild was out of sight between you handing the container to Fairchild and Fairchild handing it to Scott Hall?"

"Yes. I left Fairchild behind when I went over to Heritage Square to meet you and Al and Trish."

"So the fake Fairchild had plenty of opportunity to apply the poison to the meal."

"Oh, god, yes." With tears running down her cheeks, she said, "If only I'd dragged Fairchild along with me, he might not have had a chance to do it."

I put an arm around her shoulders. "Don't beat yourself up over that. You had no way of suspecting that somebody was trying to kill Vinnie."

"I know I didn't, but still I feel guilty about it."

"The killer would have found a way to poison the stick even if you'd kept him with you. This was a well-planned operation. For all we know the delivery man could have added the poison before giving it to you. Have the cops questioned him?"

"That detective pulled him into the office and talked to him for quite a while this morning," Ellie said.

"But she didn't arrest him?"

"No she didn't," Ellie said. "He came out looking like he'd been water boarded and hung by his heels to dry but she didn't arrest him. Now I hope you don't have any more questions for me. I've been dealing with this awful thing all day and I'm pooped." Twin streams of tears began rolling down her cheeks.

"Go home and make yourself a big gin and tonic," I said. "I'll call you later if I have more questions."

She wiped off the tears with her finger tips and scurried away like a rabbit running from a hound.

"Tough day for poor Ellie," Al said.

"She needs to go home and unwind," I said. "And you need to come with me."

"Where to?"

"How soon they forget," I said with a sigh. "You owe me a Pronto Pup from this morning."

* * *

"THAT'S HORRIBLE," MARTHA TODD said. The image on the TV screen had shifted from Trish Valentine reporting live from Heritage Square at the Minnesota State Fairgrounds to the tape of Vinnie Luciano's dramatic death throes on the Heritage Square stage. "What an awful way to die."

We were seated side-by-side on the sofa watching the evening news. Draped across our laps was Sherlock Holmes, my large, black-and-white, formerly male cat.

Sherlock had come to my doorstep looking for a handout almost ten years ago. Finding a soft touch, he'd never left. He bore no identification, so Al's wife, Carol, suggested Sherlock Holmes as an appropriate name for a cat living with an investigative reporter. The name was no big deal. I knew he wouldn't come when I called no matter what words I used.

Martha Todd had been much more difficult to acquire. We both carried so much baggage from ruined past marriages and broken relationships that commitment was difficult for us. Consequently the progression from friends to lovers to engagement had moved at a turtle's pace. We'd been lovers for nearly six years when Martha moved in to share my tiny one-bedroom apartment. Several months later I worked up the courage to buy a ring and pop the question.

Now we were searching for a larger place to live. The apartment had been quite roomy for me and Sherlock, but Martha's arrival created a severe shortage of closet and cupboard space. As a lawyer, Martha had to look sharp every day, so she brought in a stash of clothing that far outnumbered my one suit, two sport coats, and a week's supply of shirts, trousers and ties. She also brought in an array of dishes and cooking utensils that boggled the mind of a man who'd been surviving with a coffee pot, a single non-stick frying pan and a microwave.

The oven timer's buzz told us that the supper hot dish was ready. Martha rose, and I watched her walk away toward the kitchen. Watching Martha walk away, especially when her backside is clad in anything snug, is one of life's greatest erotic pleasures. Martha has an ass that can only be described as molded by the gods.

Conversely, watching Martha approach from the front is one of life's greatest artistic pleasures. She is lithe and moves with the grace of a ballet dancer. Being half Cape Verdean, she has a coffee-with-cream complexion, dark flashing eyes, jet black hair and a thousand-watt smile.

I was hoping to avoid further conversation about Vinnie Luciano's spectacular demise, but Martha was full of questions. "Who in the world would want to kill Vinnie?" she asked. "He was one of the best-liked, most generous men in the city. I've heard that he gave money to all kinds of charities."

"That's the sixty-four-million-dollar question," I said. "It's the first one I'm going to work on tomorrow. I'm going to start quizzing his employees and friends to see if they've got any ideas on who might have a motive."

"Won't the Falcon Heights police be doing the same thing?"

"They should be, but I haven't worked with the Falcon Heights police before, and I'm not sure how much information they'll release to the media. Also, sometimes people will tell a reporter something they won't tell a cop."

Chapter Four

The Hunt Begins

D ON O'ROURKE AGREED with my plan to question Vinnie Luciano's employees and friends, so I headed for King Vinnie's Steakhouse Thursday morning. I arrived at opening time for lunch, 11:00 a.m., hoping to talk with the person most likely to know everything—the bartender. Instead, I found a note on the door stating that King Vinnie's was closed until further notice because of the owner's death. I should have known.

As I turned away from the door, I met a man in a dark-gray three-piece suit coming up the steps. "It's closed," I said. "Until further notice."

"I should've known," the man said. "It's just such a habit to come here that I didn't even think about it."

"You eat here often?"

"Just five days a week. I try to get here in time to have a beer before lunch and shoot the shit with some of the other regulars at the bar."

"Ever see or hear anything that might be a reason for murder?"

"I saw and heard lots of stuff that could lead to murder, but not of Vinnie. I'm Charlie Freeman by the way. I've got a law office just up the street."

I had figured him for a lawyer. Who else goes to lunch in a three-piece suit when it's eighty-five degrees in the shade?

"Mitch Mitchell," I said. "I'm a reporter for the *Daily Dispatch*."

"You wrote the story in the paper," Charlie said. "Sounded like you were right there when Vinnie died."

"Almost as close as I am to you. It was an awful thing to watch. You say you saw things in Vinnie's that could lead to murder?"

"Well, not literally I guess. But there were some pretty hot arguments sometimes. Luckily, Vinnie had a way of cooling things off without pissing off either side."

"Maybe that wasn't always true. Maybe somebody carried a grudge after one of those arguments."

"Maybe, but I don't know who that would be."

"Do you remember who was involved in the last big argument you saw Vinnie stop?"

"Oh, jeez, that would have been last week on Monday. Or maybe Tuesday. One of the guys was another lawyer, David Cook. Got an office downtown, but he drives out to King Vinnie's two or three times a week. He's kind of a hothead, especially when it comes to politics. Big spender for the Republican party."

"Do you remember the other guy's name?"

"No clue. It was the first time I'd seen him in Vinnie's. I remember somebody said he was a high mucky-muck with the Teamsters."

"Well, thanks. I think I'll go have a chat with Mr. Cook."

"Don't tell him I sent you," said Charlie Freeman.

*   *   *

OBVIOUSLY I COULDN'T WALK in on David Cook, PCP, and ask him if he'd sent a poisoned Square Meal on a Stick to Vinnie Luciano. I decided to use a ploy that always worked. I'd tell him I was doing a roundup of comments on Vinnie's death from people who knew him well, then slide into some questions about Cook's argument with the Teamster official.

Cook's office was on the skyway near Seventh and Wabasha, only about three blocks from the *Daily Dispatch*. I walked through the entrance into a reception area with a door on each of the three other walls. A heavyset woman with white-tinged dark hair sat at a reception desk in front of the middle door. A small bronze plaque identified her as Margaret. Margaret looked up at me, put on a perfunctory smile and asked if she could help me. We went through the usual routine of me identifying myself and asking to see Mr. Cook, and she asking what I wished to see him about.

"It's about Vinnie Luciano," I said.

"The restaurant owner who died at the fair yesterday?" she said.

"That's right."

"I don't know that Mr. Cook has anything to say about Mr. Luciano."

"I believe he might be willing to help me with a comment about Mr. Luciano's death. It'll only take a minute." I didn't think David Cook was the killer, but the man he'd argued with was a possibility. I was hoping to get his name.

Margaret sighed, picked up the phone, tapped a number and spoke to her boss. She sighed again when she put down the phone. "He says you can go right in." She waved toward the door directly behind her.

I thanked her and went into David Cook's domain. The office contained two matching upholstered chairs and an over-stuffed sofa. The floor was thickly carpeted in burgundy, and the walls were lined with books, framed documents, and photos of David Cook with political figures, all of whom were Republicans. David Cook sat in a large leather chair behind a dark walnut desk. He wore a navy blue suit but no vest.

Cook rose, held out his hand for shaking across the desk, said it was a pleasure to meet me and motioned me toward one of the chairs. "So, you're looking for a statement of my reaction to Vinnie's death?" he asked when I was seated.

"That's the main reason I'm here," I said. I flipped open the reporter's notebook I was carrying and prepared to write.

"Vinnie was a dear friend and a wonderful host, and I shall miss him terribly," Cook said. "My sympathies go out to his wife and family. I can't imagine who would do such a horrible thing or why. I only hope the killer is brought to justice quickly."

Let's see, how many clichés was that? I count five.

"Thank you," I said. "Now the other reason I'm here is that I've been told you had a hot and heavy argument with somebody in King Vinnie's last week. I'm wondering if—"

Cook's face turned red as he cut me off. "Who told you that?"

"Reporter's privilege," I said.

"Fuck that. Are you implying I had something to with what happened to Vinnie?" He stood up, and I thought he might come around the desk and attack me. Charlie Freeman had been right about David Cook's temper.

Cook was the size of a pro football linebacker, so I also rose to be ready if he charged. "Not at all," I said. "I'm wondering if you know the name of the man you were arguing with."

"You think he might be involved?"

"It's possible. Anyway I'd like to talk to him—get his reaction. Do you know who he is?"

"He's Fred McDonald, head of the local Teamsters Union."

"I take it you were arguing politics?"

"Damn right we were. Left-wing liberal bastard thinks he's entitled to everything under the sun at the taxpayers' expense. Actually, I wouldn't be surprised if he was involved in the murder. He walked out in a huff after Vinnie broke us up. Said we'd both be sorry. And you know the Teamsters can be real hard-assed."

"I do. Thanks for your time and the information. I'll make sure your statement gets into a story about Vinnie's death."

"Don't tell Fred McDonald that you got his name from me," Cook said.

As I passed Margaret on the way out, I said, "Mr. Cook was very helpful. Thanks for your assistance." She did not say, "You're welcome."

*   *   *

I SWUNG BY THE *DAILY DISPATCH* office to find out where Fred McDonald could be found and to make a routine phone check with Falcon Heights Detective K.G. Barnes. The first was easy; the second had me gritting my teeth.

"We're investigating the murder of Mr. Vincent Luciano," Barnes said when I asked if there were any new developments in the case.

"It would be front-page news if you weren't," I said. "What I'm looking for is anything new since yesterday's chat with Fairchild."

"We're investigating the murder of Mr. Vincent Luciano."

"And have you learned anything additional since we last spoke?"

"We have nothing for the media at this time."

"No medical examiner's report on the official cause of death?"

"We have nothing for the media at this time."

"Any estimate when you will have something? Like maybe the medical examiner's report?"

"No, Mr. Mitchell, we do not. Have a nice day," Barnes said as she hung up.

"Bitch," I said as I put down my phone. Apparently working with the Falcon Heights KGB was going to be as much fun as dealing with the original Soviet version. Unless I'm taking notes, I tend to doodle when I'm on the phone. I had almost drawn a complete hammer and sickle during the conversation with KGB.

"Was that our friendly detective with the scary initials?" said Al, who had perched on a small open space on the corner of my desk while I was talking.

"The one and only," I said. "If they still made vinyl records, she'd be cracked."

"Repetitious is she?"

"Talking to her is like watching the movie *Ground Hog Day* only not half as much fun. Plus she uses the royal 'we' while she's telling you nothing."

"Sounds like a royal pain in the ass."

"You can say that again."

"Sounds like a royal—"

"Stop! I didn't mean it."

"Just keeping you sharp for dealing with the KGB," Al said. "How about lunch?"

"That's the first positive thing I've heard today," I said. "Lead on to the cafeteria, and I'll tell you about the people I've met so far."

* * *

I DON'T KNOW WHAT I expected from Fred McDonald, but it wasn't the big smile, crushing handshake and "it's great to meet you" that welcomed me when his secretary escorted me into his office. I'd approached with the usual story about doing a roundup of comments about Vinnie Luciano, and McDonald, a rugged-looking man in his early fifties, had invited me in.

"I read your piece on Vinnie's death and damn near puked," McDonald said. "Great writing. Made me feel like I was right there beside Vinnie while he was twisting and thrashing around. But how in hell could you stand there and watch all that?"

"I had to look away during the worst of it," I said. "But Al Jeffrey, the photographer, watched the whole thing. Maybe looking at it through a camera lens made it less real."

"I know you're looking for a comment about what a great guy Vinnie was, but you're in the wrong place. I barely knew the man."

"You weren't one of the so-called regulars?"

"A week ago Monday was the first time I ever went into the place. And I'll never go back, Vinnie or no Vinnie. I didn't like the atmosphere, if you know what I mean."

"Now that you mention it, I understand that you were involved in quite a scene that day." As I said this, it occurred to me that if this man had arranged for Vinnie's horrible death that he might do the same for a snoopy reporter.

"Yeah, I got into it with that asshole rightwing lawyer over the crap that the Republican legislature's doing. What's his name? Cook, I think it is."

"Yes. David Cook." Oops, I'd all but said straight out that David Cook had steered me to this office.

"So what about it? You think that argument had something to do with Vinnie getting poisoned?"

"I understand Vinnie broke up the battle and I wondered if you thought Cook might have been mad enough at Vinnie to set up something like that."

McDonald laughed. "No, you didn't. That asshole Cook told you I threatened him and Vinnie when I went out the door, didn't he?"

I was trapped and I felt my face getting warm. "He did," I said, confirming my previous booboo.

"Well, he's full of shit. I yelled a few things because I was pissed but it was just blowing off steam. I ain't your killer, Mitch. I don't know shit about poison."

"I didn't think you killed Vinnie. I just wanted to get your slant on the incident." I was hoping McDonald would buy this lie, but the look on his face told me he did not.

"Did Cook tell you I had something to do with Vinnie's murder?"

"No, nothing like that. He just said you yelled that both he and Vinnie would be sorry."

McDonald laughed again. "If he's worried about that I bet he won't be eating anything on a stick next time he goes to the fair."

I joined in the laughter. "Could be," I said. "Well, I guess I'll be on my way. Thanks for your time."

"Nice meeting you, Mitch," McDonald said. "Don't take any wooden food on a stick." He was still laughing as I went out the door.

"How'd it go with the Teamster king?" Al asked when I got back to the office.

"I made a royal ass of myself," I said.

"I've always said you were a self-made man."

I still really wanted to talk to Vinnie's bartender. If anybody had seen or heard anything suspicious it would be him. My problem was I didn't know his name. Nor did I know the name of anybody else who worked at King Vinnie's. I expressed my frustration.

"What about that guy you said you met at King Vinnie's?" Al said. "The one who eats there five days a week. He probably knows the bartender's full name, date of birth and place of residence."

"You're right," I said. "He said he always starts off with a beer and shoots the shit with the regulars at the bar. I could kiss you."

"Not here. Don already thinks we're connected at the head." This was true. Although I was four inches taller than Al, Don O'Rourke called us the Siamese twins, which I kept reminding him was politically incorrect, and said we were joined at the funny bone—our skulls.

I looked up Charles Freeman, PPC, in the phone book, called the number and got his secretary. She informed me that Mr. Freeman was with a client and took a message. I was shutting down my computer, preparing to go home, when he finally called.

"Of course I know the bartender's name," Freeman said. "It's Ozzie."

"Thanks," I said. "What's his last name?"

"Ooh, that's a little tougher. I should know it. Ozzie . . . Ozzie . . . Ozzie . . . Bergman. That's it. Ozzie Bergman. Now I remember. His real first name is Leonard but he goes by Ozzie because he hates that name. Lives on the West Side."

I thanked him and hung up without asking for Ozzie's date of birth. I was afraid Freeman would know it.

Another trip to the phone book. I found the bartender's number under Bergman, L.O., and punched it in. After seven rings I got a message saying no one could come to the phone just now. I declined the invitation to leave a message. Talking to Ozzie would have to wait until tomorrow.

Chapter Five

Bar Buddies

I WAS GREETED AT HOME with a rib-crunching hug and a long, luscious kiss from Martha Todd.

"You're home early," I said when I'd caught my breath. Martha, a lawyer, usually works a longer day at the firm of Linda L. Lansing, Attorney at Law. Linda L. Lansing, also known as Triple-L, was the city's top defense lawyer and a longtime friend of mine.

"I took the afternoon off to go apartment hunting," Martha said.

"Any luck?"

"Lots of luck. All bad. You should see some of the dumps in our price range."

"Maybe we have to up the range."

"We can't up it too much or we'll be on the same diet as Sherlock Holmes."

"I have a raise coming in January. We can scrape up the extra rent until then." Our problem was exacerbated by a deadline for clearing out of our apartment. We had given our landlord sixty days notice three weeks ago and we were required to be out by October first. Our available hunting and moving time was now down to five weeks.

"My billable hours are increasing. I'll look at some higher buck places next time I go out." Martha was building her list of clientele as a newbie at Triple-L's firm. She had changed jobs in May when her previous firm wanted her to open a new office for them in Fargo, North Dakota. Triple-L's job offer, purposely timed to coincide with my marriage proposal, had persuaded Martha to stay in St. Paul.

"What's new on Vinnie's murder?" Martha asked.

"Nothing," I said. "I got nowhere with the people I interviewed and the Falcon Heights investigator is stonewalling the media."

"Is that the one who calls herself KGB?"

"The same. She's as tight-lipped as her namesake."

"Maybe you can infiltrate the enemy camp," Martha said.

"What do you mean by that?" I asked.

"Schmooze her a little bit. Make her think you're on her side."

"You won't get jealous if we become buddies?"

"Not as long as you both keep your clothes on. Remember, I've decided to trust you forever and always." She raised her left hand and flashed her engagement ring.

"I'll keep it strictly professional forever and always." I decided to seal that promise with a kiss, one thing led to another and we ate a very late supper.

* * *

MY FIRST CALL FRIDAY MORNING went to Ozzie Bergman. After some hemming and hawing, he agreed to meet me at the restaurant where he "needed to check on things." I was to knock on the back door at ten o'clock, and he would let me in.

"Make sure nobody sees you," Ozzie said. "Don't park out front."

"Who would be there to see me?" I asked.

"I heard there were some TV reporters staking out the place for a few hours yesterday. I guess they were hoping to catch one of us going in."

I promised to be careful, hung up and went about some other chores, including a phone check with Detective K.G. Barnes.

"We have nothing for the media at this time," she said.

"Look, I'm on this story for the duration, which means we'll to be talking to each other every day until you catch the killer," I said. "Can we maybe get together for lunch or something to get a little better acquainted?"

"Why would we do that?"

Time to try Martha's strategy. "To build up some trust in each other. After all, we're both on the same team."

"We've never thought of our self as being on the same team as the news media. It's usually quite the opposite, so we don't think getting better acquainted with you or anyone else in the media is a good idea. Have a nice day, Mister Mitchell."

"Bitch!" I said as I put down my phone. Apparently I said it pretty loud.

"Someone of the female gender giving you a hard time, Mitch?" asked Corinne Ramey, the reporter sitting at the next desk. Many modern newspapers have tucked their reporters into cubicles, but our newsroom is still wide open because Don O'Rourke wanted it that way. Our old-fashioned city editor said he needed to be able to see which reporters were present and what they were doing.

"Hard as a stone wall," I said. "And, yes, it is a female. She happens to be in charge of the Vinnie Luciano investigation."

"So how's that going?"

"Thanks to Ms. Stonewall, nobody knows."

* * *

True to his word, Ozzie Bergman opened the back door of King Vinnie's Steakhouse at 10:02 when I knocked. He was what you'd expect in a steakhouse bartender: pushing sixty, balding with a ring of white hair at ear level and carrying a paunch that looked like he'd been sampling too much of the merchandise on tap.

"You sure nobody saw you?" he asked.

"There's nobody to see me," I said. "They must have given up."

"Probably off chasing the next fire engine. Those TV guys are worse than lawyers running after business."

I bit back a response to the slam on lawyers, recalling that before falling in love with Martha I'd reveled in telling lawyer jokes. "Have you worked here a long time?" I asked.

"Since we opened twenty-five years ago," Ozzie said. "Me and Vinnie was like cousins. Maybe brothers even."

"*Vinnie and I*," I said.

"How's that?"

"Nothing," I said, wishing I'd swallowed the reflex grammar correction. "Being so close with Vinnie must make it even rougher than just losing a boss."

Ozzie nodded and looked away.

"If you've been here every day since this place opened, you must have talked to just about every person who has ever come into the bar. Do you have any idea at all who might have wanted Vinnie dead?"

Ozzie shook his head. "Not really. Vinnie treated all our customers like family and everybody liked him. Even most of our competitors were buddies with Vinnie."

"You say most of your competitors. Were some of them not such good buddies with Vinnie?"

"There were a couple of jerks that envied our business. Hey, this ain't goin' in the paper is it?"

"Oh, no. This is what we call background. What you tell me won't be printed but it might help me find the killer. Who were these jealous competitors?"

"Well, there's Oscar Peterson at the Northern Exposure for one. And Luigi Bunatori at the House of Italy for another. But that don't mean they'd murder Vinnie."

I choked back my bad grammar reflex and said, "They're involved with food. They're the kind of people who'd think of poison."

"Oh, Christ, I can't believe they'd do anything like that."

"It's worth checking them out. Are there any customers you think might have had a grudge against Vinnie?"

"I don't know," Ozzie said. "Maybe a couple. There's one guy used to be a regular that's never come back after Vinnie threw him out for starting a fight. And there's that Teamster bum that got into it with one of the lawyers last week. Told Vinnie he'd be sorry. He's a nasty son of a bitch."

"I've actually talked to him," I said. "He claims he was just blowing off steam."

"He blew off a hell of a lot of it on his way out of here. I half expected him to come back with some goons and try to bust up the place."

That didn't sound like the Fred McDonald I had interviewed but I made note of Ozzie's remarks for future reference. "Do you know the name of the regular who never came back?" I asked.

"Oh, shit, that's a long time ago. Vinnie never forgot a name but I'm not that good at it."

"If you think of it later, give me a call," I said and handed him my card. "That's quite a record for a businessman—twenty-five years and only two competitors and two customers who didn't like him."

"Then there's his cousin Vito," Ozzie said.

This got my attention. "What about him?"

"He flat out hated Vinnie because Vinnie fired him."

"From here?"

"Yeah, from here. Where else? They started the business together as partners but Vito was drinking up the profits and insulting the customers so Vinnie said either shape up or ship out.

He didn't shape up, so Vinnie paid him off for his share of the business and shipped him out. Told him to stay the hell away."

"And has he stayed away?"

"Pretty much. He comes back maybe once a year, usually drunk, and tells Vinnie he's a rotten bastard."

Now here was a solid suspect. I wondered if KGB knew about him. "Have the Falcon Heights police talked to you?" I asked.

"No," Ozzie said. "I haven't heard from them."

"You'll probably be hearing from a detective named K.G. Barnes. She's not the most pleasant cop you'll ever meet."

"I'll keep my guard up. Thanks for the warning."

"Thanks for your help. And remember to call me if you think of that former customer's name or anything else that might help."

Ozzie escorted me to the back door and I heard the locking bolt slam into place behind me. I got into my car and drove out the alley and onto West Seventh Street. A Channel Five television truck was parked across the street from Vinnie's front door.

* * *

A FEW MINUTES BEFORE LUNCH I received a call from Detective K.G. Barnes, informing me that the Falcon Heights medical examiner would hold a press conference in the police station at 1:00 p.m., perfect timing to allow TV breaking news to interrupt all the daytime viewers' favorite soap operas.

"I'll be there," I said. "And that lunch invitation is still open for tomorrow or any other day this week. I'll even pick up the tab on my meager reporter's salary."

"You can save your meager salary for lunch with somebody else," KGB said as she hung up.

"Bitch!" I said.

"Not stonewalled again?" said Corinne Ramey.

"Cold-shouldered this time," I said.

"Is there a difference?"

"Stonewalled is professional; cold-shouldered is personal."

* * *

ONE O'CLOCK FOUND AL AND ME joining a media mob so big that the Falcon Heights press conference had to be moved outside. This allowed Chief Victoria Tubb, Detective K.G. Barnes and Dr. Leo Longwell to stand on the top step in front of the door and gaze down upon us mere mortals on the lawn and sidewalk below.

"Feel like you're in church ready to be preached to?" I asked Trish Valentine, who was reporting live and interrupting Channel Four's regular broadcast. She was up front as always, and I'd wormed my way through the crowd with judicious use of elbows and insincere apologies to stand behind her.

"It's like the king and his consorts gazing down on the rabble," Trish said. "I wonder if they'll deign to answer questions."

"They won't if the chief is as hard-ass as Detective Barnes," I said.

Chief Tubb proved to be more helpful than KGB. She opened the session to questions after Dr. Longwell droned along for almost five minutes describing the dead man's physical injuries before leaving us without an official cause of death. This, he said, would not be available until the toxicology lab results were in.

As she often does, Trish Valentine asked the first question. "Can you speculate as to what type of poison was on the stick?" she asked.

"I'd rather not get into that until we have the toxicology report," Dr. Longwell said.

I was next. "Dr. Longwell, at the scene, one of the investigators said the victim's actions were consistent with the symptoms of strychnine poisoning. Do you agree with that observation?"

"I'm not sure which actions you mean?" said the M.E.

"The one I remember best was the arching of the back so that only the victim's head and feet were touching the stage."

"That is consistent with strychnine. However, not having actually observed the victim's struggles, I can neither agree nor disagree."

Several reporters groaned, including me. A couple of others asked the same question in roundabout ways, but the M.E. was a good dodger and nobody got an answer.

Chief Tubb called a halt, and the troops scattered. "That M.E. is so good at ducking questions he could run for governor," Al said as we walked to the car.

"He certainly had his ducks in a row," I said.

"I hope you're not suggesting the doctor is a quack."

"All I'm saying is that nothing ruffled his feathers."

* * *

WE WERE ON COMO AVENUE, passing the fairgrounds, when Al said, "I wonder how that square dance caller who handed the stick to Vinnie feels about being that close to the poison pill."

"That's a good question," I said. "I should have gotten a reaction story from him."

"Is it too late?"

"I wonder." I took out my cell phone and punched in the State Fair public relations number. Lorrie Gardner answered.

"Hey, Lorrie, this is Mitch," I said. "Is that square dance caller who was there the other day still performing?"

"Scott Hall?" she said. "Yes, his club is dancing every day at 10:30 and 2:00. They've moved from Heritage Square over to the Bandshell because Scott said he got the creeps being on the stage where Vinnie died."

"Can't say I blame him. Think he'd do an interview about how it felt to be that close to a dying murder victim?"

"I could run up and ask him; I think they're still dancing up there. He's usually very good about talking to the media. I wish I had more people—"

"Okay," I said, not wanting to hear an entire list of her wishes. "Just scoot up there and see if he'll talk to us. We'll swing in and park by the Admin building and meet you there."

"The little Admin parking lot is full and you can't park on the grass," Lorrie said.

"We'll find a spot. And the first thing I'll do when we get there is run over and get a Pronto Pup."

"Do you eat Pronto Pups all day long?" Lorrie said.

"Pronto Pups are good any time of day. Can I bring you one?"

"God, no! I'd be burping all night."

"Some people don't appreciate fine dining," I said.

We turned north onto Snelling Avenue, drove into the fairgrounds through the Dan Patch Avenue gate and parked on the grass beside the Admin building. Al stayed by the car to intercept Lorrie while I went looking for a Pronto Pup.

"Bring me one," Al said. "It's the only thing I can eat on a stick after Tuesday's little demonstration."

When I returned with our mustard-slathered treats, I found Al and Lorrie in her office, where he was showing her some of the photos he had shot of Vinnie doing his dance of death. It was even hotter inside than outside. "Don't you have air conditioning?" I said.

"It doesn't work in this weather," Lorrie said. "That's why the boss lets me dress for a day at the beach. And Scott says he'll talk to you when your mouth is empty of Pronto Pup."

"Hot dog! Come on, Al, let's go out into the fresh, cool, eighty-five-degree air," I said.

We found Scott Hall taking down his sound equipment at the rear of the stage. His dancers, dressed in matching red and white outfits, were beginning to straggle away. Al followed me onto the stage, and we introduced ourselves to the caller, who was decked out in a red Western-style shirt with white trimming, a white tie, white pants and black cowboy boots. The same white ten-gallon hat he'd worn when celebrating the origin of the Square Meal on a Stick completed the ensemble. Not a drop of sweat was visible on his face.

"You guys were there for the, uh . . . you were there when Vinnie died, weren't you?" Hall said.

"That's right," I said. "We were right at the foot of the stage, almost as close to Vinnie as you were."

"And you want to know my reaction to what happened to Vinnie?"

"It would be an interesting addition to the follow story today."

"Well, does the fact that I can't step onto the same stage two days after the fact give you any clue as to how I feel?"

"Lorrie says being on that stage gave you the creeps," Al said.

"It actually made me feel like puking," Hall said. "I can still see Vinnie gasping for breath and going through those awful contortions. I've even dreamt about it. Woke up soaked with sweat and yelling. Scared my lady friend half to death. The worst thing is I feel kind of guilty because I'm the one who handed him the stick."

"Speaking of the devil, are they trying to sell those things?" I asked.

"Hell no," Hall said. "Who'd buy one after everything that's been on the news and in the paper? I can't even look at a fried potato without thinking about what the meat on that stick was wrapped in."

"You shouldn't blame yourself for handing the stick to Vinnie," Al said. "You had no way of knowing that it was loaded with strychnine."

"Anyway, I'm still shook up about the whole thing," Hall said. "It's the kind of shock that never seems to go away."

"Well, we'll go away and let you get packed up," I said. "Thanks for your comments and your time."

"No problem," Hall said. I much prefer "you're welcome," as a response to "thanks," but I smiled and shook his hand. "Oh, hey," he said. "The president of our club is still here. Erik Erickson. You should meet him. He was onstage, too, and he might give you a comment."

Hall waved to a man in his mid-fifties with a receding hairline and the beginnings of a pot belly. "Hey, Erik, come on over." Like all the male dancers, Erickson wore a red Western-style shirt, white tie, white pants, and white shoes. I remembered seeing him standing behind Hall on the day of the murder, and I had a feeling I'd also seen him somewhere else not dressed for dancing.

We shook hands all around, and I asked Erickson the name of the club.

"We're the Oles and Lenas Square Dance Club," he said.

"Are you kidding me?" I asked.

"No way. The traditional Minnesota Scandahoovian jokes are all about Ole and Lena so the founders thought it would be fun to name the club after such well-known personalities."

Hall told Erickson that Al and I were looking for reactions to Vinnie Luciano's death. "You were there," Hall said. "Do you want to say anything?"

Erickson stiffened and thought for a moment before he said, "It was the most god-awful thing I've ever seen. I was horrified by what was happening. In fact, I had to get off the stage. My wife said she almost fainted." He pointed across the stage to a red-haired woman at least fifteen years his junior. The top two buttons of her blouse were unfastened, and, sharp-eyed reporter that I am, I observed that her cleavage was a match for Trish Valentine's.

"Thanks for your time, Mr. Erickson," I said. "I've been thinking I've seen you somewhere dressed in regular clothes. Do you work downtown or have you come into the newsroom for something?"

"My day job is in the drug store on Wabasha Street. You might have seen me there," Erickson said. "At night I'm the artistic director of the Parkside Players Theatre."

"The one in the basement in Lowertown?"

"That's the one."

"That's where I've seen you. My fiancée and I have season tickets. You always come out onstage to tell us how much we're going to love the show, point out the emergency exits and remind us to turn off our cell phones before the curtain goes up."

"Hey, nice to meet a subscriber," he said. "I wish there were more of you."

"Tight budget?"

"Deficit budget. I've stopped taking what little salary I was getting and we're still running in the red. Oh, God, don't put that in the paper."

"I won't," I said. This was not the time for this tidbit, but I was pretty sure our entertainment editor would be making a follow-up phone call to the director.

"Thanks. We're working on plans for a fund drive and a premature story could really kill us."

"I wouldn't want to do that. You do some really good stuff there. I'll see if I can scare up some more customers for the coming season."

"I'd appreciate that. We can use every warm body we can find."

Erickson turned and went back to his wife. I turned to Scott Hall and made the obvious observation: "Erik's wife looks a lot younger than he is."

"That's because she's a lot younger. She's his second wife," Hall said. "One of those mid-life switches you hear about. Joyce started coming to our classes as a single and wound up as Erik's partner in more than just a square."

"What happened to his first wife?" Al asked.

"She promenaded away with the house, the two kids and one of the cars. Erik gave up a lot to get Joyce."

"The trophy wife," I said. "Is she worth what he paid?"

Hall shook his head. "I wouldn't know. She's a good dancer, but Roberta was, too. Beyond that—no comment."

"Dance floors and bedrooms don't mix?"

Again he shook his head. "Like I said: no comment."

I thanked the caller again for his help, and Al and I walked to the car. I was reaching for the door handle when another mental light came on. "Should we have one for the road?" I asked.

"My turn to buy," Al said as he started toward the nearest Pronto Pup stand.

* * *

BACK AT THE OFFICE, I decided to make one more call to Detective K.G. Barnes in Falcon Heights. I got her voice mail with a promise to return my call. I left a message noting that my deadline was 5:00, which was less than an hour away.

I put off some other calls in order to keep the line clear and wrote what I had collected about the reactions of Scott Hall and Erik Erickson to Vinnie Luciano's dramatic demise. What I needed to complete the story was a progress report from the Falcon Heights police.

Al swung by and asked if the cops were making any progress on the case, night city editor Fred Donlin asked when my story was coming, and I watched the hands on the wall clock move toward five. The clock hands were at 4:51 and I was doodling a horizontal stick man with his back steeply arched when my phone rang. I picked it up anticipating the return call from KGB.

"It's Morrie," said a dreary male voice. "I need your help."

Somehow I stopped myself from shouting, "Shit." Morrie was one of those mentally unbalanced callers who plague newspaper offices in search of impossible solutions to imaginary problems. He always seemed to call when everyone was rushing to meet a deadline and for some reason he often asked for me.

"I don't have time right now," I said. "Call back in an hour." I knew I'd be gone home by then.

"This is really bad," he said. "It's the Russians again. They're beaming their radar at me right through the walls." Morrie was a little white-haired man who lived with a little white dog in a radar-resistant brick apartment building in Lowertown, near Erik Erickson's theater. He'd been complaining about the Russian radar for years despite all our efforts to convince him that Russia had no radar that could reach St. Paul.

"It'll have to wait," I said. "Lock yourself in the bathroom and call back in an hour." I put down the receiver and saw the minute hand advance to 4:52. Almost immediately, the phone rang again. This time it was KGB.

"What's new on the Luciano murder investigation?" I asked without the customary, "Good afternoon, *Daily Dispatch*, Mitchell." There wasn't time to observe formalities.

"Our investigation of Mr. Luciano's murder is continuing," KGB said.

"I'm sure it is. Do you have any leads on a possible suspect or person of interest?"

"We can't comment on that at this time, Mr. Mitchell."

"Have you asked Vinnie's family about any enemies he might have had or anybody who was mad at Vinnie?"

"We have."

"And did they give you any help?"

"We can't comment at this time."

"Have you interviewed anyone who has been helpful?"

"We can't comment at this time."

This was not going well. "What can you comment on?" I asked.

"We can say that the investigation is continuing," she said.

"This isn't news. It would be news if you weren't continuing the investigation."

"We're not in the news business, Mr. Mitchell."

"You are in the news business because you make the news reporters report, Detective Barnes. We can even help each other. I've been known to swap information with the police when I have something they don't."

"If you have something we don't, we'd recommend you tell us, Mr. Mitchell. Withholding evidence can put you in front of a judge."

"I'll remember that," I said. "And I hope you'll help me keep abreast of the investigation. We could have lunch and talk about it."

"Our department will issue media bulletins at appropriate times. In the mean time, we bid you goodbye, Mr. Mitchell." The line went dead before I could wish her a good day.

"Bitch!" I said as I slammed down the phone. "Double bitch!"

"Stonewalled again?" said Corinne Ramey.

"Again," I said. "I've been stonewalled by cops before, but never this bad."

I went to work with what I had, pausing only to debate whether to say Falcon Heights police "declined to comment" or "refused to comment." I decided to give them one more chance and went with "declined."

I pressed the key that sent the story to Fred Donlin. Three minutes later Fred appeared before me and said that except for the quotes from the square dance caller, my story was a piece of crap. I agreed and promised to have something better the next day.

"The funeral is tomorrow morning, and I've got the names of some people who might have wanted Vinnie dead," I said. ""I'll start talking to them on my own. I'm ready to give up completely on that stonewalling bitch at the Falcon Heights PD."

"Tomorrow better be better or Don might make the next funeral yours," Fred said as he turned and went back to his desk. I assumed he was speaking figuratively, but even that left me with grave concern.

*   *   *

FRIDAY NIGHTS OFTEN found Martha and me enjoying Carol's superb cooking as guests at the Jeffreys' dining room table. Because dinner seating for six (Al and Carol had two children, Kristin, eighteen, and Kevin, sixteen) ranged from awkward to ridiculous in our shoebox apartment, we were looking forward to hosting scores of return dinners when we moved to larger quarters.

On the short drive to the Jeffreys' house in the city's Midway district, I told Martha about meeting Erik Erickson and learning that Parkside Players Theatre was in financial trouble.

"I hope they don't go under," Martha said. "They do the kind of plays you can't find anywhere else."

Parkside Players' seasons always featured several works that larger theaters with big budgets couldn't risk producing because they didn't attract a mass audience. The Parkside facility was tiny, with about a hundred seats arranged around three sides of a postage-stamp stage. "Intimate" was the critics' description of this theater, which was in the basement of a converted warehouse with 1894 engraved in a stone above the entrance. The casts were composed of unpaid community actors, and I had assumed the rent was low.

"I told him we'd talk it up with our friends," I said.

"I think their opening production is *Waiting for Godot*, which isn't the best show to sell to newcomers," she said. "As I recall from seeing it in college, things move very slowly onstage while the audience is waiting."

The possible demise of Parkside Players was also discussed at dinner because Al and Carol had season seats next to ours. We decided to try to arrange a theater party for the season's first production. Carol looked up the schedule and confirmed that the opening production was *Waiting for Godot*.

"The first show was tonight," she said. "We must have tickets for next weekend, so I guess we won't have time to round up a party. Anyway, the promo says it's a timeless tale of mankind's frustrations."

"Sounds more like a time-wasting tale of audience boredom," said Al. "I'm getting tired just waiting to see it."

Chapter Seven

Looking for Vito

I HATE THESE DAMN THINGS," Al said as a man in a black suit that looked way too warm for the weather waved us into a parking place in the church parking lot. We were working on Saturday morning because, like most *Daily Dispatch* reporters and photographers, we had a rotating day off in addition to every Sunday. Al and I are on the same rotation—the current week we'd been off on Monday, the next week it would be Tuesday and so on through the calendar.

"Me, too," I said. "But this one is a big deal for the city and Don wants full coverage. Plus we'll get to see at least one of the suspects, good old Cousin Vito."

"How will we know which one is Vito?"

"We'll look over the family gathering, and we'll each vote for a possible Vito."

"What if we don't agree?"

"Then I'll veto your Vito."

"Any chance for an override?"

"Only if two-thirds of the Luciano family says I'm wrong."

We arrived fifteen minutes before the service was scheduled to begin, assuming Vinnie's funeral would draw a full house. We were correct. The church was already nearly full, but we managed to squeeze into a pew in the next to last row. We were so far back and behind so many heads I was afraid we wouldn't get a good look at the family when they filed in. I had visions of Trish Valentine, always the early bird, sitting somewhere near the front row, but at her truncated height I'd never be able to see her.

49

Just before the service began, I stood up, stretched and made a 360-degree scan of the crowd. Up near the front sat the mayor, three city councilmen, a half dozen of St. Paul's most prominent lawyers and a couple of judges. As one of the city's premier restaurateurs, Vinnie had a buffet line of friends in high places. A few rows further back, the professional sports world was represented by the general manager of the Minnesota Twins, the president of the Minnesota Wild and the vice-president of the Minnesota Vikings.

"The Timberwolves are missing," I said, referring to Minnesota's pro basketball team.

"They usually do," Al said.

As I turned to face the rear, I spotted Detective K.G. Barnes of the Falcon Heights Police Department standing beside the open door. I surmised her primary mission was the same as our secondary mission: to check out any possible persons of interest who might attend the funeral. I paused and stared at KGB for a moment, hoping to connect, but she never met my gaze.

Everyone rose when the family members arrived and my concern about not being able to see them proved to be valid. I caught the tops of the tallest heads, but had no way of identifying any of them.

Al leaned over and whispered, "So, how are we supposed to spot cousin Vito?"

"Beats hell out of me," I whispered. "We should have got here when the mayor and the council members did."

"They probably had reserved seats," Al said.

Our dilemma was solved halfway through the service by Cousin Vito, bless his heart. He made identification easy for us by going up front to speak when the officiating priest called for comments from family and friends. I observed a clear resemblance to Vinnie in Vito's profile and hairline. Vito stood a tad taller and his fringe was noticeably darker, but he had plenty of weight to throw around.

"Vinnie and me grew up together," Vito said after introducing himself as Vinnie's loving cousin. "We played together as kids, raised hell together as young bucks and went into business together as grownup men. We didn't always agree about everything when we was workin' together, but we had a lot of fun and we did a damn . . . I mean a *darn* good business at the restaurant. I always missed workin' beside Vinnie after I left the restaurant and went on to other things. And I'll miss him even more knowin' that I ain't never gonna see him again in this world." With that, cousin Vito wiped an invisible tear from each eye and returned to his seat.

As the priest began his final incantation, Al jumped up and dashed for the door so he could get a picture of the pall bearers carrying the casket out of the church. I exited at a more leisurely pace and joined Al at the foot of the steps.

"Guess who was already here when I got out," he said.

"Do I get three guesses?" I said.

"Only one, and it had better be Trish Valentine reporting live."

"My god, even the dead can't get away from Trish Valentine reporting live."

"Just three things you can be sure of: death, taxes and Trish," Al said.

* * *

THE FOURTH THING I could be sure of, or I thought I could, was finding Martha Todd cooking up something special for Saturday dinner when I arrived home after filing my story and having coffee and doughnuts with Al. Not so this Saturday. The only thing on the kitchen counter was a note that said Martha had gone to look at some apartments.

I was on the couch, half-dozing half-watching an exhibition football game when Martha came home sometime after five. I hauled myself off the couch to greet her and noticed she was dragging her feet a bit. When I opened my arms, she threw her body against mine, wrapped her arms around my neck, hanging like a floor-length necklace, with all of her 120 pounds on my shoulders.

"Tired?" I asked. Again the ever-observant reporter.

"Pooped," Martha said.

"Any luck?"

"The usual."

"All bad?" I said as I dragged her to the couch and sat her down beside me.

"You got it."

"Can I get you something to drink? Ginger ale? Root beer?" I'd have offered something stronger but you don't keep booze in the home of a recovering alcoholic. I've been a faithful participant in Alcoholics Anonymous meetings since going through rehab eight years ago.

"Just let me sit for a while," Martha said. "I've been climbing stairs and looking under sinks all afternoon. And we have to be out of here in thirty-three days. But who's counting?"

"Maybe I can help with dinner. What are you planning to make?"

"Reservations. You're taking your exhausted lover out to dinner tonight."

"I can handle that. Any place in particular?"

"Some place with a glass of wine for me and no sports TV for you."

"The utmost in cruelty, making me watch nothing but you while you're sitting there bibbing wine." I've reached the stage where I can watch others imbibe without jealousy or desire. Well, maybe a little twinge of jealously.

"I'll be happy to trade," Martha said. "You take over the apartment hunting and I'll take you to a restaurant with giant TVs on every wall."

"Suddenly a place with wine and no TV sounds really good."

It was Saturday night and the restaurants with wine and without TV were full. We wound up settling for an 8:30 reservation at a dimly-lit restaurant in south Minneapolis. We arrived at 8:15 and finally were seated at 9:15 in the center of a packed dining room with a noise level that bordered on painful.

"Can you stand the noise?" I said at nearly a shout.

"I can if you can," Martha said at equal volume.

"It's either the noise or McDonald's."

"Noise? What noise?"

When my eyes had adjusted to the semi-darkness, I looked around the room for familiar faces—a reflex acquired by every reporter. One never knows what useful information might be gleaned from observing who is dining with whom.

Checking in all directions, I saw no one I recognized. Or did I? There was something vaguely familiar about the man with the dark moustache and flashing smile at a table against one wall. His companion was facing almost straight away from me, but her long red hair reminded me of someone. They were laughing and nodding a lot, and their faces nearly touched as they leaned across the table to hear each other above the dining room din.

"What are you staring at?" Martha asked.

"Try not to be too obvious, but take a look at the redhead and the guy with the big smile over by the wall at your left," I said. "See if they look familiar to you."

Martha turned her head with the subtlety of a striking rattlesnake and studied the pair for a moment. "Nope," she said. "Neither one rings a bell."

"I swear I've seen both of them someplace. His face and her hair are familiar but I can't think where the hell it could be."

Even after our food was set before us, I couldn't keep myself from taking occasional glances at the smile and the redhead. Who were they? Did I really know them from somewhere?

"Hello," Martha said when we were halfway through our entrees. "Remember me? I'm the lady you came in with."

"Oh, sorry," I said. "I don't mean to ignore you but that couple is driving me crazy. I just feel like I should know them."

"Why don't you go over and say hello?"

"Oh, right. I can start with, 'Hi guys, I'm just wondering who you are.'"

Feeling duly chastised, I turned my attention to Martha, but I kept the mysterious couple under surveillance out of the corner of my eye. When they stood up to leave, the woman turned toward us and I saw her boobs I realized who I'd been watching.

"It's the square dance caller from the State Fair," I said. "His name is Scott Hall. I didn't recognize him with his hat off and his clothes on."

"And the redhead is his wife?" Martha said.

"Yeah, the redhead is his wife." I was about to wave a hand at them when the reality light in my brain went on. "No, wait," I said. "The redhead is the dance club president's wife." I was glad I hadn't waved.

"So she's married to somebody else?" Martha said as the couple went out the door.

"Her husband runs Parkside Players. They've got a show tonight so that's where he is while she's dining with the club caller."

"Do you think there's some hanky-panky going on?"

"I've been told that square dancers don't mess around," I said. "Whatever's going on, it's none of my business." But I filed the couple's liaison in the memory corner of my brain. As previously noted, one never knows what information might be useful at a later date.

Chapter Eight

Northern Exposure

WHAT A HELL OF A WAY to start a Monday morning I thought as I punched in the number of the Falcon Heights Police Department. "Detective Barnes, please," I said to the officer who answered.

"The detective is in a meeting," he said. "Can I take a message?"

I had my doubts about getting a response. I couldn't picture KGB taking the time to call and say, "We have nothing for the media at this time." I left the message anyway.

Al arrived at my desk with the day's first cup of coffee as I was putting down the phone. "Any word from the Falcon Heights Dragon Lady?" he said.

"She's in a meeting," I said. "Probably telling everybody in the department to say nothing to the press. I left a message but I'm not holding my breath until she calls."

"You could suffocate while you wait. That woman's got a manic phobia about reporters and photographers."

"Manic or womanic?"

"Unisex, like the bathrooms."

"Well, in her own way she's flush with success. But enough about the bitch. How did your book signing go?" Al's first book of photos had been released by the publisher the previous week, and his Sunday afternoon had been spent signing copies at Barnes & Noble. The book was a collection of Al's personal scenic photos, candid people shots and portrait work, along with a selection of his best shots for the newspaper.

"My hand isn't cramped from signing books, but it went okay," he said. "I met a lot of people, including too many who don't read the paper."

"They'd never heard of you?"

"They'd never heard of the *Daily Dispatch*. Some said they get all their news from TV and a few, god help us, said they just listen to talk radio."

"That's a great unbiased source."

"I do have one fan, though," Al said. "A woman named Willow bought six books, for herself and her family and friends, and she kind of hung around all afternoon. Talked to me when no customers were at the table."

"Willow?" I said. "Willow what? The Wisp?"

"Don't have a clue. When I signed her book she said make it to Willow. Later on she asked for my card and I asked about her last name, but she said just call her Willow."

"Is she some kind of performer? Like Prince?"

"Didn't sound like it from the chitchat. Mostly she wanted to talk about me and how my photos show my feelings about this and that."

"Your feelings? Maybe she's a psychologist," I said.

"Better a psychologist than a psychopath," Al said.

"Maybe she is a psychopath. You said she bought six of your books."

"I told you they weren't all for her. I signed five of them to other people."

"Any of them have last names?"

"You only address them to first names. You know that."

"Well, I'm glad you had a nice time with Willow," I said. "If you run into her again you should find out more about her family tree."

"Like I said, I tried to go out on a limb but she stumped me," Al said.

Before I could branch out on this discussion my phone rang. To my amazement, it was KGB. Without so much as a "how are you," she informed me that Doctor Leo Longwell, the medical examiner, had determined the cause of Vinnie Luciano's death to be strychnine poisoning.

"So your first observation was correct," I said. "Congratulations."

"The doctor will be e-mailing his full report to all the media within the hour," KGB said.

I tried again. "As I said, your first observation was correct."

"We have no comment on that. Have a good day, Mr. Mitchell."

I shook my head as I put down the phone. "Talking to KGB is like talking to a computerized robot," I said to Al.

"Maybe she needs rebooting," he said.

"I'd love to reboot her. Right square in the ass with my size twelve boot."

"Well, I need to butt out to an assignment," Al said. "See you at lunch?"

"I'm thinking about eating at the Northern Exposure, where the owner supposedly does not like Vinnie Luciano."

"Too rich for my blood. And I can't justify it on my expense account."

"I can and I will," I said. "See you whenever."

The ME's e-mail arrived a few minutes later, giving me the basis for a story. After sending the finished piece to Don O'Rourke, I followed up by walking to his desk and telling him where I'd be having lunch and why.

"Better wait to talk to Oscar until after you eat," Don said. "If he poisoned Vinnie he might slip something into your coleslaw."

"Not the coleslaw," I said. "He's very proud of the coleslaw. He's more likely to sprinkle strychnine on the French fries."

The Northern Exposure, in a high-buck district on Grand Avenue, had one of the city's pricier luncheon menus. The owner,

Oscar Peterson, grew up in Norway and his speech bore a strong Scandinavian influence. In fact, his accent would make him the perfect caller for a square dance club named for Ole and Lena.

Oscar always greeted his customers at the door with a wide smile and a vigorous handshake before passing them on to the hostess for seating. I mimicked his joviality and said I hoped he'd stop at my table while I was there, and he promised he would. I was about halfway through my batter-fried walleye with fries and coleslaw when Oscar plopped down in the chair across the table.

"So how ya been then, Mitch?" he asked. "Ain't seen ya here for a long time."

"Been keeping busy," I said. "If you'd move your restaurant down to Sixth Street you'd see me more often."

"Yah, I s'pose I'd get more business downtown, but I kinda like it up here. Does somethin' special bring you in today then?"

I took a sip of coffee before I answered. "I'm working on the Vinnie Luciano murder story. I'm gathering the reactions of prominent people who knew him."

"Oh, yah? Well, I don't know I'm so prominent, but my reaction is I won't miss the old bastard."

"Why's that?"

"He was greedy. He gobbled up all the business from the goddamn politicians and sports teams in the city and didn't leave nothin' for nobody else. You probably don't want to print that."

"You don't think all those people went to King Vinnie's by choice?"

"He went after 'em," Oscar said. "He was like a goddamn Marine recruiter. Sucked up to them with a lot of special deals and that kinda stuff. He coulda left a few for the rest of us, ya know. And now he was goin' into the State Fair to boot."

"You have a State Fair booth, don't you?" I asked.

"You bet'cha. And I aim to protect it."

I took a bite of walleye, chewed it and swallowed. "How were you planning to protect it from Vinnie?" I said.

Oscar frowned. "You ain't thinkin' I'd be crazy enough to kill my competition now, are ya, Mitch?"

"I'm just asking what you'd do for protection."

His voice got louder. "That's my business, and it ain't for the press. But you can bet'cher boots it don't include no murder."

"*Any* murder," I said in a reflex blurt.

"What'd you say?"

"Nothing important. I'm glad to hear you wouldn't commit murder, Oscar."

"You better believe it, Mitch," he said. "Now I better get back to the door. You enjoy your lunch then and don't worry about the check."

I thanked Oscar for his time and for picking up the tab, and he walked away. I wanted to believe him, but the quick denial without an actual accusation left me unconvinced. But what the hell—the walleye and the coleslaw were delicious and the price was right.

*   *   *

"How'd it go at the Northern Exposure?" Al asked as we sipped our late afternoon coffee in the *Daily Dispatch* cafeteria.

I replayed my conversation with Oscar and explained my uncertainty about the truth of his denial. "He got defensive real quick," I said. "A little too quick."

"So you can't write him off as a suspect."

"Afraid not. So how was your assignment?"

"Boring. Shot a grab-and-grin at City Hall with the mayor handing a plaque to the big-shot developer building that new condo tower on the East Side. The day wasn't a total loss, though."

"How so?" I asked.

"When I got back here, I had two e-mails from that woman I told you about. The one that hung around at the signing."

"Willow?"

"Yeah, Willow. Told me how much she loved the book and what a great photographer I am. Good for the old ego. I sent back a thank you note."

"Always nice to be appreciated," I said. "You can't have too many friends."

"She's sexy, too," Al said.

"That makes it even more fun."

Chapter Nine

Stonewalls and Willows

MY PROBLEM WITH ALCOHOL began a dozen years ago when my wife and baby boy were killed in a collision with a jack-knifing eighteen-wheeler. I began pouring down the booze to blot out the pain but the drunken haze only increased the agony. I had sunk deep into an ever-darkening pit when Al and Carol persuaded me to go to rehab. Since then I've stayed dry with the help of an Alcoholics Anonymous group that meets within walking distance of my apartment every Monday night.

My most reliable crutch at AA is Jayne Halvorson, the mother of two teenage daughters who fled to St. Paul from an abusive husband in North Dakota. Jayne and I chat over a glass of ginger ale at a neighborhood bar called Herbie's after every Monday night meeting. More often than not, Jayne can look at a problem that has me stymied and come up with a workable solution. For example, without her assistance (and insistence) I never would have pushed myself into a jewelry store to buy an engagement ring for Martha. The last time I'd gone out on that limb, I'd found the intended ring recipient between the sheets with an old high school boyfriend.

"You didn't sound sincere tonight when you told us that everything was going well in your life," Jayne said after the usual Herbie's small talk.

"Most things are okay," I said.

"And what things are not?"

"Only one, really. The detective from the Falcon Heights PD. I can't get anything out of her for a story about Vinnie Luciano's murder. Not even a hint as to whether she's looking at a suspect or a person of interest. Normally, investigators will let out little scraps of information as the case develops, but this one's lips are clamped as tight as a pit bull's jaws on a mailman's leg."

"Have you tried schmoozing her with the old Mitch Mitchell charm?" Jayne said.

"I've tried the 'I'm your buddy' smile, I've tried flattery, I've tried the old teamwork routine, I've tried asking her to lunch," I said. "It's like banging my head against a steel door."

"Is she that way with all reporters?"

"Apparently. I haven't seen any comments from her on TV or in any other paper."

"So it's not personal?"

"No, I think it's psychological. Maybe she's been burned by a reporter, or maybe she's just paranoid."

Jayne took a long swig of ginger ale. "Maybe it's time to go over her head."

"What do you mean?" I said.

"Talk to the chief. Describe to him how other departments—St. Paul PD, for example—deal with the press and tell him you would appreciate the same courtesy from the Falcon Heights PD."

"The chief is a her, not a him, and I suspect she might be as tough to deal with as KGB."

"KGB?"

"Those are the investigator's initials, and they fit her personality. She goes by K.G. Barnes. I don't know what the K and the G are for."

Jayne drained her glass. "Maybe the chief will surprise you if you approach her diplomatically."

"Maybe," I said. "It's worth a try."

"Remember, the key word is 'diplomatically.'"

"You know me."

"That's why I'm reminding you." She put enough money on the table to cover her half of the tab and stood up, signaling it was time to go home.

* * *

MARTHA GREETED ME with the usual hugs and kisses, and Sherlock Holmes welcomed me by winding himself around my ankles until I pushed him away with my foot. After Martha and I swapped stories about our days' work—her day had been much more productive than mine—we sat down to watch the ten o'clock news.

The TV was flashing the usual montage of car crashes, fires, and violent crimes, so I was half dozing when Martha said, "Oh, look, there's Al."

There was his back anyway, at the presentation of a plaque to a developer in the mayor's office. The voice describing the event was that of Trish Valentine, who was shown a moment later wearing a blouse with three open buttons at the top. It must have been really hot in the mayor's office.

"Al has all the fun," I said. "He gets to stare down Trish's cleavage and he gets e-mails from a woman who thinks he's the greatest photographer since Ansel Adams."

"Al is getting e-mails from a woman?" Martha said.

I told her about Willow hanging out at Al's book signing and her two follow-up e-mails praising his work.

"Does Carol know about this woman?" Martha asked.

"Don't know. Anyway, it's no big deal."

"It might be bigger than you think."

"Al is not going to run away with Willow just because she likes his work."

"I'm more concerned about Willow running away with Al," Martha said.

A Killing Fair

I decided that this was not the time to mention Al's description of Willow as "sexy."

*　*　*

TUESDAY WAS MY DAY OFF and I had two options. One, I could hunt for an apartment; two, I could go to the State Fair. This was a no-brainer—no landlord would have a Pronto Pup stand in his yard, and we still had a whole month to find a new place and move. I figured I could justify my choice to Martha by talking to Lorrie Gardner about the aftermath of Vinnie Luciano's dramatic death on the fairgrounds.

In deference to Lorrie's concern about parking on the grass, I left my car way up behind the grandstand in the Fox Lot and hiked about three blocks in eighty-degree heat to her office in the Admin Building. On the way, I snagged my first Pronto Pup of the day, and I had just nipped the last bite off the stick when I greeted Lorrie at her desk. She was wearing white shorts and a skimpy blue tank top that left almost as little to the imagination as a bikini. Obviously the air conditioning hadn't been fixed.

"What brings you out here again?" she asked. "Besides Pronto Pups, that is."

"Wanted to see how you're doing," I said. "Are you over the shock of the Square Meal disaster?"

"I still can't touch anything on a stick. Which is good for my waistline because I used to try anything and everything, but it's not fun to get the shivers every time I walk past the stage at Heritage Square. I might have to stay away from that part of the fairgrounds for the rest of summer unless—"

"How about the square dancers?" I said, shutting off the torrent. "Are they still doing their thing on the other stage?"

"Oh, yes, of course they are. Scott still has them dancing up a storm twice a day."

"How can they do that every day? Don't any of them work?"

"A lot of them are retired. Didn't you notice all the white hair? The ones still working take a personal day or a vacation day. It's not always the same couples dancing every day. They switch off and—"

"But Scott's here calling every day?" I said.

"He's one of those high-tech types who work at home," Lorrie said. "He does something with numbers; I'm not sure what exactly, so he can set his own hours."

"Lucky him. Is his wife one of the dancers?"

"Scott's not married. I think he was married once but it didn't work out. I don't know the details and I don't want—"

"So he's divorced?"

"I guess. Why are you so interested in Scott?"

"I'm a reporter. I'm interested in everybody. If you'll recall, I asked first about you."

"Oh, right. You did ask about me. Thank you for that."

"You're welcome. And now I'm asking about Tommy, the kid who got whacked on the head and lost his Fairchild suit to the man who delivered the poison."

"Tommy quit the next day," Lorrie said. "He was shook up pretty bad. His father was bullshit about the kid getting clubbed. Said he was thinking about suing the State Fair but so far we haven't heard from any lawyer."

"Think Tommy would talk to me about what it's like to be personally involved in a spectacular murder?" I asked.

"I guess you could ask him. I've got his phone number. I can give it to you if—"

"Please. I'd appreciate it."

She wrote Tommy Grayson's phone number on a scrap of paper, talking all the while about the difficulty she'd had finding a replacement Fairchild with the fair already under way. I took the paper, squelched her verbal stream with a "thank you" and set off to buy another Pronto Pup. It was, after all, almost time for lunch.

* * *

"HOW WAS YOUR DAY OFF?" I asked Al on Wednesday morning as he arrived at my desk bearing two cups of coffee.

"It was okay," he said. "I got some stuff done around the house but mostly tried to stay out of the heat. Oh, and I got three more e-mails from my Number One fan."

"Willow?"

"Who else? She's just full of praise for the book, and she's finding deep meanings I never thought about in some of my shots."

"Sounds like your relationship with Willow is beginning to take root."

"Well, it doesn't hurt to branch out and make a new friend once in a while."

"Does Carol know you're branching out with a new friend you happen to think is sexy?" I asked.

"It's not really worth mentioning at home," Al said. "We're just having a little Internet fun. So, what did you do yesterday?"

I told him about my trip to the State Fair, my consumption of two Pronto Pups and the chitchat with Lorrie about the square dancers and their caller. "I didn't tell Lorrie that Martha and I saw the caller dining with the club president's wife in the Red Mill Saturday night."

"Oh, yeah? You haven't told me about that either. Where was the club president?"

"He's the owner and artistic director at Parkside Players, remember? They had a show that night, so he must have been there."

"Wonder if he knew who was having dinner with his wife."

"I should have gone over to the caller yesterday morning and asked."

"A dedicated reporter who wants all the news that fits in print would have done that."

"That news might not have been fit to print. Anyhow, this dedicated reporter figured quizzing Lorrie was enough business to conduct on his day off. I was really there for a Pronto Pup and a walk through the dairy barn." Having grown up on a southern Minnesota dairy farm, I still have an affinity for Holsteins and Ayrshires that draws me to the State Fair dairy barn every year.

"Okay. So, what's up today? Anything I can tag along on?"

"Well, I get to start off my day by calling KGB," I said. "Would you like to take my place on that one?"

"Deliver me from ever talking to that woman again," he said. "Guess I'll go see if the boss has any exciting assignments for me."

"I'm hoping to have lunch at Luigi's House of Italy. It's not as pricey as Northern Exposure."

"If the timing works out, I'll join you."

"Okay. Don't take any wooden e-mails."

"Only if the wood is from a Willow."

I drained my coffee cup, took a deep breath, picked up the phone and punched in the Falcon Heights PD number. The man who answered said Detective Barnes was not available and offered to take a message. I asked where Detective Barnes was and he said this information was not for release to the press. I sighed and left a message.

I was making some additional routine phone checks when Don O'Rourke appeared at my side. "I need you to cover the police beat," he said. "Augie called in sick this morning."

This meant spending the rest of the morning in the press office at the police station. I'm often sent to fill in as police reporter when Augie Augustine is felled by one of his bouts with a chronic illness commonly known as a hangover. Usually this is fun because I get to go through the night reports and write about the weird problems encountered by police officers during those hours.

This day was no exception, starting with a report about a drunken man who was arrested while raising hell with customers and employees at a mini-market the previous morning. He appeared in court in the afternoon, pleaded not guilty and was released into the custody of his girl friend. Shortly after midnight he was arrested again—this time for beating up the solicitous girl friend with her hair dryer. You know the old saying: no good deed shall go unpunished.

I had just punched the computer key that sent my story to Don when Homicide Detective Curtis Brown walked into the office.

"Being spanked again?" Brownie said. The standing joke between us was that being sent to the police station was punishment for a reporting mistake.

"That's right," I said. "I'm being punished for not having solved Vinnie Luciano's murder."

"Hey, what's with that case anyway? Your last two stories didn't say a damn thing," Brownie said.

"That's because there's not a damn thing to say. I haven't found the smoking gun—or in this case the dripping poison bottle— and I'm getting absolutely nothing from the Falcon Heights police."

"Is their investigator that tight with her reports?"

"She's so tight she makes you look like Santa Claus." Brownie was infamous for his caution when talking to the media, but during a homicide investigation he would release enough tidbits to keep the story alive.

"I'll have to more careful," Brownie said.

"God save us from that," I said.

"Watch it, Mitch. You could be booked on a charge of praying in a public building."

"I'd pray out loud on the Capitol steps if it would loosen the tongue of Detective K.G. Barnes."

"Please do whatever it takes. Vinnie was a VIP in this city and some of us in the department would like to know what's going on with the homicide investigation."

"Maybe you could talk to Detective Barnes, cop-to-cop."

"Good idea," Brownie said. "But I have a better one," he added with a smile. "Have a good day, Mitch." Brownie turned and went out the door before I could ask about his idea.

My cell phone rang at about 12:45, just as I was wrapping things up at the police station. It was Al, saying he could pick me up with a staff car for lunch. The House of Italy was on Payne Avenue, a short ride from downtown to the East Side.

The House of Italy was smaller in both dining area and menu prices than the Northern Exposure. The owner, Luigi Bunatori, and his wife, Francesca, lived above the restaurant and sometimes invited special guests to eat in their private dining room. These special guests were usually politicians looking for a quiet place to discuss city and state issues.

Luigi Bunatori's custom was to greet male customers with a bone-crushing handshake, wave in the general direction of the dining room and say, "Sit anywhere there's a clean table." When we were met at the door by a tall, blonde woman, we speculated that Luigi was entertaining someone special on the second floor. The hostess who pointed us toward an empty booth confirmed this suspicion but said she was not permitted to identify the special guest. I said I hoped we could chat with Luigi for a few minutes, and she promised to relay the request.

I had finished a cup of minestrone and was starting on my meatball sandwich when Luigi arrived at our booth. He slid in beside Al, facing me.

"How was the soup?" Luigi asked after shaking hands all around. We both said it was wonderful and he gave us a big smile. "So, Amelia says you want to chat with me. What's it about?"

"We're still working on the Vinnie Luciano murder story," I said. "I'm just wondering about your reaction to his death."

"Me?" Luigi said. "Why should I have any reaction to Vinnie's death? Vinnie and me had nothing in common."

"You and Vinnie's both draw a lot of high-profile customers," I said. "I thought maybe you considered him a competitor for that sort of business."

"Are you kiddin'? How could a little place like this compete with a huge operation like Vinnie's? You could put this whole restaurant into King Vinnie's kitchen. They got their crowd and we got ours, and ours is a hell of a lot smaller. King Vinnie's is way out of my league."

"Did Vinnie ever try to lure away any of your crowd?" Al said.

"Jesus, you guys are asking as many questions as that detective from Falcon Heights," Luigi said. "What's with the inquisition any way?"

"You were questioned by Detective Barnes?" I said.

"Yeah, I think that's what she said her name was. A real bitch, that woman. So now what am I, some kind of suspect in Vinnie's murder just because I was at the fair that day?"

"You were at the fair?" I said. "Were you where you saw Vinnie die?"

"Christ, no," Luigi said. "I wouldn't go anywhere near where that asshole was showing off. Pardon my French."

"You didn't like Vinnie?" Al asked.

"I don't like all these questions," Luigi said. "Like I told that detective, I had nothin' to do with Vinnie Luciano, dead or alive. Now if you'll excuse me, I'll get back to my guest." He stomped away and disappeared through the door leading to the stairs.

"Take your time with your sandwich," I said. "If we hang around long enough we might see his guest leave."

So we dawdled and had a second cup of coffee. We dawdled some more and had dessert and a third cup of coffee. We were about to give up the stakeout when two middle-aged men wearing dark business suits emerged from the stairway door and walked briskly to the exit.

"I should know the guy on the right," Al said. "Who is he?"

"Mark Peterson," I said. "The attorney general of the state of Minnesota."

"Good to have friends in high places."

"Especially if you're suspected of taking somebody down," I said.

Chapter Ten

The Chief Problem

THE MESSAGE LIGHT on my phone was blinking. I pressed the play button. "This is Detective Barnes," the message said. "Call us." Oh, goody, the royal "us." And her voice was cold enough to freeze the Mississippi River in August.

I punched in the number and was immediately transferred to KGB. "Hi," I said when she answered. "It's Mitch from the *Daily Dispatch*."

"Are you proud of yourself?" she said.

"That's a strange question. Why do you ask?"

"I thought you'd be bursting with pride after going over our head."

"Going where? I'm sorry, but you've lost me." Not to mention mixing a plural modifier with a singular noun.

"Going over our head and getting the St. Paul police chief to talk to our chief about releasing information. Are you proud of that?"

Oh, my god, I thought. Brownie's better idea. "I never asked him to do that," I said. "If the city chief called your chief, it wasn't my idea." Technically this was true.

"So you're an innocent man?" KGB said.

"Absolutely," I said.

"And we both know that this country's jails are full of innocent men, don't we, Mr. Mitchell?"

"I'm telling you the truth, Detective Barnes. You're giving me credit for having way more influence with the police than I actually have."

"Really?" she said. It was more of a snort than a question.

"Really," I said. "Reporters can only dream about having that kind of power."

"Well, it looks like your dream has come true and your pajamas are wet. But the fact is there haven't been any developments in this case to report. If you don't believe us, we'll transfer you to Chief Tubb and you can ask her in person."

I didn't appreciate having my figurative dream turned into a wet one so I decided to go on the offensive. "What about the people you've been talking to?" I said. "For example, is Luigi Bunatori a suspect, or a person of interest or what?"

There was a moment of silence before she answered. "What makes you think we talked to Luigi Bunatori?"

"He said you did. Can you confirm that? I won't publish his name."

Another moment of silence. "You can say we have talked to a person who knew the victim," KGB said. "You can even say we've talked to several persons who knew the victim. However, they are not suspects. These were informational interviews."

"So they're not even persons of interest?" I said.

A third momentary pause. "One of them is."

"Would that be Luigi? As I said, I won't publish the name."

"That's all we're saying at this time," she said. "We're not identifying any individual as fitting any category, Mr. Mitchell, and Chief Tubb will back us on that. Now, are there any other questions?"

"Not at this time," I said. "Thanks for the call."

"Have a nice day," KGB said. She made that routine signoff sound like the curse of the mummy's tomb.

I ended the call, and without even putting down the receiver, I punched in the private number for Detective Curtis Brown. After two minutes on automatic hold, the Muzak was interrupted with, "Homicidebrown."

"Dailydispatchmitchell," I said. "Tell me, how did you persuade your chief to call the chief at Falcon Heights?"

"When did that happen?" Brownie asked.

"Very recently. KGB sounded really pissed about it but she did pass out a tiny crumb of information."

"Well, what a lucky coincidence for you. I guess the chief has a really strong interest in that case."

"Anyway, thanks for the assist."

"I don't know what you're talking about. Have a good day, Mitch."

So, if Brownie was denying putting the bug in the chief's ear, no way would I blow his cover. But I would mention to Al that we could use a flattering shot of Brownie at the next homicide scene.

I wondered who else KGB had questioned. Fred McDonald of the Teamsters had laughed me out of his office before I could ask about talking to the investigator. Oscar Peterson of the Northern Exposure had clammed up and walked away before I could ask about meeting with the cops. And even if they hadn't talked to KGB before I got to them, there had been plenty of time for a subsequent meeting. Was there a diplomatic way of getting back to McDonald and Peterson and inquiring? I couldn't think of one.

And there was still another possible suspect to consider. What excuse could I use to meet with Vinnie's cousin Vito. It was too late to use the reaction story scam on him. He'd expressed his reaction, whether it was genuine or not, at the funeral.

Somehow I had to dig up something for a story the next day. Readers' interest in the Vinnie Luciano murder was waning because I'd written so little about it. Already my stories had been moved from page one to the Local section front. Soon they'd be put in the back pages with the truss ads, which, as Don often told reporters, was the dead-end depository for stories that lacked reader interest.

I did not want my stories to be in the back pages with the truss ads. Come to think of it, I wasn't sure the paper still carried truss ads.

* * *

MARTHA GOT HOME LATE, wearing a weary look and bearing a box emitting a strong smell of pizza. She had gone to look at an apartment after work and was too tired to cook. She opened the box to reveal a two-way pizza—one side vegetarian for her and the other half crammed with sausage and pepperoni for me.

Martha would have been willing to end the hunt by making a deposit on this apartment, but she was aced out by a another hunter. While the rental agent was showing Martha the kitchen, a woman who'd looked at the apartment earlier in the day called to say she'd take it.

"That's a bitch," I said. "You finally find a winner and somebody grabs it right out from under your feet."

"Story of my life," Martha said. "But the agent said she's got something else I might like just as much. I told her we've only got thirty days left in this apartment, and we made a date to look at it Saturday so that you can come along."

"Wonderful. Nothing like togetherness on the weekend."

"Togetherness is especially good when you're as sick of looking at apartments as I am."

"I've noticed that the pressure of the hunt is wearing you down." Martha had been dropping off to sleep the minute she hit the bed, which wasn't her usual pattern.

"If we put what's left of the pizza in the fridge and go to bed right now, I might not go to sleep so fast," she said.

We did and she didn't.

* * *

"ANY MORE E-MAIL BARKS from your favorite tree?" I asked Al as we sipped coffee in the *Daily Dispatch* cafeteria Thursday morning. I had put in a call to KGB, who once again was "not available" according to her telephone guardian, and decided not to wait by the phone in breathless anticipation of her response to the message I'd left.

"A couple," Al said. "Willow is psychoanalyzing my pictures, one by one, trying to find what she calls their deeper meaning. She also offered to buy me lunch today. Do you think I should go?"

"Does she know you're married?"

"I think I've made that clear."

"So maybe she's after the depth of your psychological meaning and not the shallowness of your physical body?"

"I doubt she's after this body. But I think I'll pass on the lunch invitation."

"You're probably smart keeping this a cyber friendship," I said. "Wives have been known to get jealous and do unspeakable things to husbands they suspect of sharing more than a sandwich with another woman."

"Carol wouldn't do anything unspeakable," Al said. "She'd be speaking the whole time she was stabbing me."

"Sharp words to go with a sharp knife?"

"You get the point."

The light on my phone was blinking when I returned to my desk. I checked the message, expecting to hear KGB's icy voice. Instead the caller was a man who said his name was Ozzie and rattled off a number.

"Ozzie?" I said out loud. "Who the hell is Ozzie?"

"Sorry," said Corinne Ramey, who was at the nearest desk. "I don't know who Ozzie is."

"I was talking to myself," I said. "Sorry I was so loud."

"Isn't talking to yourself one of the first signs of dementia?" she said.

"I'd be crazy to answer that," I said as I punched in the number for Ozzie Whoever He Was.

The voice that answered said, "Vinnie's Steakhouse, Ozzie speaking."

Of course. It was Vinnie's bartender, Ozzie Bergman. Was forgetting the names of people you've interviewed another sign of dementia?

"This is Mitch at the *Daily Dispatch*," I said. "What's up?"

"You said to call you if I had anything interesting," Ozzie said.

"I did. What have you got?"

"A new boss."

What the hell? Could Vinnie's family have sold the restaurant that fast? "What happened?" I asked. "Who is it?"

"Vinnie's lawyer read his will to the family yesterday. Would you believe he left the restaurant to his cousin Vito, the guy he kicked out twenty years ago?"

"You're kidding. Why would he do that?"

"Don't know," Ozzie said. "Vinnie's oldest boy, Louie, called and told me about it this morning. Said it was a kick in the ass to him and his brother and sister. Last they knew, they were all named in the will to get equal shares in the restaurant."

"So this must have been a recent change?" I said.

"I guess. Louie said the kids are thinking about contesting the will."

"Have you talked to Vito since you got the news?"

"He ain't been in. Me and Max, the manager, are still running the joint."

"Max and I," I said.

"What about you and Max?"

"The correct way to say that is . . . oh, forget it. I'm having verbal knee-jerks."

"Who'd you say is a jerk?"

"Nobody's a jerk—except maybe me." I asked Ozzie for phone numbers for Vito and Louie. After reciting the numbers, he said, "Hope this helps with what you're doing."

"You don't know how much," I said. I thanked him and smiled as I hung up. I now had a story for the next day and a reason to contact cousin Vito. And cousin Vito now had a clear motive for murder.

Chapter Eleven

Will Power

It's a goddamn outrage, that's what it is." Louie Luciano was shouting so loud I had to hold the phone three inches away from my ear. "The son of a bitch must have tricked Pops or blackmailed him somehow. There's something crooked going on here. I know damn well there is."

"Well, there's murder for one thing," I said. "Is Vito capable of that?" I had started my day by calling Louie for a reaction and I was getting an accusatory blast that would require a bit of editing for publication.

"That old bastard is capable of anything," Louie said. "I'm not saying Vito killed Pops, but I sure as hell think he did something dirty to get Pops to change his will."

"You mentioned blackmail. How could your dad be blackmailed?"

"Plenty of ways. You've got no idea what goes on behind the scenes in the restaurant business."

"Such as?"

"Persuasive offers to inspectors for one thing. Under-the-table cash deals with suppliers for another."

This was getting better and better. "By 'persuasive offers to inspectors' do you mean bribes?" I said.

Louie was silent for a moment. "I ain't taking this any farther with you," he said in a quieter tone. "If you print anything about inspectors I'll deny I ever said it."

"Okay, let's go off the record for a minute. If I promise not to quote you in the paper, will you tell me what you mean by persuasive offers?"

Louie paused again before he said, "I mean crossing the inspectors' palms with cash to get them to look the other way if they find a minor violation or two. I ain't saying Pops ever did that, but it can be done."

"How would Vito know if Vinnie did that?" I asked.

"He worked at King Vinnie's for five years," Louie said. "And I bet you anything he kept tabs on what Pops was doing there even after Pops kicked his ass out." Again he was shouting and I moved the phone away from my ear.

"Okay, back on the record. When did your dad change his will?"

"Not even two months ago. The new one is dated June 10th."

"So what are you going to do about the will?"

"Me and my brother and sister are going to meet with a lawyer today to talk about contesting the goddamn thing. The son of a bitch ain't getting away this shit."

I choked back my response to his grammar and said, "What time are you meeting the lawyer?"

"Four o'clock. Why?"

"I plan to call you to find out what you decide," I said. "Or can I count on you to call me?"

"I guess I can call you," Louie said. "Unless the lawyer thinks I shouldn't."

"If I was your lawyer I'd want the public to know about the lawsuit."

"Well, you ain't my lawyer so I'll see what he has to say about it."

I gave Louie the numbers for my office phone, cell phone and home phone, and wished him the best of luck.

When I put the phone down I realized my head was throbbing, probably from being subjected to Louie's high-volume remarks. Confident that the headache would go away quickly, I walked over to Don O'Rourke's desk and told him what I had coming for a story.

"About time you got something worth printing," Don said. "Make it sing."

Before starting to write, I called the Falcon Heights PD to get a comment from Detective K.G. Barnes. I was told Detective Barnes was not available at this time. Surprise, surprise. I left a message saying I was looking for her comment on Vinnie Luciano's will.

The return call from KGB came less than a minute later. This actually was a surprise.

"What about the will?" she asked without wasting time identifying herself.

"Is this Detective K.G. Barnes?" I said.

"You know it is. What about the will?"

"Do you think it has a bearing on Vinnie's murder?" I said.

"We don't know anything about the will," she said, using that damn royal "we" again. "Why should it have anything to do with the killing?"

So the tight-lipped detective of Falcon Heights hadn't been told about the will. I was tempted to play her game and invite her to read about it in the paper. But I wanted her reaction, so I explained that Vito Luciano had recently replaced Vinnie's children as inheritor of Vinnie's Steakhouse.

"Are you sure of that?" KGB said.

"As sure as I am that walleyes poop in the river," I said.

"That's disgusting."

"What, that Vinnie cut the kids out of the restaurant?"

"No, your gross comment about the walleyes."

"Didn't mean to shock you," I said. "Just trying to clearly illustrate a point."

"The illustration is very clear and very disgusting," she said. "Now tell us how you think Vito getting the restaurant affects the murder investigation?"

I wondered if she was being deliberately obtuse or if she was as dumb as that sounded. "Don't you think that gives Vito a motive for murder?" I said. "And isn't the timing—only about seven weeks after the will was revised—just a little bit suspicious?"

"We think that's a pretty long stretch."

"Don't you think it's worth questioning him?"

"We've already questioned Vito."

"Really? As a family member or a person of interest?"

"As we told you previously, we're not identifying anyone as anything at this time. Now if you have no more questions, we'll say goodbye and have a nice day."

"I didn't say I have no more questions," I said.

"Goodbye and have a nice day," said KGB.

When I put down the phone, the headache was still there. If anything, it was more intense. Talking to KGB had that effect on me.

"Bitch!" I said.

"Stonewalled again?" said Corinne Ramey.

"Not completely," I said. "This time she did drop me a pebble."

"Maybe next time she'll give you a rock."

"Only if she can bounce it off my head."

When I'd finished writing my story, my head still felt like a rock the size of a Buick really had bounced off it, so I hunted through the jumble in my desk drawers for a bottle of aspirin that had to be there somewhere. The hunt proved as futile as a pack of hounds pursuing a fox with a rocket on its tail. Apparently I had consumed the last pill and forgotten to renew the supply. I told Don about my problem and asked if I had time to visit the drug store on Kellogg Boulevard, about three blocks away, before my next assignment.

"We can probably live without your butt in your chair for twenty minutes," Don said. "While you're out, take a run up to

Candyland and bring back a bag of caramel corn." Candyland, which produces the world's sweetest and tastiest caramel corn, is a couple of blocks farther up Kellogg.

"That'll take at least another ten minutes," I said.

"We'll suffer through it. Bring a big bag." He dug out a ten-dollar bill and thrust it toward me.

"Can I keep the change as a tip?"

"My tip would be to remember that I'm your boss," Don said.

"Good tip," I said.

The painkiller display was at the rear of the drug store, close to the pharmacy counter. As I plucked a bottle of the cheapest aspirin off the shelf I heard a male voice from behind the counter say, "Hey, Mr. Mitchell, how ya doing today?"

The owner of the voice had an oversupply of flesh on his belly and a shortage of hair on his forehead. He looked familiar, but a lot of people look familiar to me, and I couldn't quite place him. "Hi," I said. "I'm, uh, doing fine."

The man laughed. "I'll bet you don't know me with my clothes on," he said.

"Would I know you with them off?" I asked.

"You'd know me in square dance clothes. We met at the State Fair the other day. I'm Erik Erickson, president of the Oles and Lenas. Remember?"

I did remember. I also remembered seeing his wife having dinner with his club's caller in a dark and distant dining room a few nights previous. "Oh, yeah, sorry," I said. "You do you look different without the red-and-white getup."

"Yeah, well this is my day job. I try to make enough here to cover what I'm losing with Parkside Players."

"I hope you'll get to where you're breaking even. My fiancée and I are doing our best to help. We're coming to see your show tomorrow night."

"Great. You know, there's a bar upstairs from the theater. Maybe you'd like to join me and my wife for a drink afterward."

"Maybe," I said. "There'll be four of us. Al, the photographer you saw at the fairgrounds, and his wife will be with us." Had I really heard this educated man say "me and my wife?"

"We'll have a party. Just hang around in your seats until I get things squared away after the show. You can keep Joyce company while she waits."

She didn't need additional company a week ago, I thought. I thanked Erik for the invitation and said we'd see him then. As I walked up Kellogg toward Candyland, I wondered if Joyce would recognize Martha and me as fellow Saturday night diners.

* * *

THE WORKDAY WAS DONE and I was sitting next to Martha ready to watch the 5:30 news when I realized the Luciano family had not called about their meeting with their lawyer, which should have been finished by this time. I took my cell phone into the kitchen and punched in Louie's number.

The woman who answered told me that her dad was away at a meeting.

"Do you know where I can reach him?" I asked.

"Probably in O'Halloran's bar," she said. "That's where they usually meet." She gave me Louie's cell phone number, and I thanked her, signed off and called the number.

"Yeah?" said the voice that answered.

"Louie?" I said.

"Who else would answer this phone?"

"Good point. This is Mitch Mitchell at the *Daily Dispatch*. What did your family decide about contesting the will?"

"We're suing his ass," Louie said. "We're gonna get our restaurant back from that thieving bastard."

"Who is your lawyer?" I asked.

"The Bulldog."

"Doug Riley?"

"You got it," he said. Doug Riley was known as the Bulldog because when he got a grip on a case he didn't let go until he'd won at least a piece of what he was after.

"Is he there with you?" I asked.

"Yeah, we're all getting shit-faced together."

"Can I talk to him?"

"Why not? He's just coming out of the john. I'll hand him the phone."

"Hey, Mitch, how are ya?" Riley said. "Hang on a second while I finish zipping up my fly." Riley was as smooth as olive oil in court but not so much in person.

I quizzed the lawyer long enough to confirm the family would be contesting Vinnie's will and to get the details on when they were filing. When we finished, I said, "Will you do me one favor?"

"What's that?" the Bulldog asked.

"Don't call the TV stations."

"Why would I call those morons?"

"Good point. Thanks for your time."

I walked back into the living room and sat down next to Martha. "Why do you have that cat-who-swallowed-the-canary smile on your face?" she asked.

"I just got a fresh lead for tomorrow's Vinnie Luciano story," I said. "And I'm the only reporter who's got it."

Chapter Twelve

New Lease on Life

M Y PLAN TO INTERVIEW Vito Luciano Saturday morning went down the drain when Augie Augustine again called in sick. Apparently he'd had a really rousing Friday night party with his buddy Jim Beam and was paying for his fun with a headache and nausea. I was called upon to co-pay for his binge by filling his chair at the police station.

The best story in the reports file involved a bank robber who really treasured his Milwaukee Brewers baseball cap. Posing as a polite customer, he took off his Brewers cap and laid it on the counter when he greeted the female teller. The robber left the bank with a sack full of money in his hand and nothing on his head, but he returned to pick up the cap long after the teller had hit the alarm. The forgetful Brewers fan was still adjusting his cap when two cops with weapons at the ready blocked his second exit. You can't make this stuff up.

Before I wrote the police stories, I knocked out a piece about Vinnie Luciano's family suing to contest his will. Eddy Gambrell, who sat in Don O'Rourke's chair on Saturday, was delighted to get something fresh on the Luciano story. "I hear the Falcon Heights cops aren't giving you much to work with," Eddy said.

"Their investigation seems to be moving with the speed of a glacier," I said. "If they don't turn up something pretty soon they'll have to put Vinnie's murder in their cold case file."

My work day ended at one o'clock, and my real day started an hour later when Martha and I approached a two-story brick duplex on Lexington Avenue. We were scheduled to meet the rental agent, Rosie Reynolds, who was going to show us the vacant side of the duplex and, if we decided to take the unit, introduce us to the resident on the other side.

"Looks nice," I said as we waited for Rosie. A porch with a wooden rail ran all the way across the front. The white paint on the rail was clean and fresh and the gray paint on the porch floor wasn't chipped or scuffed. The white doors and window casings also appeared to have been painted recently, as did a gray wooden handicapped ramp beside the porch steps.

"What's with the ramp?" I asked.

"Don't know," said Martha. "Rosie didn't mention that."

"Maybe ADA requires it for all rental units. You're a lawyer, you should know."

"You're a reporter, you should find out."

A few minutes later, we were sitting on the porch steps, half dozing in the eighty-something heat, when a black BMW pulled up behind my blue Honda Civic. A short, plump woman who I guessed to be in her early fifties stepped out and joined us at the foot of the steps. She was dressed for the weather in a scoop neck dress made of almost see-through material.

"Mitch, this is Rosie," Martha said. "Rosie, this is my fiancé, Mitch."

"You write for the paper, don't you?" Rosie said as she gave my hand a vigorous shake. I confessed that I did.

"Who do you think killed that guy at the fair?" she said. "There hasn't been much about it in the paper since the day it happened."

"That's because we haven't found out much about it," I said. "I don't have any idea who did the killing and the Falcon Heights cops don't either."

"It's scary," Rosie said. "Makes you think twice every time you bite into something on a stick out there."

"The Pronto Pups are safe. At least the dozen I've sampled so far this year were."

"You eat those things? The grease they fry'em in is older than I am."

"That's what gives them their unique flavor," I said. "Your plain old corn dog cooked in fresh oil can't compete with a real honest-to-god Pronto Pup."

"Could we look at the house please?" said my vegetarian fiancée. "Listening to comparisons of cooking grease has my stomach rolling like a cement mixer."

"My opinion is cast in concrete," I said.

Rosie gave me a long look and groaned before taking a key from her purse, unlocking the door and waving us in. "We'll take the tour and then stop in next door to meet the neighbor," she said. The bit about meeting the neighbor raised a question in my mind. Would we have to past muster with this person in order to rent the place?

Entering the broad, high-ceilinged foyer was like walking into a steaming swamp. As previously noted, the outdoor temperature was at least eighty degrees. The air trapped inside the closed up duplex must have been close to a hundred.

"Does this place have central air?" I asked as I wiped a sudden outbreak of sweat off my forehead.

"No, but it has window units on both floors," Rosie said. "Obviously we don't run them when the house is empty."

"Obviously," I said.

Rosie led us through the house, pointing out the beauty of the oak woodwork and the number of tall windows that allowed a lot of light to enter. *And*, I thought, *a lot of cold air to enter in the winter*. On the first floor were a living room with beige wall-to-wall carpeting, and a kitchen, a dining room and a half-bath with beige linoleum floors. Upstairs were two pale-blue-carpeted bedrooms that shared a tiled bathroom, where the temperature was several degrees hotter. I saw air conditioners in the windows of only the dining room and the larger bedroom.

When we returned to the first floor, Rosie asked if we wanted to see the basement.

"Is it cooler there?" I asked.

"It always is," Rosie said.

"Let's go." We descended the stairs and found the basement to be both cool and damp. It contained a water heater and a furnace, both fueled by natural gas, and a scattering of trash that hadn't been swept up after the previous renter's departure. Rosie saw me eyeing the trash and promised to get it cleaned up before we moved in.

"Both the water heater and the furnace are practically brand new," Rosie said. "They were installed between renters three years ago." I grunted my approval.

We climbed the stairs to the main floor and again were immersed in a sea of hot, stale air.

"Does the air conditioner in the dining room cool this whole floor?" I asked.

"Pretty much," Rosie said. "Please don't be obsessed with the temperature. Remember you're in St. Paul where it's winter most of the year."

I mopped my dripping face again and said, "Well, this isn't winter and I am obsessed with the temperature."

"You know it cools off right after Labor Day, and if we take this place we can't move in until October," Martha said. "Next summer we can put fans in the kitchen and the living room. The big question is: do we take it?"

"Can we go out on the porch to discuss that?" I said. A drop of sweat was tickling the tip of my nose and my shirt was as soggy as a long-haired dog in a dunk tank.

"We can," Rosie said.

Out on the porch, I could almost feel my sweat glands relaxing and my pores closing to their normal eighty-degree circumference.

"Any questions?" Rosie said.

We already knew that the rent didn't include the cost of either heat or electricity, and we'd guessed at the amount of the required deposit. Including the estimated additional expenses of heat and electricity, the total was at the tip-top of our housing budget, but we had decided we could afford it without having to steal tidbits out of Sherlock's bowl for breakfast.

"What about the walls?" Martha asked.

"What about them?" Rosie said.

"They're all white. Can we paint them?"

"I believe you can at your own expense."

"Fine," Martha said. "I like to paint." She turned to me. "Do you want to go home and talk about it or do you want to grab it?"

"If you like it, let's grab it," I said. I was reasonably pleased with what we'd seen and I knew how tired she was of house hunting. "As long as you'll do the painting—"

"We'll take it," Martha said.

"Wonderful," said Rosie. "I'm sure you'll be very happy here. Now, why don't we go next door and meet your new neighbor?"

What was this obsession with the neighbor? Meeting him or her seemed to be a standard part of the house tour. Oh, well, what the hell? We followed Rosie to the other front door and stood beside her as she rang the bell.

Several minutes passed with no response, but Rosie stood patiently without ringing the bell again. I was about to suggest that nobody was home when the door opened halfway and a deep voice said, "Afternoon, Rosie."

The voice came from waist level, so I looked down, expecting to see an unusually short man, a dwarf maybe. What

I did see was a woman looking up at us from a motorized wheelchair. Her skin was the darkest I'd ever seen on an African-American face, her coal black hair billowed in an elegant Afro, and her upper body looked sturdy and erect. She wore a pale green sleeveless blouse that revealed a pair of well-muscled arms, which were folded across her chest. Her facial expression made it plain she was wondering why we were bothering her.

"I want you to meet your new neighbors," Rosie said. "Zhoumaya, this is Martha Todd and Warren Mitchell, who have agreed to rent the other unit. Martha and Mitch, this is Zhoumaya Jones."

The name struck me as something out of a Neil Simon farce. "Zhoumaya?" I said. "Jones?" My tone of incredulity suggested that Rosie might be pulling my leg.

"You got a problem with that?" said the deep voice from the wheelchair. Her brown eyes, sharp as chips of flint, were locked on mine.

"Oh, no," I said. "No, no. None at all. Sorry if it sounded like that."

Her eyes softened and the corners of her mouth turned up slightly. "Want me to spell my name for you?"

I shook my head. "Not necessary."

"I'll do it anyway. It's J-O-N-E-S." This was followed by a long, loud laugh.

The laughter threw me even farther off base, but I forced myself to join in. "Thanks," I said when the hilarity ended. "I'll write that down."

"So what's your real name?" Zhoumaya asked. "Is it Warren or is it Mitch?"

"It's both. I mean my family—my mother and my grandma—and strangers call me Warren, and my friends call me Mitch. Well, actually my grandma calls me Warnie Baby, but I don't encourage that."

"And which should I call you?"

"I hope you'll call me Mitch." I certainly wanted this woman to see herself as a friend.

"Mitch it is," Zhoumaya said. She turned her face toward Martha. "And what shall I call you?"

"Just Martha," she said. "I don't have any nicknames."

Zhoumaya turned her attention back to me. "I've seen your name in the paper."

"Yes, ma'am," I said. "I'm a reporter."

"I'm not ma'am," she said. "I'm Zhoumaya."

"Sorry. Yes, Zhoumaya, I'm a reporter." God, I was stumbling all over myself in front of this woman.

Zhoumaya opened the door all the way. "Why don't you come in and sit down," she said. "I have the air on in the living room and I shouldn't be holding the door open."

We accepted the invitation with gratitude and she spun the wheelchair 180 degrees on the spot and led us into the cool of the living room. This half of the duplex was a mirror image of the one we'd just agreed to rent. I settled into a comfortable tiger-striped armchair and surveyed my surroundings. The floor was hardwood, partially covered by a multi-colored, African-looking area rug—a vast improvement over beige carpeting. The furnishings also had an African look and the sky-blue walls were decorated with paintings of African scenes.

Zhoumaya saw me looking around like a kid in a toy store. "We came here from Liberia to get away from the fighting. My late husband owned a shipping business in Monroeville so we were able to bring most of our stuff." She smiled and added, "His name was Doliakeh Jones."

"Spelled J-O-N-E-S?" I said.

"That's right. You're beginning to understand Liberian names." I was also beginning to like my new neighbor.

Glenn Ickler

Naturally I was curious about her husband's death—I doubted it was from old age—but didn't feel comfortable asking about it. Zhoumaya must have sensed this because she opened the road to questions by saying, "Doliakeh became late in the same accident that took away my legs."

"What happened?" I asked.

"We had a crazy accident with our motorcycles." My eyebrows must have gone up because she said, "Yes, believe it or not, we began riding motorcycles many years ago. Doliakeh was on a bike when I met him, and he got me started on my own before we were married. Anyhow, we were riding out in the country north of the Cities, going along about sixty or so, when boom—a tree fell across the road in front of us. Doliakeh was in the lead and he hit the tree head-on. I skidded into it kind of sideways trying to stop. We both went flying when our bikes flipped. He was killed on the spot and I broke my back. That was on Labor day, so it will be three years next week."

"What made the tree fall down?" Martha said. "Was it really windy?"

"There was no wind at all," Zhoumaya said. "The tree was hollow and it just picked that time to fall down."

"Awful," Martha said.

"Amazing," I said.

"Like somebody once said, timing is everything," Zhoumaya said. "I've been in this contraption ever since."

"You get around very well," Rosie said.

"Hey, I've got me a racing chair with a big old red flag on it and I've been working out in it on the street. I'm looking to do a marathon—maybe Boston next spring."

"Good for you," Martha said.

"That's wonderful," Rosie said.

"How are you going to work out when the winter weather hits and the street is full of snow?" I said.

93

"I go to Florida right after Thanksgiving and I don't come home until April Fool's day," Zhoumaya said. "I've got a ground floor condo down there, and I can roll right out the back door onto a bicycle path."

"Problem solved," I said. "You should be in great shape by April."

"I'm in great shape right now." She flexed both arms at shoulder level and the biceps looked strong enough to propel a truck, much less a wheelchair. "In fact, I might chuck this motorized job and get a self-propelled model for inside the house."

"I'd keep the motor," I said. "There must be days when you don't feel like Hercules."

"Plenty of those," she said. "But you two must have better things to do than sit here listening to my problems. You satisfied with the place next door?"

"Pretty much," I said. "The landlord's a little sloppy with the maintenance—there's trash in the basement from the last renter—but with some fresh paint on the walls we can make it look like home."

I heard Rosie suck in a lungful of air and I turned toward her to see her face getting red. I was about to tell her not to worry about the trash when Zhoumaya spoke.

"You think the landlord's maintenance is sloppy?"

"A little," I said. "But we can live with that."

"Well, good," she said. "Then suppose you write me a check for the first and last month's rent and a damage deposit."

"Write *you* a check?"

"Didn't Rosie tell you? I own this building. I'm your sloppy landlord."

Now I sucked in a breath of air and felt the red blood rising in my face. "I'll write the check as soon as I pull my foot out of my mouth," I said.

"You do that. And I'll make sure that the trash is gone by the time your check clears the bank."

"It's no big deal."

"Oh, but it is. It's not every day that I'm called sloppy."

Martha came to my rescue with her checkbook in her hand. "How much do we owe you?"

"I should add a ten percent surcharge for the insult, but I'll let it go this time," Zhoumaya said. She named a figure that exceeded our guess, and Martha sucked in a lungful of air and wrote the check. Zhoumaya Jones, the wheelchair marathon wannabe, was officially our landlord.

Chapter Thirteen

The Play's the Thing

ONCE READ A NEWSPAPER review of a play that began: "Unfortunately, I had a very poor seat. It was facing the stage." I had seen that play from an equally poor seat and agreed wholeheartedly with the critic.

Our seats at Parkside Players Theatre that Saturday night weren't quite that bad, but it was a performance I would rather have missed. In fact, if we hadn't promised to have drinks with the artistic director and his wife after the performance, our little group of four would not have returned to our semi-poor seats after the intermission.

I knew in advance that the script was stultifying because I had seen *Waiting for Godot* a few years before, and I would have stayed away but, what the hell, we had paid for season tickets. Plus there was always a chance that a talented, energetic cast would lift the production to a level of acceptable mediocrity. This was not to be. Apparently the dreariness of the script had infected both the actors and the director.

My eyes were glazed over and Al's eyes were closed, with his chin resting on his chest, before the first act ended. Luckily, he didn't snore. Martha and Carol at least pretended to be more attentive, sitting up straight and focusing on the inaction occurring a few feet in front of us.

None of us were looking forward to our after-theater date with Erik and Joyce Erickson. If Joyce was sitting somewhere behind us, she would probably be observing Al's state of lethargy. Erik surely would be looking for comments on the performance, so after the half-hearted bows had been taken to a quiescent audience and the stage lights had gone dark, we huddled together trying to think of something positive to say.

"The costumes were appropriate," Carol said.

"The lighting wasn't bad," Al said.

"The set was nice, what there was of it," Martha said. It consisted of a railroad track laid on a bare stage leading to a sky cyclorama.

I thought about the static people who had played the logy characters. "The actors fit their roles," I said. This could be interpreted in several ways, and I hoped that Erik would perceive it as complimentary.

We had broken our huddle and were trying to look casual in the center aisle of the empty theater when Erik Erickson appeared from backstage and hustled toward us. We exchanged greetings all around and Erik said his wife would meet us upstairs in the bar. "She saw the show when it opened last Thursday night and decided that once was enough," he said. "She's been doing her own thing since then." I thought this showed good sense on her part but I refrained from saying so.

"Wonder if he knows that her own thing includes a late dinner in a dark restaurant with a hot caller," I whispered to Martha.

"Shush," she said. "You know the answer to that."

The theater was in the basement of a late nineteenth-century brick building, two floors below the restaurant. There was a single exit for the audience, and every time Erik made his curtain speech and pointed to that exit I wondered how he was getting around the city fire code that called for more than one.

When Erik finally joined us, he led us up the stairs to the restaurant. Joyce Erickson had procured a table for six, and again there were greetings all around. Joyce's welcoming smile flickered as I shook her hand, but no one else saw the brief change of expression. She was wearing a low-cut black dress that set off her red hair and revealed a generous spread of cleavage. I couldn't help observing that her breasts were freckled, and wondering if the tiny flecks of tan went all the way to the nipples. Pure journalistic curiosity, of course.

We sat down. A waitress wearing a skirt that barely covered her buns appeared and we ordered drinks. As we'd feared, Erik's first words after we three men had watched the waitress walk away were, "So, how did you folks like the show?"

There was a moment of quiet as all four of us waited for somebody else to go first. Carol came to the rescue just as the silence reached the point of awkwardness. "I do a lot of sewing, so I noticed the costumes. Very nicely done."

"As a photographer, I always check out the lighting," Al said. "It fit the scene very nicely."

"I thought the set went with the script very nicely," Martha said.

"The actors fit their roles very, um, nicely," I said.

Erik smiled. "What you're really saying is that the show sucked."

"Well, I wouldn't go that far," I said. "But it is a tough script to work with."

"I would go that far," Erik said. "The show is boring as hell. We're struggling financially so I put it in the season to save money. You know, it has a low-cost set and only involves three actors. But I can see it was a big mistake. As you must have noticed, there were a lot of empty seats out there."

"Are you saying that the audience is staying away in droves?" Al said.

"That sums it up perfectly," Erik said. "I was hoping our production would be so good that regulars like you would spread the word, but it's been just the opposite."

"So the word being spread has been negative?" Carol said.

"Apparently," Erik said. "Like your husband said, people are staying away in droves."

"As previously noted, it is a tough script to work with," I said.

"Paul Matheny is an excellent director and all three actors have played major roles here before," Erik said. "I was sure they could pump some life into the show. Instead it's pretty much been a disaster."

"Well, there's always the next show," Martha said. "We've always enjoyed coming here and I'm sure we will again."

"Thanks," Erik said. "With a season opener like this, I don't know how many more shows there will be. We're losing money on this one and probably turning off some people who would have come to the next one."

Carol had her program open to the season schedule. "The rest of your season looks good," she said. "You should be able to fill those seats again."

"I hope so," Erik said. "If not, there's a guy who wants to buy us out. Cheaply, of course."

At that point, our short-skirted waitress appeared with our drinks and Martha switched the conversation to another topic.

As our glasses neared a state of emptiness, Martha rose and excused herself for a trip to the ladies room. Joyce stood up and said she'd go along. When they returned, Erik paid the tab and Al and I took care of the tip. "We should leave enough to show our appreciation for the shortness of her skirt," Al said.

"Her legs were probably the most interesting thing you guys saw all night," Erik said. "I'll have to cast her if we ever do 'A Chorus Line.'"

In Al's car, headed for our apartment, Martha told us about her trip to the ladies room with Joyce. "She told me that what we saw in the restaurant wasn't what it might have looked like."

"Did she say what it might have looked like?" Al said.

"She didn't have to," Martha said. "Her story is that Scott Hall wanted to discuss problems with the square dance club—she and Erik are the presidents—and that all the restaurants in St. Paul had long waiting lines."

"The long waiting line bit is true," I said. "That's why we were in the same place they were. Did she say what the club problems were?"

"We didn't get into that. I figured the less said about that night the better."

"Do you suppose Joyce went home and immediately discussed those square dance problems with Erik?" Al said.

"What do you think?" I said.

"I like to give people the benefit of a doubt but in this case the doubt is bigger than the benefits," Al said.

"I just hope those two don't do something that messes up either the square dance club or the theater," Carol said.

"May the dancers not break a leg and the actors always be square with their partners," Al said.

"If Joyce and the caller are careful, nothing should break up the squares," I said. "Anyway, it's none of our business." Silly me.

Chapter fourteen

Farewell to the Fair

MONDAY WAS LABOR DAY, the last day of the Minnesota State Fair. I was at my desk, trying to think of an excuse to go to the fairgrounds on company time to snag one last Pronto Pup, when Al approached carrying two cups of coffee.

"What's happening?" I asked as he handed me one cup. With his now empty left hand, he cleared a corner of my desk wide enough to accommodate his butt before he answered.

"A bunch more e-mails from Willow is what's happening," he said. "Including a photo of herself wearing nothing on top."

"We're talking bare boobs?" I said.

"You're abreast of the situation," he said.

"Are they photogenic bare boobs?"

"They're small, but I believe they're what you'd describe as 'perky.'"

I tried to picture perky in my mind. "Does she have a reason for sending you this mammalian display?"

He took a swig of coffee before he answered. "She wants me to shoot photos of her in the nude."

"Whoa! It's time to say thanks for the mammaries and goodbye, Willow," I said. "This tree is starting to look like a trunk full of trouble."

"You got that right," Al said. "But how do I chop her off?"

"You can start by putting the nix on the nude pix. That should let Willow know she's barking up the wrong tree."

"I don't want to hurt her feelings."

"So tell her that her breasts are beautiful but you're not into nude photography."

"There are a couple of nude shots in my book from a class I took before I married Carol. They only show bare butts and partial boobs but they're in there and, sure as a carp craps in the river, Willow has seen them."

"So explain that those were shot in a previous lifetime," I said. "She should understand that you're now a married man and can't go around shooting naked women willy-nilly."

"Women don't have a willy," he said. At that point, Eddy Gambrell, the assistant city editor, sitting in for Don O'Rourke on the holiday shift, yelled that he had an assignment for Al. He walked slowly to the city desk carrying his coffee and wearing a worried look.

My mind went back to thoughts of Pronto Pups, interspersed with visions of perky boobs. Voila! I had the answer. Lorrie Gardner, the State Fair's PR chief, had perky boobs. I could check out Lorrie's boobs for perkiness while I was interviewing her for a wrap-up of the fair. How was attendance compared with last year, what was the most popular food on a stick, etcetera, etcetera, etcetera?

I almost ran to the city desk and pitched this story to Eddy.

"Sounds almost as interesting as watching fudge harden," Eddy said. "But what the hell, you're not doing anything here but keeping your chair warm."

Twenty minutes later I was standing in front of a Pronto Pup purveyor at the State Fairgrounds. Two minutes after that, with my half-eaten, mustard-slathered treat in hand, I walked into Lorrie Gardner's office and was rewarded with an elegant view of her shorts-clad bottom. She was bending over at the waist, picking up a ballpoint pen that had rolled under her desk.

"Hey, Lorrie," I said.

She jerked to an upright position and spun to face me. I checked out the contours of her tank top. Yes, perky was an accurate description. "Oh, god, you're eating another one of those artery cloggers," she said.

"If it makes you feel better, I'll jog up Machinery Hill to wear off the fat and calories," I said.

"You'd wear off a lot more running up the steps on the grandstand about twenty times. What brings you out here today?"

"The need of one last Pronto Pup and an overwhelming desire to see you one more time before you fade into that after-the-fair-is-over limbo you disappear into."

"I take a week off and then start helping plan next year's fair. You can come see me any time."

"It's not the same in cold weather," I said. The temperature in the room was well into the nineties, so the aforementioned shorts were brief and her tank top was minimal.

Lorrie looked down at her partially bare perkiness. "Next year, air conditioning."

"No way. Your hot weather costumes are a permanent exhibit."

She tried to look offended but failed. "Surely the editor didn't send you to the fair merely to eat junk food and harass the help."

I explained my skeletal story idea and we talked about the fair for the next fifteen minutes. Among the things I learned was that food on a stick sales dropped sharply the day after Vinnie Luciano's death but recovered in time to threaten the record twelve-day high.

When Lorrie ran out of numbers and laudatory adjectives, she asked about the Luciano murder investigation. I told her about my battle for information with Detective K.G. Barnes and said I'd developed some suspects on my own.

"I hope they catch the killer," Lorrie said. "Watching Vinnie lying there twisting and jerking was the worst moment of my life."

"Vinnie's, too," I said.

* * *

HOLIDAY OR NOT, my AA group met that night, and I had my usual follow-up chitchat with Jayne Halvorson in Herbie's Bar. Jayne nodded along as I poured out another commiseration over the official police silence on the Vinnie Luciano murder case. I expected sympathy and advice in return, but instead she changed the subject.

"Tell me something good that's happened to you recently," she said.

I thought a minute. "I had two Pronto Pups at the State Fair today." I chose not mention the additional pleasure of seeing Lorrie's perky boobs and provocative butt.

"See, life isn't all bad. Anything else good going on in your life outside the newsroom?"

"Oh, yeah," I said. "We found a new apartment. Actually Martha found it, but I went along to look at it and help make the decision. Diplomat that I am, I also managed to insult the landlord."

"How'd you do that?" Jayne said.

I told her my comment about sloppy maintenance and the surprising response I'd received. "Zhoumaya took it amazingly well," I said. "Lucky for me, she seems to have a sense of humor."

"Her name is Zhoumaya?"

"Believe it or not. It's Zhoumaya Jones."

"You're kidding?" Jayne said. "You're renting from Zhoumaya Jones?"

"You know her?"

"Everybody in City Hall knows who she is." Jayne works in City Hall for the Parks and Recreation Department. "Her husband was a major agitator for immigrants' rights, from the mayor's office down to the janitorial staff. He was killed in some freak motorcycle accident a couple of years ago. I'm surprised you didn't know about his work. His name was D.B. Jones."

In fact, I had heard of D.B. Jones. Our City Hall reporter had written about his immigrant rights campaign several times and

Al had photographed him. "Of course," I said. "Zhoumaya told me her husband's name was Deli . . . something Jones. I never made the connection to D.B."

"Well, Zhoumaya has made some connections in City Hall since D.B.'s death. She's picked up where he left off on the immigrants' rights thing. She has to work mostly by phone and e-mail because she doesn't drive, but she knows what's going on. Check out her Facebook page."

"I don't do Facebook, but this sounds like a connection I should make in person. Maybe our man in City Hall isn't getting all the news."

"You probably won't get much more. From what I hear, Zhoumaya likes to be anonymous and work behind the scenes—unlike her husband, who loved to take his issues to reporters."

"Whatever," I said. "I'm glad I mentioned her name to you. It would be stupid for me to live next door to her and not try to pick up some stories."

"See, life isn't all bad," Jayne said. "Now go ahead and bitch some more about the Luciano case if you want to."

"I'm pretty much bitched out. I don't know what the Falcon Heights cops are thinking, but right now my leading suspect is Cousin Vito, who inherited the restaurant after Vinnie made a recent change in his will. Problem is I don't know how to approach him. If call him up and ask for his reaction to the family's lawsuit he'll give me the standard 'no comment' and hang up."

"How about a story on whether he plans to make any changes at the restaurant. New menu, redecorate, things like that. You could start by quizzing him on his plans, then broaden it to how he felt about Vinnie and family stuff like that. You might get an inkling about his guilt feelings, if he has any."

"Jayne, you're in the wrong business," I said. "You should have been a city editor. I'll run that one by Don O'Rourke first thing tomorrow morning."

Chapter Fifteen

The Moving Finger Points

Tuesday morning found me standing at Don O'Rourke's desk, as I'd promised Jayne Halvorson I would.

"Hey, you finally came up with an angle that's worth a story," Don said after I'd made my pitch. Chalk one up for Jayne.

Contacting Vito wasn't as easy. His wife answered the home phone and said he wasn't there. She gave me his cell number, so I called that and got his voice mail. I left my name and both my office and cell numbers after the beep and went to the cafeteria to grab a cup of coffee. Al was just coming out with a cup in each hand. "You can buy tomorrow," he said as he handed a cup to me.

"What's happening?" I asked as we walked back to my desk. "And I don't mean with your photo assignments."

"You're referring, of course, to Willow, my number one fan."

"The one and only."

"Willow practically has me weeping," he said. "She won't take no for an answer on the nude shots. Even worse, she wants a naked shot of me."

"A naked shot of you? I merely *thought* she was goofy, now I know it for a fact."

"A bare fact, you might say."

"I might, but I won't." We had reached my desk and Al took his usual corner perch. "I take it you're not going to hang out with Willow."

"Not with her or for her," Al said. "Being nice didn't work, so I guess I'm going to have to be a real bastard and tell her to knock off the e-mails altogether."

"Apparently that's what it will take," I said. "Something like, 'Hi Willow, please make like the tree you're named after and leaf.'"

"Cute, but cute won't work with her. I'm going to flat-out tell her that our e-mail exchange is over and that I won't open any more of her messages."

"That should get the job done."

"Let's hope. And speaking of jobs, where are you going today?"

I hadn't thought about going anywhere, but the question gave me an idea. "I'm going to King Vinnie's Steakhouse to see if I can stake out the new owner."

"Don't you need a photographer? I'm currently without a mission, and I'm tired of listening to Sully Romanov talk about his trip to Israel." Sully was a photographer who loved both to travel and to talk about his travels.

"Check it out with the desk. I can always use a photographer."

I suggested trying the back door because it was still before opening time, so we parked behind King Vinnie's Steakhouse, right beside a black BMW. "If we're lucky, the Beemer belongs to Vito," Al said.

"I doubt if any of the hired help can afford that kind of ride," I said.

The door was unlocked and we found Vito in the kitchen with Max Triviano, the manager, and Ozzie Bergman, the bartender. When Vito saw us, he took a step back and said, "Who the hell are you?"

"I think they're from the paper," Ozzie said. He pointed at me. "That one's been in here asking questions about Vinnie and some of the customers."

"Ozzie's right; we're from the paper," I said. We introduced ourselves and I made the pitch for a story about Vito's plans for the restaurant, just as Jayne had suggested. "I've been trying to get you on the phone to set up an interview but my editor didn't want me to wait any longer so we came here hoping to catch you."

"Any plans I might have aren't ready to be put in the paper yet," Vito said. "I only just got this place a couple weeks ago, and it wasn't like I was expecting it."

"You didn't know it had been willed to you?" I asked.

"Oh, I knew that. What I'm saying is I didn't expect Vinnie to go out and get himself killed before the ink was dry. When he told me about changing the will I figured it was just an insurance maneuver."

"What do you mean by insurance maneuver?"

"I mean he was afraid those greedy kids of his might hire somebody to knock him off so they could inherit the restaurant."

"Did Vinnie tell you that?" I asked.

"He did," Vito said. "He was scared of those kids, especially Louie, the oldest."

"Did he give you any specific reasons why he was scared?"

"The kids, especially Louie, have been after him to retire and turn the business over to them. They all worked here before they graduated college. Louie's worked here the most—on and off between other jobs that he either got fired from or quit because he hated the work or the boss or both. He's just a loose cannon and the other two, Tommy and Patty, pretty much follow along with whatever screwy Louie wants. They give me the creeps, those kids."

"How old are 'those kids'?" I asked.

"I think Louie just turned forty," Vito said. "They're spaced about two years apart, so Tommy would be thirty-eight and Patty thirty-six. I might be off a year or two either way."

"Louie acted like he was surprised when I talked to him about the will. Didn't Vinnie tell the kids about the change?"

"I don't know. He said he was going to get them together and tell them all at the same time. Maybe he hadn't had a chance to do that. Louie's the only one that lives close. Tommy lives up in Duluth and Patty is way the hell off in Wisconsin somewhere. She's married to a goddamn Packers fan."

"Oh, my god, how could she do that when the Vikings do so much business with King Vinnie's?" Al said.

"Some people got no loyalty," Vito said. "Anyway, that's all I know about Vinnie's will."

"Are you aware that the kids are contesting it?" I asked.

"Yeah, I heard about it," Vito said.

"What's your reaction?"

"No comment. Talk to my lawyer."

"Who is that?"

"Guy by the name of Andrew Morris. Works for Linda Lansing's firm downtown. You probably heard of it."

I had heard of it. The firm was owned by the best criminal defense lawyer in the Twin Cities, Linda L. Lansing, also known as Triple-L. And, as previously noted, Martha Todd was employed there.

* * *

BACK AT MY DESK, I ran down my list of people who might have put out a hit on Vinnie Luciano. The newest addition was Louie Luciano and his siblings. Also featured were Fred McDonald, the angry Teamsters leader; Oscar Peterson and Luigi Bunatori, restaurant competitors who were jealous of Vinnie; and of course Vinnie's cousin Vito.

Vito was still my favorite. With the revised will bequeathing him the steakhouse, he had the most to gain.

But Louie and his gang were also worthy of consideration. If they really hadn't been told about the revision of the will, they might have seen the Square Meal on a Stick introductory show as a prime opportunity to get rid of their father. And even if they knew about the change, they might have been angry enough to kill Vinnie and take their chances on contesting the will.

Vito's choice of law firms was also interesting. In addition to having strong representation in the fight over the will, he would have the top defense lawyer in town in his corner if he was charged with anything criminal.

What about Oscar and Luigi? They both had motives and, being in the food business, they might think of food as a dispatching agent. I'd keep them on the list.

Fred was a distant runner-up. He'd had a run-in with Vinnie, but there was no long-standing enmity. Maybe it was time to drop him.

My primary question was: Who knew about the dog-and-pony show introducing the Square Meal on a Stick far enough in advance to hire a hit man who'd have time to disguise himself, poison the food and deliver it to the stage?

Maybe the State Fair's public relations director could answer that question. Too bad the Pronto Pup stands were closed for the season.

Meanwhile, I had some more questions to ask.

Chapter Sixteen

Clueless in Falcon Heights

What do you know about Andrew Morris?" I said to Martha Todd as we sat down to watch the news that evening.

"Andy is a colleague in our firm," Martha said. "Why do you ask?"

"Andy is representing Vito Luciano in the suit over Vinnie Luciano's will," I said. "Which no doubt means that he drew up the will that cut out Vinnie's kids."

"Andy is a very good lawyer. I'm sure he'll give Vito a very good chance to win. Beyond that, I can't talk to you about a colleague."

"How good is very good? Where would you rank Andy on a scale of ten?"

"I'm not going to get into that," Martha said. "I especially won't discuss this with you because you'll be covering the story."

"Must you be so damn ethical?" I asked.

"Would you love me as much if I wasn't?"

"I'd love you if you were pushing little old ladies in front of buses and suing the city for their pain and suffering."

"You would not. You'd have Al following me with a camera to catch me in the act of pushing, and you'd be writing about the corrupt ambulance chaser who was stealing the taxpayers' money."

"It's a moot point," I said. "You're incorruptible."

"But I'm extremely loveable," she said.

"Is there time to demonstrate that before supper?"

"I thought you'd never ask," she said. "I was just about to call out for pizza."

"Hold that call," I said. She held the call and I held her until well past our normal dinner hour.

*   *   *

WEDNESDAY WAS MY DAY OFF, but I couldn't resist driving to the State Fairgrounds to see Lorrie. I could have quizzed her by telephone, but it was turning into another hot day and I was curious about her choice of clothing. With the fair no longer running, parking was no problem. I pulled in between the only two cars standing on the blacktop next to the Admin building.

Lorrie was wearing shorts and a T-shirt, but the shorts went halfway down her thighs and the T-shirt was a couple of sizes too large. Her ensemble looked like a semi-inflated balloon hanging above two shapeless sacks. For this I could have phoned.

"Aren't you roasting in all those clothes?" I asked. "It must be ninety degrees in here."

"My armpits are swimming, but some big shots from downtown are coming in. I thought I'd better cover up a little," Lorrie said. "What brings you out here when you can't stuff your face with Pronto Pups?"

"Your stunning, magnetic beauty. And a question about the Square Meal on a Stick."

She tugged at the bottom of the T-shirt so that it stretched taught across her breasts, confirming that they were still perky. "You're so full of B.S. that I wish I had boots on, but I'll try to answer your question."

"It's a two-parter: How far in advance did you advertise the Square Meal introduction program and did you mention Vinnie Luciano's name in the promo?"

"Oh, god, let me look." She opened a desk drawer, pulled out a thick Manila file folder and started flipping through the contents. Three-fourths of the way down the pile she pulled out a sheet of paper. "Here's the press release. It's dated August 18, the Thursday before the event, which was on Wednesday. My aim was to get a note in the Sunday papers and a mention on the weekend TV news shows."

"And did you succeed?" I asked.

"Let me check the clips." She pulled out another Manila folder and started flipping. "Okay, we did get a couple of lines in the *Sunday Dispatch* calendar of events."

"Did it mention Vinnie?"

"It did. It says the new treat was created by Vinnie Luciano, owner of King Vinnie's Steakhouse. Why are you asking?"

"I was wondering where Vinnie's killer found out about the program, and how much time he had to concoct a murder scheme and hire the guy to carry it out."

"I guess that's your answer," Lorrie said.

"Was the *Sunday Dispatch* the only paper that carried the story?"

"It's the only clip I have. Apparently the editors in Minneapolis didn't think it was worth the space. There's also a note in here that Channel Four mentioned the unveiling of a new treat on a stick on their Sunday evening newscast, but I don't know if they mentioned Vinnie or not."

"Maybe Trish Valentine, reporting live, would know."

"You could ask her. I'm sure you wouldn't mind including a trip to see her in your quest for stunning, magnetic beauty."

"You're right," I said. "I wonder where she's reporting live today."

"She's always where the action is," Lorrie said. "I'd head for the nearest fire or crime scene."

"Good advice." I waved goodbye and went home to my air-conditioned apartment. I'd done enough legwork on my day off. Besides, I had orders from Martha to start packing in preparation for our move to Zhoumaya Jones's domain. Sherlock Holmes helped by constantly winding his body around my ankles while I was putting stuff into boxes.

*   *   *

EVER THE MASOCHIST, I started my day on Thursday with a call to the Falcon Heights Police Department. To my amazement, Detective Barnes was at her desk. My call was immediately transferred and KGB surprised me further by wishing me a good morning.

"Good morning to you," I said. "You're sounding very upbeat this morning."

"The day is young," she said. "We missed hearing from you yesterday."

"Didn't anyone call you about the Luciano case?"

"A very sweet young lady did in fact call us. She was quite willing to accept our statement that we had no new developments for her. No quibbling, no quarreling, no trying to squeeze out something that wasn't there."

"And your point is?" I said.

"That we appreciate a cooperative attitude on the part of the media, even when we are unable to reward it with news about pursuing a suspect or a so-called person of interest," said KGB.

"Are you suggesting I've not been cooperative?"

"We're merely commenting on the demeanor of yesterday's caller. It's up to you if you wish to make a self-comparison."

I wished to punch her in the face until her nose was poking out through the back of her head. Gritting my teeth, I said, "Have you anything new to report to this humble and cooperative reporter today?"

"Actually, we have," she said. "We have questioned a number of Mr. Luciano's family members, friends and business associates and have found nothing to lead us to the perpetrator of the crime. We are of course continuing our investigation but we are without sufficient evidence to bring charges against anyone at this time."

"You don't think cousin Vito Luciano had sufficient motive to get rid of Vinnie?"

"We don't have any evidence that Mr. Vito Luciano acted in that manner."

"What about Vinnie's children? He'd been refusing their requests to retire and give them the restaurant, and they thought they were still in the will. Didn't they have strong motivation to get rid of dear old dad?"

"Again, we have no evidence that would lead us to that conclusion."

I was getting more and more annoyed with her use of the royal "we." "So where does leave all of you?" I said.

"We—and we're referring now to the police department here, not just this detective—will continue the investigation and would like to speak with anyone who might have information pertaining to Mr. Luciano's death. We would appreciate the inclusion of our phone number and e-mail address in your story, Mr. Mitchell."

"You know me. Always cooperative in the fullest."

"We thank you for that, Mr. Mitchell. Have a nice day."

I started to respond but the line was dead. I put down the phone and sent an e-mail to Don O'Rourke. "Here's your head for the Luciano case: 'Stonewalling cops hit stonewall.' Story to follow."

I looked over at Corinne Ramey sitting at the next desk. "Hey, Corinne, did you call the Falcon Heights cops about Vinnie Luciano yesterday?"

"Yes, I did," she said. "Detective Barnes politely told me that there were no new developments in their ongoing investigation."

"Detective Barnes thought you were very sweet about it."

"Sweet?"

"Just one sugar lump short of a full bowl."

"That bitch," Corinne said. "I'll show her something sweet the next time I call."

*   *   *

"WHAT'S NEW?" Al asked as I plopped down facing him at a table in the lunchroom.

"The KGB actually said something beyond '*nyet*' this morning," I said. "She more or less admitted their investigation was going nowhere and they've run out of people to question."

Al thought for a second before he said, "Stonewalling cops hit stonewall?"

"That's exactly the head I suggested to Don."

"Ah, great minds run in the same goofy grooves. So where does that leave us for stories and pix about the murder of St. Paul's leading restaurateur?"

"It leaves us with whatever we can dig up and photograph on our own."

"If we keep digging we should have a scoop," Al said.

"Or we'll be deep in a hole," I said.

"I might need a hole to hide in."

"From your bare-breasted cyber friend Willow?"

"You got it. She keeps on sending e-mails saying we should get together and talk about our relationship."

"You have a relationship?"

"She says we do. I told her I was finished swapping e-mails with her, and I haven't answered her last six messages, but she

116

still won't go away. And she attaches that same topless photo to every message."

"How do you know it's the same photo every time?" I said.

"I check it out," Al said.

"You're keeping abreast of the situation?"

"Who wouldn't?"

"Only a boob. But this is more than having fun and singing about 'Willow, titwillow, titwillow.' I think you've got yourself a stalker. Maybe you could get some kind of restraining order."

"I don't want to mess with that. I'll just keep ignoring her messages and opening the attachments."

"I'd also watch my back if I were you."

"Are you serious? You think she'd try to do something physical?"

"Stranger things have happened."

Chapter Seventeen

Baring Up

MY FRIDAY BEGAN with a call from Douglas Riley, informing me that he had filed a lawsuit in the name of Vinnie Luciano's three children contesting Vinnie's most recent will and testament. "Louie said you'd be interested," the lawyer known as the Bulldog said.

"Thank you. I'm extremely interested," I said. "Who does this leave in charge of King Vinnie's Steakhouse?"

"Good question," he said. "According to the law, it's Vito, but we've put a provision into the suit forbidding him from making any changes in the business or selling anything connected to the restaurant until the question of ownership is settled."

"Could Vito close the restaurant?"

"No, the restaurant must remain in operation."

"What happens if Vito runs it deep into the red while the lawsuit drags on?"

"We've included a provision that puts a neutral accountant in charge of the books so Vito can't skim off the profits or intentionally run the business into the ground."

"How about unintentionally?"

"We don't think he's stupid—just crooked as a spiral staircase."

"Can I use that quote?" I asked.

"Be my guest," Riley said. "Any more questions?"

"I can't think of any right now but I may be calling you back." He gave me his phone number and wished me a nice day.

Linda L. Lansing's office phone number was on my speed dial. I called it and asked for Andrew Morris. The call was transferred and an upbeat voice said, "Hi, Mitch, how are you this morning?"

I realized I had met this man at a retirement party for one of Martha's colleagues in July. We did the "I'm fine, how are you, I'm fine routine," and then I asked if he had a comment on the legal challenge to Vinnie Luciano's will.

"Did Vito tell you to call me?" he asked.

"He did," I said. "He said he has no comment and referred me to you."

"Well, I'm sorry but I can't comment until the suit is filed."

"It was filed this morning. Doug Riley just called me."

"Oh, jeez, they've got the Bulldog?"

"They have. They're very serious about this. By the way, Riley says your client is as crooked as a spiral staircase."

"That sounds like Riley. I'm not responding to personal slurs."

"Are you responding to the challenge?"

"Not at this moment," Morris said. "I can't comment until I see what they're saying. How about I call you after I've had a chance to read it?"

"I knew you'd say that but I had to make the call."

"Whatever. Probably won't get back to you until Saturday. I've got a full plate in front of me this morning."

"Don't forget about me," I said.

"If I do you can sic Martha Todd on me," he said.

"You'll be sorry if I do. She'll make the Bulldog look like a puppy."

I doubted that talking to Detective K.G. Barnes would be worth the effort but I made the routine call. She was, of course, in a meeting. However, she called back in less than ten minutes.

"Did running your plea for information have any results?" I asked.

"We got several calls," she said. "Unfortunately, none were productive"

"Were all of them kooks?"

"We never classify our callers as anything but concerned citizens, Mr. Mitchell."

"Any of them confess to the murder?"

"We can't comment on the content of the calls other than to say they were not productive," KGB said.

"I have a tidbit for you. This morning Vinnie Luciano's children filed a suit to throw out the new will."

"Thank you, we'll make a note of that."

"Even though you think ownership of the restaurant isn't a motivating factor in the murder?"

"Even though. A person never knows, do we?" I silently tried to sort out the grammar in that sentence.

When I gave up, I said, "Nice talking to you, detective. I'll check in again tomorrow."

"We're always happy to be of assistance. Have a good day, Mr. Mitchell." As if that bitch cared about my day.

I had one more call to make. I went to the cafeteria, bought a cup of coffee and returned to make that call.

"Homicidebrown," said St. Paul Police Detective Curtis Brown.

"Dailydispatchmitchell," I said in my matching one-word response.

"Hey, Mitch, how've you been?" Brownie said. "Sorry we haven't had any work for you lately."

"I've been missing you. It's time for another killing in St. Paul."

"Are you calling to report one?"

"Not this time. But I am calling to ask for help on one that is growing colder by the day."

"And would you be talking about a certain event at the State Fairgrounds?"

"I would be." I took a sip of coffee during his reply.

"I read your piece yesterday saying the Falcon Heights police haven't turned up one damn suspect," Brownie said. "They must be crapping their pants with nothing to show for their work on the murder of a prominent guy like Vinnie."

"They don't sound too concerned about it," I said. "But I have some suspects even if they don't."

"Yeah? Who?"

"I can't tell you, but would it be possible for me to find out if Vito Luciano and Louie Luciano have rap sheets on file? This is strictly for background—it won't be in the paper unless they're arrested, in which case I'll go through channels." Another sip of coffee.

"Vito and Louie, huh? Well, those two are worth checking. I hear that both of them were after the restaurant like two lonesome sailors chasing the only whore on the dock. Do you know that Louie and his brother and sister are contesting the will?"

"You heard that already? They just filed this morning."

"My grapevine is long and fruitful," Brownie said. "You guarantee the stuff you want is for background only?"

"Swear it on a stack of stylebooks," I said. I was counting on the mutual trust Brownie and I had built up over almost ten years.

"I'm doing this only because I'm as interested in solving Vinnie's murder as you are. I'll get back to you. Have a good day."

My day was getting better. The filing of the lawsuit gave me a fresh story lead and the background on Vito and Louie might give me some insight as to how either of them would go about setting up a killing. My mood was getting mellow when Al appeared with no coffee in his hands and a frazzled look on his face.

"What's up?" I asked.

He did not take his customary seat on the corner of my desk. "When I came in just now, she was standing outside the front door."

"Willow?" I said.

"Who else? Luckily, I saw her before she saw me, and I turned around and came in through the skyway." More than forty of the blocks in downtown St. Paul are interconnected by a skyway at the second-story level. A person can walk all over the core of the city without ever having to go outside. This is a great boon during the winter when the temperature at street level is down to zero or below.

"Now are you convinced that she's a stalker?"

"Okay, I'm convinced. What should I do?"

"I'd get a restraining order keeping her away from this building. And, come to think of it, away from your home, too."

"You think she'd go to the house?"

"It would be the next step if she can't catch you here," I said. "Imagine Carol opening the door and finding Willow standing there—maybe with no clothes on."

"I can barely imagine Carol's reaction. She doesn't even know Willow exists."

"Maybe it's time to give her the naked truth. It might head off an unpleasant surprise."

"I'll have to think about that. Meanwhile, do you know a good lawyer?"

"I live with one of the best," I said.

"I can't go to Martha and tell her I've been carrying on an e-mail exchange with a nutty woman," Al said.

"She already knows."

"You told her about Willow?"

"Everything but the bare titties. She'll never say anything but I'm sure she'll advise you to tell Carol right away."

"I'll take that advice under advisement," Al said. "What's Martha's phone number?"

*   *   *

"DID YOU HEAR FROM AL today?" I asked Martha after greeting her with a hug and a kiss as she came through the apartment door.

"I did," she said. "I got him on track to get a restraining order tomorrow but there are two problems with it."

"Can you talk about them without breaking attorney-client privilege?"

"If I don't tell you I'm sure he will. Number one, we don't know Willow's last name, so the order might not hold up in court, and number two, we don't know where she lives. The order will have to be served on the street, assuming she can be found."

"They might try the *Daily Dispatch* front door tomorrow morning," I said. "Al spent the day going in and out through the skyway because she was standing there big as life this morning."

"What about you?" Martha asked. "Did you see her when you went out?"

"I didn't see anyone who looked like the picture Al showed me. I never left the building until four o'clock, and at some point she had to get tired of standing there. She'd need to eat or drink or go find a bathroom eventually."

"Sometimes obsessive people can suspend normal body functions for incredible periods of time. We had a case where a stalker waited outside the stalkee's house for three days without food or water."

"What about . . ."

"Must have done it in the dark if it ever became necessary."

"Didn't the stalker's target call the cops?"

"She had no restraining order and he was on a public street. He finally passed out, so she went to court, got an order and took a cop with her to hand it to the creep as she went back into her house."

"Did you advise Al to tell Carol about Willow?" I asked.

"I most certainly did," Martha said.

123

"Did he do it?"

"Who knows? We'll find out pretty soon because we're invited there for dinner."

From the conversation at the Jeffrey home it was obvious that Al had not said anything to Carol about his problems with Willow. This made for some tension at the dinner table any time the conversation touched on any of our activities during the day. Once Carol asked Martha if she was dealing with any interesting new cases, and Martha's coffee-with-cream complexion darkened a shade as she replied that she had acquired kind of a kooky new client but could not discuss it with anyone. Al found it necessary to go into the kitchen for coffee at that point.

We were eating dessert—wide slabs of cherry pie with mounds of vanilla ice cream—when the doorbell rang. Kristin jumped up and trotted to the door. We heard the door open, and a second later we heard Kristin scream. Her face was as red as the cherries in the pie when she came running back into the dining room.

"Mom, there's a naked woman standing on our porch," she said.

Al was up and heading for the door like a human cannon ball.

"Get her last name and address," I yelled.

Martha kicked me hard in the left shinbone under the table.

Chapter Eighteen

Means and Motive

THE JEFFREY ABODE was not where I wanted to be for the next half hour, but that's where I was and there was no getting out. Carol was rip-shit with all of us—Al, me and Martha—for having, as she said, "conspired to keep her in the dark about that crazy woman." The storm finally subsided after we all apologized for the third time, and both Martha and I convinced Carol that we had done everything but twist Al's arm to the breaking point to persuade him to tell her about Willow.

As for Willow, she hadn't stayed long. With his cell phone in his hand, Al had given her fifteen seconds to leave his property before dialing 911. She had laughed, but had turned away and strolled to her car, emphasizing every measured step with a swing of her bare buttocks. I confess I watched every undulation over Al's shoulder, and was as startled as he was when Willow stooped and gave us a ten-second moon shot before going around to the driver's side of the car.

"Now what?" Carol said as she finally sat down.

"Restraining order," we three said in unison.

"Are you going to hand it to her the next time she shows up naked on our porch?" Carol asked.

"We'll find a quick way to serve her," Martha said. "We sure don't want her showing up here again. Poor Kristin."

Poor Kristin had retreated to her bedroom after some soothing and apologizing from all of us. Kevin, on the other hand, had volunteered to answer the door the next time Willow rang the bell.

*   *   *

AFTER AN IMMATERIAL half day of work on Saturday morning, I helped Martha pile some boxes into the car and drove to our new apartment. Zhoumaya Jones had told us we could start moving stuff in at any time so we decided to get started.

We had no key, so I rang Zhoumaya's doorbell. "Well, look who's here," she said in her gravelly voice. "Come on in while I round up a key."

We stepped inside as she spun her wheelchair around and rolled ahead of us to the living room. "Sit yourselves down," she said. "I'll be back in a minute. How about some iced tea?" We said iced tea would be very nice and she wheeled away to the kitchen. She returned with a tray holding three glasses of iced tea and our apartment key on her lap.

"Oh, Zhoumaya, I could have helped with that," Martha said.

"Don't need help," Zhoumaya said. "I've been practicing my balancing act for occasions like this."

"Are you still into marathon training?" I asked as I plucked two glasses off the tray. I handed one to Carol and took a long drink from the other.

"I am, and nobody's run over me yet," Zhoumaya said. "Yesterday a guy slowed down beside me and his passenger leaned out the window and asked if I wanted a tow."

"I'd be scared to death to be on the street in a wheelchair," Carol said.

"I've got a great big old neon orange flag on a stick so people can see me real good," Zhoumaya said.

"You're okay as long as drivers use it as a warning and not as a target," I said.

"Aren't you the jolly one," Zhoumaya said. "I'll bet you see that glass you're holding as half empty, not half full."

"Actually it's only three-eighths empty," I said. "My job as a reporter has trained me to see the negative side of things."

"That's too bad. Speaking of job, your last story about poor Mr. Luciano's murder was pretty negative."

"You mean the one about no suspects and nobody left to question?"

"That's the one. There was a lot of talk about it in City Hall that day. Is that murder going to go unsolved?"

"Not if I can help it. I'm still digging at it."

"He always thinks he's better than the police," Martha said. "And sometimes he's even right."

"That's not always a good thing," I said. "I've been shot, kicked in the groin, whacked on the head and almost drowned a couple of times by killers Al and I exposed."

"Well, be careful of what people give you to eat while you're exposing this one," Zhoumaya said.

I held up my glass of tea and said, "Should I be worried about this?"

"If you should be worried, you're already too late," she said.

We finished our tea with no dire consequences, took the key and went to the door. As we turned to say goodbye, Zhoumaya said, "You can keep the key. And you don't have to check on the basement. That sloppy landlord has gotten rid of all the trash down there."

I felt my face grow as warm as an egg in a kettle of boiling water as I thanked her.

* * *

MONDAY MORNING FOUND ME back in the police station. Augie Augustine had called in sick and Don had caught me on my cell phone as I was getting into my car. I had suggested maybe Augie could use some outside assistance with his health problem and Don had said Augie had personal problems that were none of my business.

Thus chastised, I dug through the weekend police reports and came up with a real doozy to start the day. It seemed that a man was drinking alone in his apartment when his girlfriend forced her way in, screaming curses and accusing him of cheating on her. He locked himself in the living room and she knocked a wall down, threw a television onto the floor, smashing it, and dumped a case of beer on the floor, with several bottles breaking. The report said there also were blood stains on the wall.

The man tried to run down the stairs to get away but the girlfriend picked up a stool, chased him and hit him with it. Police charged the woman with assault and battery with a dangerous weapon (the stool), burglary with an armed assault, and malicious mischief causing more than $250 worth of damage.

The man was also charged with assault and battery because the woman's hand was cut while he was scuffling with her. Life in these United States—you can't make this stuff up.

I had finished dealing with the reports and was slurping on my second cup of coffee when Detective Curtis Brown walked into the office. He greeted me, laid two sheets of paper on my desk and said, "You didn't get these from me."

"Get something?" I said. "Nonsense. I haven't so much as talked to you for several weeks."

"Keep that in mind," Brownie said as he turned and left the office.

The first sheet dealt with Vito Luciano. It showed a couple of arrests for speeding and one for driving while intoxicated. Next came the biggie: doping horses at the Canterbury Park race track in connivance with a chemist who worked at 3M Company.

The doping case was four years old. It had gone to a grand jury, which failed to indict either Vito or the chemist because of lack of evidence. However, it was noted that Vito and his chemist buddy were barred from the track by the Minnesota Racing Commission.

Fascinating. Was said chemist still in St. Paul? Could said chemist concoct a potion to poison a Square Meal on a Stick? The first question might be answered by a call to 3M. Answering the second would require some finesse in a conversation with Vito Luciano.

The second sheet dealt with Louie Luciano. Three speeding tickets, a driver's license suspension, a domestic violence charge that was dropped, and the grand prize: an attempted murder charge that resulted in a fine and three years probation. Louie had choked a neighbor nearly to death during an argument over cutting trees along their property line. The man had protested after Louie cut down three tall trees on the neighbor's side of the line in order to improve Louie's television reception. The court also had ordered Louie to replace the trees.

I thought a phone call to the neighbor might be interesting. His name was Edgar Palmer and his address was no longer next door to Louie when I found the listing in the phone book. I called the number and a woman answered.

I identified myself and asked for Edgar Palmer. She said he was at work and would be home about 5:30.

"Are you his wife?" I asked.

"Yes," she said. "What's this about?"

"It's about Louie Luciano nearly killing your husband two years ago. I notice you've moved out of that house."

"We moved after Louie poisoned our dog," she said. "We didn't think it was safe there anymore."

"Louie poisoned your dog?"

"We couldn't prove it was Louie, but somebody poisoned Lucky and who else would it have been. Louie had been really nasty to us ever since the fight about the trees. Our daughter was being treated for hemophilia at the time, and the sleazy so-and-so knew that Lucky was her best friend."

"That's terrible. How's your daughter doing?"

"She's recovered, thank you," she said.

"Do you know what kind of poison killed your dog?" I asked.

"We took Lucky's body to the vet. He said it was strychnine."

I restrained myself from shouting "bingo," calmly thanked Mrs. Palmer for the information and said I wouldn't need to talk to her husband.

"Has this got something to do with Louie's father's murder?" she asked.

"One never knows," I said. "But I'm going to find out."

"I hope you can put that rotten bastard away for life," she said.

With the help of Mrs. Palmer's revelation that strychnine killed her daughter's dog, maybe I could.

My next call went to 3M. After pressing my way through a multitude of menu numbers, I finally connected with a human female who asked how she could direct my call.

"Doctor Philip Lymanski," I said.

"One moment." A phone began ringing and after the fifth ring a man said, "This is Doctor Lymanski."

He was still on the scene, available to assist Vito Luciano if needed for the concoction of a deadly sandwich filling. However, I wasn't prepared to talk to him yet. "Oh, sorry," I said. "Wrong number."

I almost let out a war whoop when I put down the phone. Now I had two bona fide suspects with motives for murder and the means to kill with chemicals. Should I call KGB and tell her everything I'd learned?

Chapter Nineteen

Narrowing the Search

O f course I wasn't going to tell KGB. Why should I? What had KGB ever done for me?

Now the question was where and how to start. My two suspects had the means and the motive but how could I find out if either or both had the opportunity.

Should I come on like gang busters with Vito, tell him I knew about the horse doping charge and challenge his association with Dr. Philip Lymanski? Or should I try to finesse a discussion about horse racing, doping and chemists? How could I present this in terms of a story for the paper?

Or should I start with Louie by confronting him with the strychnine poisoning of the Palmers' dog? That might be risking strangulation. Maybe I should play it cagey with Louie and try to find out where he was on the day of—and the day before—his father's murder? And again, how could I turn this line of questioning into a story?

I posed these questions to Jayne Halvorson as we drank our glasses of ginger ale in Herbie's after our Monday night AA meeting. My plan was to consult with Jayne that night, run it past Martha when I got home and get Al's opinion the next morning before doing whatever the hell I thought would work.

As always, Jayne took her time responding. After several sips through her straw, she suggested telling Vito and Louie that I was planning to write a story about when Vinnie Luciano's loved ones last saw him and what they were doing when they learned of Vinnie's death. This would also require interviewing

Vinnie's wife and the other children to camouflage my real intent, but it could even make a legitimate story.

"Brilliant," I said. "I knew you'd come through with an idea. Prominent victim's family recalls his last hours. You're wonderful."

"And I'm only charging my usual fee," Jayne said.

"I'm paying the tab for your ginger ale?"

"That's right. But I'm having seconds."

"I think I can cover it."

On the sofa at home, with Sherlock Holmes straddling our laps, I repeated the conversation to Martha and asked for her opinion.

"My first opinion is that you should be careful how you approach those two guys," Martha said. "The word around my office is that Vito has connections with some pretty nasty people, and it's obvious from what you've told me that Louie has an explosive temper."

"I'm with you there," I said. "I don't relish being ambushed by a friend of Vito's or having Louie's hands around my neck."

"The only thing around your neck should be my arms."

"I'm also with you there. Why don't we try a little of that?"

"Here or in the bedroom?"

"The bedroom is much more comfortable. Plus we can get naked first," I said.

"Naked in the bedroom it is," Martha said. And naked in the bedroom it was.

*   *   *

I DIDN'T SEE AL until lunchtime on Tuesday because he'd been sent out to shoot a semi-trailer rollover on Interstate 94 in the eastern suburb of Lake Elmo. Some idiot had cut off the truck, forcing the driver to take evasive action that threw the trailer out of balance. The whole eighteen-wheel rig came to rest on its side, blocking all westbound lanes leading into the Twin Cities at rush hour. Oh, yes, the trailer's load of cornflakes was also spread across a wide patch of the highway. The only good news was that the truck driver wasn't hurt.

"Did you pick up a few boxes of cornflakes?" I asked when Al joined me in the cafeteria.

"My kids are fixed for breakfast until they graduate from college," he said.

"No Willow lurking at the door?"

"No sign of her. Maybe she finally got the message. Anything new on the King Vinnie front? The KGB making any progress?"

"The KGB reported only that she had several more calls from tipsters and that 'we' are following up. But wait until you hear what I've got going."

When I finished my tale of acquiring the Vito and Louie rap sheets and my subsequent actions, Al said, "So now what?"

"Don has his doubts about my story idea, but he finally gave me the go-ahead. I've already set up an interview with Vinnie's wife for this afternoon. That seemed like an innocuous way to start. And of course I need a photographer to take a mug shot."

"Got any photographers in mind?"

"Only one. The slip is already written and we're meeting the grieving widow in her home on Mississippi River Boulevard at two o'clock."

"Don really bit on this?" Al said.

"I think Don knows what I'm really after—that it's about trying to smoke out the killer. But Vinnie was his next-door neighbor, and he's really pissed at what little the Falcon Heights cops have done."

* * *

Vinnie Luciano had lived in a well-kept Tudor style house on the high bluff overlooking the Mississippi River. The spectacular view across the river included Fort Snelling, a nineteenth-century outpost originally built for protection against Indian raids. The fort had been turned into a tourist attraction, complete with men in Civil War era soldier costumes who fired a real 1860s cannon for the visitors. As we walked from the car to the front door, I wondered if the cannon shots could be heard in the Lucianos' front yard.

Sophie Luciano met us at the door and ushered us into the living room. Like her late husband, she was short and wide, and her straight black hair was sprinkled with gray. She wore a black dress appropriate for a recently widowed woman and sensible black shoes. The only pieces of jewelry she wore were her engagement and wedding rings.

She waved us toward two armchairs, both of which were upholstered with bright elaborate patterns, and offered us iced tea. We accepted and she brought three glassfuls from the kitchen on a tray. After passing out the tea, she sat on a wide, floral-print sofa facing us, with a glass-topped coffee table in between. The only items on the table were the morning paper and a *National Geographic* magazine, both squared up with the edges of the table.

After we offered our condolences, she nodded and said, "You were there, weren't you? When Vinnie died?"

"Yes, both of us were as close to Vinnie as we are to you right now," I said.

"That's the only reason I'm talking to you," Sophie said. "I've been keeping away from the media, but I want to ask you about his last moments. What they showed on TV looked so awful, like he was in terrible pain."

I didn't like where this was going. The thought of recounting Vinnie's writhing death throes to his loving wife brought a knot to my stomach.

Al saved my day. "I think he was beyond pain," he said. "I was very close because I was shooting pictures and it looked to me like he was unconscious and not feeling a thing." *Liar*, I thought.

"I had that same feeling," I said. "His body was moving but he seemed to be totally out of it."

"You're not just saying that to comfort me?" Sophie said.

"No, no," we said in unison.

"That's really how it looked close up," Al said.

"Thank you," she said. "I never imagined that my husband would die like that. So horrible."

I needed to change the subject quickly so I asked when she'd last spoken with Vinnie and we moved along into the interview. Her description of the couple's last hours together was so mundane I was barely listening until Sophie mentioned that three days before the murder Louie had been visiting while Vinnie was bragging about the Square Meal on a Stick.

My brain snapped to attention when I heard that. "Did Vinnie mention when he was introducing it at the fair?" I asked.

"Oh, yes, he gave us the full story, including where it was happening," Sophie said. "He was really hyped about showing off that crazy square thing, and he thought doing it at Heritage Square with a bunch of square dancers was a great gimmick."

"What did Louie think of that 'crazy square thing,' as you call it?"

"Louie thought it was a great idea. Asked Vinnie what time the show was starting so he could try to get off work and be there."

"And was he there?" I asked.

She thought for a moment. "I don't really know. I don't recall that he's ever said anything about being there. I guess you'll have to ask him."

"I'll do that," I said. Oh, baby, would I ever.

* * *

"AREN'T YOU ASHAMED of lying to the poor woman like that?" Al said as we walked to the car.

"Like what?" I asked.

"Telling her he was out of it, having no pain."

"You told the same lie. 'Beyond pain,' you said."

"Good thing she didn't have a lie detector."

"I have a feeling she detected both of our lies and chose to accept them."

"No lie?" Al said.

"Nothing but the truth," I said.

We parked the car in the company garage, and were almost at the front door of the *Daily Dispatch* when we saw her. Willow, wearing a high-necked, ankle-length pale blue dress, was leaning against the wall beside the door. Luckily she was looking in the opposite direction. We flattened ourselves against the wall and backed away. When we were out her sightline, we turned and high-tailed it around the corner. We went into the nearest skyway entrance and made our way to the office, with Al grumbling about the inefficiency of the system that hadn't yet produced a restraining order.

"Maybe the lack of a last name is causing a problem," I said. "Martha found her on Facebook after we got home last night and she goes by Willow and nothing else."

I called Martha at her office and learned that the order had been issued after some discussion of the name. "It's just a matter of finding her to serve her," Martha said. "There's no home address listed anywhere for someone whose name is just Willow."

"Well, she's camped outside the *Daily Dispatch* front door as we speak," I said.

"I'll call the police and tell them," she said. "Is she wearing any clothes?"

"She's wearing a baby-blue dress that goes from her neck down to her ankles."

"Too bad. She'd be easier to spot if she was still in her baby pink birthday suit. Anyway, I'll send the cops. Bye, sweetie, see you at home."

Chapter Twenty

Take Your Choice

O F COURSE WILLOW HAD MOVED away by the time the officer with the restraining order reached the *Daily Dispatch*. Al learned of the service failure Wednesday morning via e-mail—from Willow. She sent an apology of sorts for her unclad appearance at Al's front door. It ended with, "I don't know what got into me, but I wish it was you." She included the standard bare boobs attachment and added a photo of her bikini-waxed crotch with her legs spread. Al called me into the photo department and showed me the new anatomical view of Willow on his laptop. "It looks like she took this one herself, holding the camera at arms' length," he said. "See how the angle isn't quite straight? She was tilting the camera a little to one side."

"My god, quit critiquing the photography and kill that thing," I said. "What if you get hit by a car or something, and the cops pick up your laptop and find this kind of crap on it? They'll send you to Sandstone for five years." Sandstone is the site of a federal prison in northern Minnesota.

"Jeez, I was going to make a big print and enter it in this year's Guild contest," Al said. The Twin Cities Newspaper Guild sponsors an annual contest for various categories of newspaper work. "It might take first prize in the self-portrait division."

I looked again at the fleshy pink tunnel and said, "You could call it 'Opening the Gates of Hell.'"

"I'd sure catch hell if Carol ever saw it." He pressed delete and the voluminous vagina vanished from view.

After my routine phone check with Detective Barnes, who said "we" had nothing new but were following up some additional telephone tips, I was sent to the University of Minnesota to cover a Board of Regents meeting. This stuffy event wiped out my morning, but I had some time to chase Vinnie Luciano's killer after lunch. I decided to start with Vito, so I managed to grab Al and we drove to King Vinnie's Steakhouse hoping to catch the new owner on the job.

We were in luck. Vito was mingling with the remainder of the afternoon crowd, most of whom had consumed a late lunch heavy on the liquid side. We took Vito aside and I explained the phantom story we were working on.

Vito's face turned scarlet. "Jesus H. Christ!" he said, loud enough to catch the attention of everyone still in the dining room. "Don't you guys ever quit? Vinnie's been dead for what? Three fuckin' weeks? Let it alone for god's sake."

Could this be a guilty conscience talking? "People are still interested," I said. "Vinnie had a lot of friends in this town. It's a natural human interest story."

Vito scowled at me for an uncomfortable moment before replying. "Tell you what, Mr. Reporter. If you promise never to come to me lookin' for anymore half-ass stories, I'll answer your questions for this one. Fair enough?"

"Fair enough."

Vito led us to his office, waved us into two guest chairs facing his desk and closed the door. He walked around the desk, sat down and took a cigar box out of his top right drawer. He offered us each a cigar and we both said, "No thanks." He bit off the tip of a big, black one, applied a wooden match to the business end, blew out a cloud of blue smoke, and leaned back in his chair.

"Fresh from Cuba," Vito said. "Sure you won't join me?"

We shook our heads in unison and I thought about Don O'Rourke's funny bone joke about us being joined at the skull.

"So, what do you want to know?" Vito said, emitting another blue cloud. Out of the corner of my eye, I saw Al's camera flash.

"Well, let's start with the day Vinnie died and work backward," I said. "Were you at the fair that morning?"

"Never go near the fair," he said. "That place is a fuckin' zoo, pardon my French. Too many people, and I wouldn't touch any of that crap they're sellin' in the name of food out there."

"Not even a Square Meal on a Stick?"

"If I never hear of that piece of shit again it will be too soon."

"So you didn't go to the grand introduction of your cousin's invention?"

This brought a huge puff of smoke. "No way in hell was I goin' there."

"Did you know about the Meal . . . uh, Vinnie's concoction before the program?"

"How could I not?" Vito said. "That's all he talked about for a month before the fair started. He had this marvelous idea and the idiots at the fair bought it. He tried to get me to taste it and I told him to shove it where the sun don't shine."

"So you knew about the project even before Vinnie's big show at the fairgrounds?" I said.

"That's what I said. He talked about it so much I was ready to kill him. Oh, hey, don't put that in the paper. Those dumb-ass cops in Falcon Heights might take it the wrong way."

"You think the Falcon Heights cops are dumb?"

"They ain't turned up even a suspect much less caught the killer. What else are they but dumb?"

I wanted to agree, but I also wanted to stay on the main subject. "Did you know when and where the ceremony was going to be held?" I asked.

"Christ, yes. He thought that doin' it on the Heritage Square stage with a bunch of square dancers was the slickest sales gimmick since that pill maker started puttin' horny people into twin bathtubs. He tried to get me to come and watch, but like I said, I don't go near the fairgrounds while it's full of dumb-ass people."

"So you knew what time the show was starting?"

Another major cloud of smoke went up. "Of course I did. Why do you keep askin' about the goddamn program anyway? I thought this story was about the last time I saw Vinnie alive."

Oops. Better get on to the announced topic. "It is about that. Sorry. I got sidetracked on what happened that day. It's still pretty fresh in my mind."

"Lucky you. I'm just damn glad I wasn't there. The shots I saw on TV were enough to make you puke."

"So, getting back to the main story," I said. "You seem to have been spending quite a bit of time with Vinnie this summer."

"We were gettin' to be like cousins again, the way we used to be," Vito said. "We started gettin' together after he called me and said he was changin' his will because he was afraid of Louie. Looks like he had a good reason to be."

"You think it was Louie that had him killed?"

"That's who my money is on. Can't convince that dumb-ass detective, though."

"You've told her you think it was Louie?"

"Hell, yes. He didn't know the will had been changed, and he was so hot to get that restaurant that his ass was on fire. He's been out of work since last January when he got canned for grabbin' his boss by the throat." Another piece of information to put in my file on Louie.

"So, what did you and Vinnie do as cousins, besides changing the will?" I said.

"Oh, we did this and that," Vito said. "A little golf. Some card games. We went to the casino down at Prairie Island one time. Vinnie won a few bucks playin' blackjack and I lost my ass at the roulette wheel."

"Ever go to the races at Canterbury Park?"

I wanted this to sound innocent but it drew a blast of cigar smoke. "No, we didn't. If you'd been readin' your own paper a few years back you'd know I can't go there no more."

"Sorry. I forgot about that. Now I remember the story: you and a chemist friend got into some kind of trouble out there."

"They claimed we was dopin' the horses, but they couldn't get us indicted. The chicken-shit bastards at Canterbury banned us anyway."

"Are you still buddies with the chemist?"

A quick puff of smoke. "Haven't seen him since the grand jury hearings," Vito said. "Why are you askin' about him anyway? He's got nothing to do with me and Vinnie."

"Sorry. I tend to wander off the beaten path sometimes. So tell me about the last time you saw Vinnie. What were you doing?"

"We played golf and had a couple drinks the day before he died. He beat me by ten strokes but that was no reason to kill him, in case you're thinkin' I might have had something to do with it."

"I'm not thinking anything like that," I said.

"Bullshit you're not," Vito said. "You're suspicious as hell because I got the restaurant. Well, go ask Louie what he was doin' the day of the murder and see what you think then. Now I got work to do so I'll say goodbye to you gentlemen and wish you a good day."

"And a good day to you," Al and I said in unison, and we headed for the car.

"So what do you think?" Al asked as we drove out of the parking lot.

"He's still high on my list," I said. "The way he hesitated before he said he hasn't seen the chemist since the grand jury proceedings made me think he was blowing more than pure cigar smoke."

* * *

THURSDAY WAS MY DAY OFF. I spent the morning packing stuff for our move and wondering if Corinne Ramey drew the short straw for calling KGB. I could barely resist calling Corinne and asking, but I had promised myself to stay completely away from the Luciano murder case for at least one day.

To my surprise, the Luciano murder case came to me. Early in the afternoon I received a call from Louie Luciano, who asked in an angry voice why I was pestering his mother about his father's death.

I explained my cover story to Louie, and added that I was intending to call him the next day.

"Why not do it now?" he said. "I want to hear what you're asking."

"Fine," I said. "Hang on a minute while I get my notebook."

As usual I started working backward from the time of Vinnie's death. "Where were you while your father was introducing his new product?" I asked.

"Where I usually am during the week," he said. "At work."

Vito had said he was unemployed. "Where do you work?" I asked.

"I'm working for Swenson's Lawn and Garden Service on Payne Avenue. That morning I was cutting the grass at a big house in North Oaks." North Oaks is a suburban collection of big houses owned by a collection of people with big bucks.

"Kind of a hot day for cutting grass," I said.

"You do it when the customer wants you to," Louie said. "I was on a riding mower so it wasn't so bad."

"So you weren't able to get to your father's show at the fairgrounds?"

"No way. And after what happened, I'm glad I wasn't there. It looked like shit on TV."

"It looked even worse close up."

"My mom said that you said he wasn't in no pain when he was flopping around on the floor. Is that really what you think?"

"I really don't know whether he was in pain or not," I said. "His eyes were closed so he might have been unconscious."

"But he might have been in pain?" Louie asked. He almost sounded hopeful.

"I'd like your mom to think he wasn't."

"Yeah. Me, too. So now what?"

"So, did you see your dad the day he died or the night before?"

"No. Last time I stopped by was Sunday morning for Mom's sourdough pancakes. She makes them for breakfast every Sunday, and I eat 'em by the dozen. That morning Pop was like a little kid bragging about that crap on a stick. Wanted me to take off work and be there for the program, but I said only if he gave me a day's pay. He just laughed at that."

"That was your last conversation?"

"Pretty much. He didn't want to talk about anything else."

"What did you want to talk about?" The restaurant maybe?

"Nothing special. Just not about a stupid thing he was selling at the fair."

"Were you doing anything special with your dad in the days before he died?

"We didn't see each other that much. He was always busy at the restaurant, like usual."

"Are you saying he wasn't there for you very much?"

"I'm saying he was always busy with the goddamn restaurant."

"How about when you were in trouble? Was he there for you then?"

"What are you talking about? Who said I was in trouble"

"Weren't you arrested for choking your next door neighbor?"

There was a moment of silence before he said, "Who told you that?"

"A person who called me."

"Fuckin' Eddie. Did Eddie call you?"

"No, I swear to you that Edward Palmer did not call me, and I'm not going to tell you who did."

"Little rat fink. I'll bet it was Eddie."

"It was not Eddie. But obviously what I heard is true."

"We had an argument and he pushed me and I pushed him and I got the blame," Louie said. "He started it by yelling at me about his poor little treezies. He should've been busted, too."

"Did your dad stand up for you then?"

"Pop was taking care of the restaurant like he always was. Mom bailed me out and came to court with me."

It was time to squeeze him a bit. "What did you say when your dad told you he'd changed the will?" I asked.

"I told you, he never said boo about changing it," Louie said. "I found out about it after he was dead."

"So you thought King Vinnie's was still willed to you and your siblings."

"My siblings? Oh, yeah, my brother and sister. We all thought that."

Time to try a quick switch. "When was the last time you were at the State Fair?"

"What? What the hell's that got to do with anything?"

"Just wondering how often you went to the fair."

"I went the first Saturday—the weekend after Pop got killed. The Back Alley Bumper Cars were playing at the grandstand. They're one of my favorite bands."

"So you're not like your Uncle Vito, who says he never goes to the fair."

"I hope to hell I'm not like my Uncle Vito in anything I do," Louie said. "Are we done yet?"

"Almost," I said. "I heard that you poisoned your neighbor's dog. Is that true?"

"You *did* talk to Eddie. No, that's not true. I've kicked the little bastard's ass when he shit on my lawn, but I never poisoned him. Eddie's a lying son of a bitch if he says I did."

Interesting choice of expletives while we're talking about a dog. "So you had nothing to do with the dog being poisoned?"

"How could I? I wouldn't even know where to get the stuff."

"Okay, forget I asked about that. What I really want to know is did you love your father."

"What the hell kind of question is that? Of course I loved my father. Every kid loves his father."

"I'm glad to hear that. I guess now we're done."

"Good. Be goddamn careful what you write about me and my mother."

"I'm always careful what I write about people."

"You better be extra careful or I'll come down to the paper and kick your ass."

"Can I quote you on that, Mr. Luciano?"

"You do and I guarantee I'll kick your ass."

"Have a nice day," I said as I put down the phone.

Okay, Vito might be right about Louie. Louie had thought he was still inheriting one-third share in the restaurant, and he'd had part of Sunday and all of Monday and Tuesday to find the strychnine left over from poisoning the dog and hire someone to take it to the fair. But where would he find a hit man? Did one of his fellow workers at the lawn service make some extra money that day? I wondered if Swenson's Lawn and Garden Service would tell me if anyone was absent on Wednesday, August 24th.

I looked up Swenson's number and made the call. A real person answered the phone and identified himself as Arne Swenson. He said yes when I asked if he was the owner of Swenson's Lawn and Garden Service, but he thought for a moment before he answered my query about absenteeism. "I don't see how it's any business of the press," he said.

"Just a routine bit of information for a follow-up story on Mr. Luciano's murder," I said.

"I don't generally talk to the press about my employees, and I don't think it's right for me to discuss who wasn't at work on any specific day. So, I'll say goodbye then, and you have a nice day."

I stared at the silent phone for a moment, cursed lightly and put it down. A moment later I smiled and picked up the phone again. I thought I knew who Arne Swenson would talk to about his employees' work records.

"Homicidebrown," said the person I'd called.

"Dailydispatchmitchell," I said.

"Hang on a minute," said Detective Curtis Brown. The minute dragged by for 360 seconds while I listened to some unidentifiable music before he said, "What's up?"

I told Brownie about my conversation with Louie Luciano and asked if he would do me a favor.

"Depends on what it is, but I think I can guess," Brownie said.

"Would you call Swenson's Lawn and Garden and request absentee records for August 24th? You could say you were investigating a case. Something about immigration maybe. Those places hire a lot of immigrants during the summer."

He thought for a moment. "It's not really kosher, but it's not really out of order either. Have you asked your pal at Falcon Heights to do it?"

"I wouldn't waste my time calling her because I already know what the answer would be."

"Okay. I'll make up some story about looking for an illegal immigrant wanted for something or other. I'll call you back."

Ten minutes later I had my answer. Two employees were absent from Swenson's Lawn and Garden Service that day. The names of the two workers who had called in sick were Louie Luciano and Francisco Garcia, otherwise known as Frankie.

Chapter Twenty-One

A Fair Day

WAS IT TIME TO TELL Detective K.G. Barnes about what I'd discovered? Or should I talk to Frankie Garcia first? No-brainer—it had to be Frankie.

I told Don O'Rourke what I had and what I wanted to do. Consequently, Friday morning found me parked on Payne Avenue, half a block from Swenson's Lawn and Garden Service at 6:45 a.m. I knew lawn service people started working early because I'd seen them on the job as I drove to the *Daily Dispatch* office, where I routinely checked in at 8:00 a.m.

Swenson's headquarters consisted of a small white office building surrounded by a parking lot filled with pickup trucks hitched to flatbed trailers full of yard work equipment. The trucks were all painted bright red and white, like the Norwegian flag, and bore a company logo on each door.

My problem would be identifying Frankie Garcia. I knew it would be useless to ask Arne Swenson to point out an employee, so I was playing it by ear—or I should say by eye—as the men arrived.

The first two workers showed up five minutes after I'd settled back in my seat behind the morning *Daily Dispatch*. Both were Hispanic. So were the next five to arrive. Number eight was Louie Luciano. He was followed by a Hispanic woman, who in turn was followed by two black men and a 300-pound redheaded white guy. Soon the men began emerging from the office and heading for the trucks. Now I had to guess which truck to follow in hopes of talking to Frankie Garcia.

Louie, bless his heart, helped me to decide. When he emerged from the office, accompanied by the monster redhead and two Hispanics, Louie was talking and laughing with one of the Hispanics. A guy this chummy with Louie would seem to be the best bet to follow. What's more, he was short and slender, about the right size to fit into Fairchild's costume. Of course if he teamed up with Louie I'd have another problem.

Again Louie helped me. He and the redhead got into one truck and the two Hispanics got into another. I ducked very low behind the newspaper as Louie drove past me, and popped up in time to see Frankie—if it was Frankie—drive out of the yard and head south. Damn. I was facing north.

By the time I'd turned around in the nearest parking lot and worked my way into the beginning of rush hour traffic, the Swenson truck was out of sight. I'd be the wrong private eye to send on a stakeout.

After risking my fenders by running two yellow lights, I caught a glimpse of bright red a block ahead of me. I managed to keep the truck in sight as it turned onto a side street, and I followed almost a block behind it as the driver wound through the East Side neighborhood. I said thank you to Arne Swenson for painting his vehicles red.

The truck finally stopped at a two-story brick house surrounded by green shrubbery, several flowerbeds and a spacious yard. I drove past, went two blocks beyond the truck, parked and walked back. By the time I reached the men, they had unloaded a riding mower and an electric hedge trimmer.

"Hi," I said. "Who do you work for?" Like I couldn't tell from the logo on the truck.

The man with the hedge trimmer shook his head. Apparently his English was as poor as my eyesight.

The man seated on the mower pointed to the truck. "Swenson," he said. "Payne Avenue. Telephone on door."

"What if I wanted to hire you for a job without paying the company?" I said. "Would you work freelance that way?"

"Work six days a week at Swenson," the man said. "No time for extra."

"Couldn't you take a sick day from Swenson? I'd pay you a little more than he does per hour. My name is Warren, by the way. What's yours?"

"Frankie," said the man. "Swenson don't like sick days."

"But you must take one now and then," I said. "You can't work all the time."

Frankie laughed. "Yeah, but I already take one this month. Better not take no more."

"What did you do? Take a day and go to the State Fair?"

"Hey, how you guess it?"

The guy with the hedge trimmer started the motor and began clipping, so I had to yell over the buzz. "Just lucky I guess. Did you take your kids?"

"Got no kids. Me and a buddy go out to the fairgrounds. Fair ain't really started that day but we watch the guys set up rides. Watchin' them put up that double Ferris wheel is better than grandstand show."

"Your buddy work for Swenson, too?" I said.

"Yeah," he said. "We both get sick together. So I better not get sick again. You want us, you call Swenson." He started the mower and was off with a roar.

Back at my car, I slid behind the wheel and called Louie Luciano's home on my cell phone. I asked Louie's wife if he had a cell phone and she gave me his number.

"You lied to me," I said when Louie answered on his cell.

"Who are you? What are talking about?" he said.

I told him that I'd talked to Frankie and learned that they were both at the State Fairgrounds on the day of his father's murder.

"Okay, I was there at the Midway," Louie said. "I thought you was asking if I was at Pop's program."

"*Were* asking, and I asked both questions," I said. There was that reflex correction popping out again. "You told me you'd only been to the fair the following Saturday."

"Okay, okay. I didn't understand the question. I didn't lie to you. I was at the fair with Frankie but we was at least a block away from Pop's program. We never went near Heritage Square. In fact, Pop was dead and in the morgue by the time we heard about what happened. I didn't know about him getting killed until Mom called after I got home."

"You didn't hear the sirens from the Midway?" I said.

"You kidding? With the noise they make setting up those rides you couldn't hear a bomb if it hit Heritage Square and blew it to pieces."

"Maybe that's true," I said. "But can anybody other than Frankie tell me everything you did at the fairgrounds that day?"

"I didn't see nobody else that I knew, if that's what you mean," Louie said.

I gritted my teeth and managed not to correct the "nobody" else. "That's what I mean. Can anybody other than Frankie verify your claim that neither of you went near your father's program?"

"You asshole. Do you think that I could've killed Pops?"

"If the shoe fits, lace it up," I said.

"Well, I didn't. And if you print that I did I'll come to your office and kick your goddamn ass all the way to the fairgrounds."

*   *   *

"You got enough for a story?" Don O'Rourke asked when I returned to the newsroom.

"I can't use any names, but I think I can do a piece saying the *Daily Dispatch* has learned this and learned that from unofficial sources," I said. "Then I'll run it past our tight-lipped buddy in Falcon Heights and see if it inspires a comment."

"Give it a shot," Don said. "Maybe it'll get the cops off their butts."

So I gave it a shot, writing that through unofficial sources the *Daily Dispatch* has learned that a person with a strong motive for killing Vinnie Luciano was at the State Fairgrounds the day of the murder, accompanied by a person whose stature matches that of the person who wore a stolen Fairchild costume while delivering the poison to the victim. I added that although both persons deny involvement in the killing they cannot provide proof of their activities at the fairgrounds.

With fifteen minutes to go before deadline, I called Detective K.G. Barnes. To my amazement, she was available immediately.

"This is what we're running today and I'd like your comment," I said. I read her the story and held the phone two inches away from my ear. I had no problem hearing KGB's reply.

"Are you crazy?" she yelled. "You can't run that."

"Give me three reasons why not," I said.

"Number one, it's libelous."

"Who am I libeling? There's no names mentioned."

"Your anonymous suspect will sue you."

"And get his name in the paper as the plaintiff in the lawsuit? I doubt it."

"We'll sue you."

"On what grounds?" I asked.

"You're meddling in a murder investigation," KGB said.

"When did that become a crime? I'm neither interfering with nor hindering your investigation. If anything, I'm helping you by uncovering a person of interest. If you want the names I'll give them to you. Got any more reasons we can't print the story?"

"Yes. You're printing unfounded rumors."

"Wrong. The story is based on face-to-face interviews with the people involved."

"How about we forbid you to print it?"

"How about I read you the First Amendment?"

"You're a crazy, out-of-control reporter chasing stories that aren't there."

"Is that the comment you want us to print?" I asked.

"Yes," she said. "No, wait. We need to talk to the chief."

"You've got five minutes to talk to her and get back to me."

"What if we can't do it in five minutes?"

"Then I'll write that Falcon Heights police refused to comment." I heard the receiver slam down and the line went dead.

"What are you grinning about?" asked Corinne Ramey, who'd been eavesdropping at the next desk.

"I just went one-up on my favorite bitch," I said. "Which reminds me, did you get to call Falcon Heights on my day off."

"I did. And Detective Barnes will never tell you how sweet I am again. I worked her over for a good five minutes trying to pry out some information."

"Tough couple of days for the KGB," I said.

Four minutes later my phone rang and I found myself talking to Falcon Heights Police Chief Victoria Tubb. "I strongly urge you not to print that story, Mr. Mitchell," she said.

"Three reasons why," I said.

"You're mucking around in something you know nothing about."

"Can you prove to me that the story isn't accurate?"

"It's all based on anonymous interviews so I don't know if it's accurate or not. My problem is that you're talking to people without police permission."

"Show me a law that says I need police permission to 'muck around,' as you so colorfully describe it."

"There's no law," the chief said. "It just isn't done. It's not, uh, it's not gentlemanly."

"It has been done before in America and it will be done in the future," I said. "Now, do you have a printable official comment on the story or not?"

"My official comment is that I have no comment on a story that to my knowledge has no basis in fact."

"That's it?"

"That's it. And I want the names of the people you've interviewed or I swear I will charge you with obstructing justice."

"I'll call Detective Barnes and give her the names as soon as the story is in print," I said. "Have a good day, Chief Tubb." This time I got to hang up the phone, but I did it in a gentlemanly manner.

As I added the chief's comment to my story, I wondered what would happen when Louie Luciano read it. Would he really come to the office to kick my ass?

Chapter Twenty-Two

Playing Hide-and-Seek

"MAYBE I SHOULD HAVE put a ban on e-mails into that restraining order," Al said as we ate our sandwiches at noon.

"Willow still baring her limbs?" I asked.

"I got the crotch shot again this morning. Along with a message that said 'this pussy could be yours, why won't you make it your pet?'"

"Tell her you have felines for nobody but your wife."

"She knows that. Still she sends her personal cat scan."

"I hope you deleted it."

"Yes, I put the cat out."

"Still no word that Willow got the restraining order?" I said.

"No, the tree still stands alone," he said. "I just hope she's serious about staying away from our house. My kids don't need another anatomy lesson."

"I'll bet Kevin would grin if Willow would bare it."

"He found the last show way too entertaining. Since then he's been running to the door every time the bell rings."

I'd heard enough about Willow, so I changed the subject to the Luciano murder case and filled Al in on my morning activities. I had given KGB the names of Louie Luciano and Francisco Garcia just before lunch. She hadn't even thanked me, which was not a huge surprise.

"Think KGB will question Louie and his buddy?" Al asked.

"She has to," I said. "If nothing else, Chief Tubby will order it."

"And then what will happen?"

155

"Unless Louie and Frankie can come up with an alibi, which would surprise me, they should be charged with murder. It looks to me like Louie supplied the strychnine and Frankie delivered it in the Fairchild suit."

"You don't think Louie carried the death on a stick to Heritage Square?"

"He could never squeeze that belly into the Fairchild costume. Frankie is skinny, the same size as the kid who got bonked on the head. They make the perfect pair of perps."

"Well, I hope the perfect perps get popped into prison by the cops," Al said.

"That act by a copper would be a proper crime stopper," I said. Al threw up his hands in surrender and left the cafeteria. I mentally patted myself on the back for my poetic triumph and went to my desk.

* * *

MY FIRST PHONE CHECK at eight o'clock Saturday morning went to the Falcon Heights police, who had not released any information to the media since receiving the names of my two suspects. Neither KGB nor Chief Tubb was available. I left a message with the desk sergeant and turned to other tasks sent my way by Saturday City Editor Eddy Gambrell.

It was after 10:30 when I realized that the Falcon Heights police had not returned my call. I called them again and this time I was immediately transferred to Detective K.G. Barnes. "We are preparing a news release for all media," she said. "You should have it in your e-mail in about fifteen minutes."

"I'll be calling you as soon as I've read it," I said.

"We'll be going off duty as soon as we've sent it," said KGB.

"Then I'll call the chief."

"She's already gone off duty. Have a nice weekend, Mr. Mitchell."

I put down the phone in an ungentlemanly manner, causing Al, who was perched on the usual corner of my desk, to jump. "You seem less than happy," he said.

"The bastards are sending out a press release and then running for cover before anyone can question them," I said.

"I assume the bastards you're referring to are your tight-lipped friends at the Falcon Heights PD."

"With friends like that no reporter needs enemies. I give them Vinnie's killers on a stick and they stick me with the same canned press release as everybody else, with no chance for questions."

"There's no gratitude in this world anymore."

"You're right. Reporting has become a thankless task."

"And photography has become a game of hide-and-seek."

"Willow's still stalking you?" I said.

"This morning she was waiting by the exit door of the parking ramp," Al said. "I saw her when I drove in so I stayed upstairs and used the exit to the skyway."

"You'd be in the pits without that skyway."

"Keeps me on the straight and level," Al said. "Straight away from Willow and a level above her head."

The e-mail from Falcon Heights arrived a few minutes later. It said that the police department had followed a newly provided lead and had detained for interrogation two persons of interest in the Vincent Luciano murder case. The two men, both still unidentified, were being held in the Falcon Heights city jail pending further questioning. There would be nothing in addition released to the public until Monday morning. This bureaucratic drivel was attributed to Chief Victoria Tubb.

"Notice that she doesn't mention where she got the newly provided lead," I said.

"Let's hope people remember that they read it here first," Al said.

"I'll be sure to remind them," I said. "At least Louie won't be coming in here to kick my ass any time soon."

* * *

On Sundays I usually call my mother and my grandmother, two widows who live together on a farm near the southeastern Minnesota city of Harmony. I do this even though I always get a lecture about my church attendance, which is actually 100 percent nonattendance, from Grandmother Goodhue, better known to friends and family as Grandma Goodie.

This Sunday was no exception to the golden lecture rule. I called after Martha and I had hauled a carload of stuff to our new home, and Grandma Goodie's first question was, "Did you go to church this morning, Warnie baby?" She has called me Warnie baby since the moment my parents named me and she has nagged me about church every Sunday since I was old enough to shave.

"I had to skip church this morning, Grandma," I said. "We needed the time to pack up some stuff for our move. October first is less than two weeks away, you know."

"You have your priorities all muddled up, young man," Grandma Goodie said. "You should be taking care of where your soul is going before worrying about moving your earthly belongings. For all you know, you could be facing the Lord's judgment in less than two weeks."

"I'm counting on the odds being in favor of my soul staying with me longer than my earthly belongings can stay in this apartment."

"You never really know when your soul will depart, Warnie baby. Think about that poor man who was poisoned with his own food at the State Fair."

"I think about him every day," I said. "I've finally figured out who gave him the poisoned food."

"I'm glad to hear that," she said. "Maybe we'll be able to come back to the fair next year then." She and my mother had stayed away from the State Fair for the first time in almost forty years because they didn't want to be that close to the scene of a crime.

"I'm sure you can. You could have come this year. There was no danger."

"We just didn't want to be anywhere near the place where that poor man died. It's scary just to talk about it. I felt really sorry for those square dancers on the stage that had to stand there and watch that man die in agony. I was a square dancer once myself, you know."

"The square dancers vanished in a hurry," I said. "There were only a few still watching by the time poor Vinnie stopped struggling."

After giving me another scolding for avoiding church, Grandma Goodie called my mother to the phone. She, too, was happy to hear that the killers had been caught, making the fairgrounds safe for women in their sixties and eighties again.

I mentioned our moving date and said, "You'll have to come up in October and see our new place."

"I suppose we could do that," Mom said. "When are you two getting married then? Have you reserved a time for the church?"

"We haven't set a date for the wedding."

"Isn't it about time you did that?"

"We've only been engaged for about six months."

"Well, it took you six years to get that far," she said. "Don't let it drag on for another six then. Your poor grandmother could be in a nursing home."

"Yes, ma'am, we'll try to get our act together before Grandma falls apart," I said.

"Don't be a smart aleck, young man."

"I'm not. But remember, Martha was away doing her scholarship payback thing in Cape Verde for almost three of those six years." Martha had agreed to work for the Cape Verde attorney general's office for three years in return for a law school scholarship in the United States.

"I suppose I'll have to give you credit for that," Mom said.

"Anyway Martha and I aren't good at rushing into things. It was hard enough for us just to get engaged."

"I know, dear. Not that I'm trying to rush you, but your grandmother and I aren't getting any younger."

"Good point," I said. "I'll mention that phenomenon to Martha."

"Again the smart aleck."

I made a note to ask Martha when she thought we might have a wedding. And if she thought it might be in a church.

* * *

AUGIE AUGUSTINE CALLED in sick early Monday morning, so again I found myself in the tiny press office in the police station. This time when Don called, I was diplomatic enough to refrain from suggesting any possible cures for what ailed Augie.

The featured police blotter story of the day was about two women who had an argument that culminated in one woman grabbing the other by the hair and slamming a door into her face. I tried to picture that as I wrote the story and had some difficulty putting the face and the door together. You just can't make this stuff up.

I was thinking about making a call to the Falcon Heights police when an e-mail from Chief Victoria Tubb arrived. The chief was informing all news media that the two persons of interest in the Vinnie Luciano murder case had been reclassified as suspects, had been arrested and were in custody. They would be brought into Ramsey County District Court at 8:30 a.m. Tuesday. They were identified as Louis Luciano, age forty-eight, and Francisco Garcia, age twenty-eight, and their home addresses in St. Paul were given. The e-mail also said that both addresses had been searched on Saturday, but it didn't say what, if anything, had been found.

I called Don at the city desk and said I would do a story as soon as I talked to either the chief or Detective Barnes.

"You sure you got time?" Don said. "I could have Corinne Ramey make the call and write the story."

"You've got to be kidding," I said. "These are my suspects and my story. There's nothing even half as important going on here at the St. Paul PD."

I got a busy signal when I called Falcon Heights police. Of course. Every newspaper, TV channel, and radio station in the Twin Cities would be calling about the chief's e-mail. I kept disconnecting and punching in the number over and over for several minutes before I finally scored. The desk sergeant sounded frazzled as he transferred me to Detective K.G. Barnes.

"Are you looking for a medal?" KGB asked when I identified myself.

"No medal, just recognition," I said. "And the answers to a couple of questions."

"We're really not answering questions."

This didn't stop me from asking. "What did you find when you searched the suspects' houses?"

"We're not releasing that information at this time."

"Did you find strychnine at Louie's house?"

"We're not releasing that information at this time."

"Do you think Frankie . . . Francisco . . . wore the Fairchild suit and delivered the lethal stick full of poison?"

"We're not releasing those details at this time."

"Are you releasing any information beyond the chief's skimpy little e-mail?"

"Not at this time," said KGB. "Have a nice day, Mr. Mitchell."

"Bitch!" I yelled as I banged down the silent phone.

A passing police officer stopped and stuck his head in the open door. "Your girlfriend driving you nuts?" he asked.

"This woman will never be anybody's girlfriend," I said.

"One of those bitches that swing both ways?"

"No, just one of those bitches who make life miserable for people who have to work with them."

"I hear you," he said and walked away.

I wrote the story, touched it up with some background material about the changing of Vinnie's will and included the tidbit that Louie Luciano's former neighbors had accused him of poisoning their dog. "Bet you didn't know that, KGB," I said as I pressed the key that sent the story to Don. Wasn't I just the smartest crime solver in the world?

* * *

THE COURTROOM WAS JAMMED with reporters, photographers, and curious citizens by 8:15 Tuesday morning. I noticed the Luciano family was split into two groups, with one clustered around Vinnie's widow and the other surrounding Louie's wife. The two camps didn't seem to be communicating with each other.

Every seat was filled so I wormed my way through the TV cameramen until I was standing behind Trish Valentine in the aisle on the left side of the room. Being behind Trish was advantageous because she was always closest to the action and she was short enough for me to see over her head.

"Glad you could make it, Trish," I said.

"Trish Valentine, reporting live," she said. "Always first where there's breaking news."

"You're as regular as an old man on a diet of prunes," I said.

"And you're as disgusting as an old dog sniffing on a hydrant," Trish said.

Our exchange of compliments was interrupted by the bailiff's call for all to rise and the appearance of the Honorable Anthony T. Thomas. After everyone who had a seat was seated, Louie Luciano and Francisco Garcia were brought in and placed front and center by a quartet of uniformed policemen. Both men wore orange jumpsuits, handcuffs, and ankle shackles. Doug Riley, the Bulldog, rose from a front row bench and announced that he was appearing for both of the accused.

Ramsey County Attorney Lawrence Brigham, appearing for the people, read the charges against the two men. Both were charged with first-degree murder and of depriving the deceased of his human rights. Frankie was also accused of aggravated assault in the clubbing of Tommy Grayson and with the theft of the Fairchild costume. I smiled at the possibility of Frankie being found not guilty of murder but doing time for stealing the big round head of a gopher.

Brigham gave a quick summary of the events at the State Fairgrounds on the day of Vinnie Luciano's murder and added an intriguing tidbit. He said that during a warranted search of Louie Luciano's premises, a container with a small portion of strychnine had been found in the garage. In my mind, this was damning evidence against Louie. Case closed.

When asked for their pleas, both Louie and Frankie said not guilty in loud, decisive voices. Riley then asked that his clients be released without bail on the grounds that all the state's evidence against them was circumstantial and neither man was a flight risk. Judge Thomas gave Riley a look that said "you must be kidding" and set bail at $250,000 for Frankie and $500,000 for Louie. The Bulldog started to respond, but the judge stopped him by banging the gavel and calling for the next case.

Al was shooting photos at the back of the courtroom when the prisoners were led out, and I saw Louie say something as he passed him. As we left the courthouse, Al told me about the encounter. "Louie said to tell you that he is gonna beat this rap, and then he's gonna beat your goddamn head in," Al said. "So I guess you'd call this giving you a heads-up."

"Think I should buy a helmet?"

"I think you'd better watch your head and your back if he's not put away for life."

"I can't see either my head or my back. How the hell can I watch them?"

"It's all done with mirrors," Al said.

Chapter Twenty-Three

Quick Turnabout

I WAS TRYING TO PUT SOME life into a story about coyotes invading the posh suburb of North Oaks Wednesday morning when Al arrived at my desk. "I got in without having to dodge Willow this morning," he said. "She got hit with the restraining order while she was standing out by the parking ramp. She just sent me an e-mail asking how I could be so mean and cruel. She says all she wants to do is be my bosom friend."

"Did she include a bosom friendship photo?" I asked.

"She sent both the bosom buddy and the crotch companion shots. I deleted everything and I'm considering burning the laptop to make sure they're gone."

"Be careful where you burn it. You could be fined for air pollution."

"I'd gladly pay a fine to have Willow pollution burned out of my life for good."

After I finished the story, I went to the cafeteria for a doughnut and a cup of coffee. Al had been sent out to shoot a seventeen-car pileup caused by a guy texting on Interstate 35, but there were several other slackers in the cafeteria with whom I could kill some time between assignments.

When I returned to my desk I found I'd killed nearly a half-hour. It was time to call Detective K.G. Barnes and try to coax her into leaking some more information about the case against Louie Luciano and Frankie Garcia. For one thing, I was wondering how big the strychnine container was and how much poison remained inside it. For another, I wanted to know if they had any evidence against Frankie beyond his presence—and denial of same—at the fairgrounds on the day of the murder. To my surprise, I was transferred to KGB immediately.

"How can we help you, Mr. Mitchell?" she said. Her tone was less antagonistic than usual. In fact, it was almost friendly. My guard went up immediately.

I asked about the strychnine and she said the details of all charges would be discussed at this afternoon's media briefing.

That startled me. "I didn't know there was a media briefing this afternoon," I said.

"Didn't you get our e-mail?" she said. "We thought that's what you were calling us about."

"When did you send it?"

"Five minutes ago. You're slipping. You usually respond in less than three."

"Sorry. I just got back from, uh, an assignment and I haven't checked my e-mail since early this morning."

"Read our e-mail," KGB said. "We think you'll agree that it could turn this whole case around."

"Sounds like I'll be calling all of you again as soon as I've read it."

"We'll be here." There was a disconcerting smugness in her voice. I said goodbye and started calling up my e-mails with one hand while I was putting down the phone with the other.

The Falcon Heights police e-mail, which was signed by Chief Victoria Tubb, said there would be a media briefing at 1:30 p.m. at the police station today to discuss a new development in the Vinnie Luciano murder case. A report to Falcon Heights police from the FBI fingerprint laboratory had identified some prints found on the purloined Fairchild costume as belonging to a male St. Paul resident with a criminal record. This man had been taken into custody late Tuesday night and was being interrogated. His identity would be revealed and the results of the interrogation would be discussed at the afternoon briefing.

I sat in stunned silence for a moment before reaching for the phone. I didn't know the Fairchild costume had been found, let alone sent out for fingerprint analysis. This could be a major break in the case against Louie Luciano and Frankie Garcia, and it was a major break the wrong way from my point of view. I punched in the Falcon Heights police number.

"That was quick," KGB said when I was transferred to her line. "Figuring in the time it took you to read the e-mail, we'd say that you're back in form, Mr. Mitchell."

"Flattery will get you nowhere," I said. "What kind of game are you playing with the press? This is the first time you've told anyone that the Fairchild costume had been found, much less sent out for analysis."

"We didn't go public with that because we didn't want the perpetrator to know we'd found the costume," KGB said.

"Where was it?"

"That's part of this afternoon's discussion."

"This could take Frankie Garcia off the hook," I said.

"And possibly Louie Luciano along with him," she said. "Depending on what our present guest tells us under interrogation this afternoon."

"Will you be water boarding him?" I wasn't serious, but I could visualize KGB doing this.

"We don't think it will be necessary to go to that extreme."

"Who is this guy? What kind of record does he have?"

"You'll hear all that in a couple hours with the rest of the reporters. All we're saying at the moment is he has an arrest sheet several pages long. Basically he's a thickheaded thug who gets looked at every time there's assault or armed robbery in the area."

"You mean when they round up the usual suspects?"

"You could put it that way."

"This could knock a huge hole in your case against Louie."

"And also *your* case against Louie," KGB said. "Remember, you're the one who convinced us to take a closer look at Louie because you're so absolutely sure of his guilt. Maybe this is why everything we turn up about Louie turns out to be circumstantial."

"I guess I'll see you this afternoon," I said.

"One-thirty on the dot. Have a nice lunch, Mr. Mitchell." She sounded much too cheerful, and I could see why. She was now one-up on me, and she would actually be pleased to shoot down my Louie and Frankie theory. It occurred to me that she'd be even more pleased if she had heard Louie's courtroom exit pledge.

I tucked my tail between my legs and went to the city desk to tell Don about the new development.

"That was a quick turnaround," Don said. "What does this do to yesterday's charges against Louie and the other guy?"

"It could blow them completely out of the water," I said. "If this new guy is really the one who cold-cocked Tommy and stole the suit, Frankie Garcia is a free man. I just hope the new guy says Louie is the one who hired him."

"Well, the best you can do for now is to update your story with as much as you've got for the running electronic edition," Don said. "Take your twin with you to the briefing. Have him get a decent mug shot of that detective you call KGB."

I wrote the update, sent it to Don, found Al in the photo department and told him about Chief Tubb's surprise announcement.

"Holy shit, if this guy confesses to clobbering Fairchild and delivering the poison, Louie's pal will walk," Al said.

"And if this guy does not ID Louie as the person giving him the poison, Louie will also walk. I'll see you in time to get to the briefing. I'm going out for a while."

"Where to?"

"I'm going to buy a helmet," I said.

Chapter Twenty-Four

Suspect on the Square

I WAS ONLY HALF KIDDING about buying a helmet. I was actually going to lunch with Martha Todd and the head of her firm, Linda L. Lansing, but if there had been a bicycle shop between the *Daily Dispatch* and the restaurant I might have stopped in to pick up a piece of protective headgear.

I've been having occasional lunches with Linda ever since she represented the defendant in a major murder trial I covered about eight years ago. Linda is a woman who draws the attention of every man in the room when she walks in. She is tall (six-two), slender (but curvaceous in all the proper places) and blonde. Our friendship has always been platonic because she has always lived with a female lover. In fact, they were among the happy couples to be officially united on the first day that same-sex marriage was legal in Minnesota.

Linda and Martha were already seated when I arrived. I'd barely settled into a chair after kissing Martha when Linda said, "Andy Morris sends his thanks to you for taking Louie Luciano out of circulation."

"Why does Andy care about that?" I asked.

"Don't you remember? Andy is representing Vito Luciano in Louie Luciano's suit to get Vinnie Luciano's most recent will thrown out. With Louie in jail on the charge of killing Vinnie, maybe the suit against Vito will go away."

"And then again, maybe not," I said. I told them about the arrest of a new suspect in the Vinnie Luciano murder case.

"Oh, god, what a circus this is turning into," Linda said. "If this new suspect really did deliver the poison he'll probably give up the person who hired him in turn for a lighter sentence."

"That's exactly what I'm thinking," I said. "And the person he names might not be Louie."

"Ouch," Martha said. "That would sink your theory and put Louie back where he could make trouble for Vito."

"For me, too," I said. "He's promised to beat my head in when he beats the murder rap."

"Maybe you should buy a helmet," Martha said.

*   *   *

As I ALWAYS DO at briefings, I slid in behind Trish Valentine at the Falcon Heights Police Station. In addition to always standing in the front row, Trish is aggressive and almost always attracts enough attention to be called on for the first question. And because the speaker is looking toward Trish when I wave my hand, I usually get to ask the second question.

"Good to see you, Trish," I said.

"Trish Valentine, reporting live," she said. "Always first with breaking news."

The briefing area was packed with print and electronic reporters and photographers when Chief Victoria Tubb and Detective K.G. Barnes entered. The chief began by reading her statement, which covered what KGB had told me about the fingerprint leading to the arrest of a man with a long police record.

The chief said the Fairchild costume had been found in a dumpster two blocks from the fairgrounds, and that a fingerprint on the head led to the arrest of Mathew Grimes, also known as Grubby Grimes; age thirty-eight, whose last known address was in a rundown neighborhood near the river in St. Paul. I wondered if there was really a house at that number or if Grubby slept under a bridge.

"Do you know where that address is?" Trish whispered.

"It's where you don't want to go without company," I said. "And I don't mean just one cameraman."

"Always first with breaking news," she said.

"Or a broken head if you go there," I said. I turned my attention back to the chief in time to hear her say that Mr. Grimes was cooperating with investigators and would be arraigned the next morning.

As I'd hoped, Trish was the first person called upon when Chief Tubb asked if there were questions.

"You said Mr. Grimes is cooperating," Trish said. "Does that mean he has named the person who hired him to deliver the poison?"

"It does not," the chief said.

"Has he refused to name the person who hired him?" I asked while Chief Tubb was still looking at Trish.

"He claims not to know the identity of the person who hired him. On the advice of his attorney, he has declined to say anything further about the transaction."

I wanted to say, "You call this cooperating?" Channel Five's reporter did it for me in a more diplomatic manner by asking in what other ways Mr. Grimes was cooperating.

"Mr. Grimes has offered to provide more information in return for further consideration of the nature of the charges to be brought against him," Chief Tubb said.

"What are the charges?" another reporter asked.

"As I just said, the charges are under consideration at this time," the chief said.

"So you're making a deal?" Trish said.

The healthy pink color of the chief's face was instantly replaced by angry red. "I wouldn't categorize our negotiations as making a deal, and neither should you. Thank you all very much for coming and have a good day." She spun and walked out, followed so closely by KGB that I suspected a Velcro attachment.

"Nice going," I said to Trish. "You drove her out of here before I could ask if they were letting Frankie Garcia out of jail."

"Oh, that's a good question. I'll have to call the chief and ask her that one."

I should have known she'd jump on that. "Always glad to help."

"Always first with breaking news." With a queen-like wave, Trish followed her cameraman out of the room.

Al met me at the door. "Is this a get-out-of-jail-free card for that Garcia character?" he said.

"Trish Valentine reporting live is going to find out for us," I said. "Thanks to my big mouth, she'll be first with breaking news."

In the car on the way back to the office I called the Falcon Heights Police Department on my cell phone. I wasn't about to wait for Trish Valentine reporting live to find out about Frankie Garcia's potential freedom. The duty sergeant answered and informed me that Chief Tubb was not taking any calls from the media. "She says to tell you she believes she said everything that needs to be said at the press conference," he said.

"How about Detective Barnes?" I said. "May I speak to her?"

"She's not available neither," he said. "Have a good day." He hung up before I could correct his "neither" with "either."

Well, at least Trish wouldn't have it in her breaking news.

"Stonewalled again?" Al said as I shut off the phone and shouted an expletive.

"I've been stonewalled so much I've got rocks in my head."

* * *

THURSDAY MORNING FOUND me once again standing behind Trish Valentine. This time we were in the courtroom, waiting for Mathew (AKA Grubby) Grimes's arraignment. "No luck asking Chief Tubb about Frankie, huh?" I said.

"My contact at the jail says they're letting him out, but I can't get anybody to go on the record," Trish said. "When it happens I'll get it first."

When Grimes was brought in wearing the usual orange jumpsuit, handcuffs and leg shackles, a man in a dark suit stepped up beside him. "Your honor, I am Daniel Ballew, Mr. Grimes's court-appointed attorney."

"Is Mr. Grimes not in a financial position to hire an attorney?" said Judge Anthony T. Thomas.

"That is so, your honor," Ballew said.

"Given the serious nature of the charge against Mr. Grimes, it would seem that he should have the best possible representation. Do you have any prior experience of this nature, Mr. Ballew?"

Ballew's face turned a light shade of red. He pursed his lips and stood a little straighter. "I do, your honor. I have successfully defended a person charged with manslaughter."

"Very well. Let us continue," said the judge.

The clerk read the charges, which were theft of material valued at more than $200, aggravated assault and accessory to murder. Grubby Grimes pleaded not guilty to all three.

After bail was set and Grubby was led away, reporters and photographers blocked the front steps, surrounded the two attorneys and bombarded them with questions.

As usual, Trish was first. "Mr. Brigham, is Francisco Garcia being released."

"Mr. Garcia will be released on reduced bail, amount to be determined, later today," said Assistant Ramsey County Attorney Andrew Brigham, who had appeared for the people.

"Has Mr. Grimes admitted delivering the food that killed Vinnie Luciano?" I asked.

"Mr. Grimes admits delivering the item but denies knowledge of its contents."

"Has Mr. Grimes identified any other suspects?" I asked.

"Mr. Grimes claims not to know the identity of any other suspects," Brigham said. "We have surveillance film of a man who looks very much like Mr. Grimes meeting a man wearing a ski mask at night in a parking lot but the masked man is not identifiable."

"Does he look anything like Louie Luciano?" the reporter from Minneapolis asked.

"I can't comment on that," Brigham said.

"Where's the parking lot?" Channel Seven's reporter asked.

"I can't comment on that either."

"Has he given you information in exchange for a plea bargain down from murder-one to accessory?" I asked.

"We have reached an agreement with Mr. Grimes and his attorney on the charge."

"Is that a yes?"

"It's all I'm going to say." He spotted a crack in the circle of reporters and, like a slippery Vikings running back, he slid through the narrow opening and accelerated toward his BMW in the parking lot.

Our attention turned to the defense attorney.

"Just what is your agreement with the prosecution?" Trish asked.

"I've been asked not to discuss the details at this time," said Daniel Ballew.

"Who asked you not to do that?" I asked.

"The court."

"Judge Thomas?" In court, the judge had seemed unaware of Ballew's existence, much less a plea agreement.

"Well, not exactly," Ballew said. "The prosecution, actually."

"So the prosecution is keeping the plea bargain a secret," said the Minneapolis reporter.

"You could say that," Ballew said.

"I will say that," said the reporter.

"We all will," I said. "And we'll challenge it."

"You have the right to do that."

"Yes, we do. So what's the defense of your client going to be? Temporary poverty?"

"As the prosecutor told you, my client had no knowledge that the material on the stick was lethal," Ballew said. "He fully believed he was being paid to deliver an item of food to the man on the platform."

"Lucky he didn't sample it along the way," Trish said.

"Yes, it is fortunate that my client is a thoroughly honest man." This brought a chorus of laughter, during which Ballew ducked through the same opening the prosecutor had used and turned on the jets toward the parking lot.

"I've got the perfect headline for my story," I said to Al on the way to our car. "Square meal killer gets square deal."

"Meanwhile, we're back to square one on who hired Mr. Grubby," Al said.

"My guess is that it wasn't Louie Luciano."

"So who are you squaring up on next?"

"My money is now squarely on cousin Vito."

Chapter Twenty-five

Starting Over

I T'S ONE THING TO SUSPECT a man of murder and quite another to prove his guilt, as was demonstrated the next morning by the subject of one of my sure-thing accusations.

Because Friday was this week's day off, I was eating a leisurely breakfast at home when Don O'Rourke called. "You had a visitor here this morning," he said. "I'd suggest staying indoors today."

"Anybody I know?" I said.

"Fellow by the name of Louie Luciano. Says he got out of jail this morning, and he's got a present for you that he needs to deliver in person."

"He promised to give me a broken skull if he got out."

"He's big enough and pissed off enough to provide one. I tried to cool him down and get an interview on his release but he barreled off looking for you. Like I said, you'd be smart to stay off the street today."

"You didn't tell him where I live?"

"I was tempted, the way you embarrassed the paper by all but convicting him in your story, but I didn't want to be an accessory to murder like your new friend Grubby Grimes." Don said.

"You're all heart," I said. "I'll try to return the favor by producing the real killer."

"Maybe you should let the cops do that. They seem to be a step ahead of you on this one."

That hurt. "As a presidential candidate once said, this is a marathon, not a sprint. We'll see who's ahead when the final arrest is made."

"As I remember it, that candidate came in a distant second in his race, so you'd better pick up your step the rest of your race. Another fiasco like this one and you'll spend the rest of your career writing weather reports and the garden news." My ear drum reverberated from the force with which he put the phone down. Don rarely displayed his displeasure with such vehemence. I suspected he had heard from the publisher.

Great. Now I had an unsolved murder to write about, a vengeful former suspect to dodge and an unhappy boss to win back. I picked up the cup of hot coffee I'd set down when I answered the phone and took a sip. It had cooled to room temperature.

I almost gagged as I swallowed the lukewarm liquid. I put the cup into the microwave and hit the one-minute button. While the machine was exciting the coffee molecules and sending them to a higher temperature I booted up my laptop. When the microwave went "ding," I took out the coffee and opened the folder on the Vinnie Luciano murder. I always copy the files from important ongoing stories into my laptop, both as backup and for use away from my desk.

Okay, it was my day off, and I should be enjoying myself. But I'd been warned to stay off the street, so what was I going to do cooped up at home? Watch daytime TV? I'd rather have Louie Luciano break my skull than sit through *Family Feud*. Might as well use the time to read through the case file and see where the review would lead me.

It led me back to Vito Luciano, the inheritor of King Vinnie's Steakhouse. Vito had denied being at the fair the day of the murder, but he hadn't offered any information as to where he was and who, if anyone, could vouch for his location. He had also denied having had recent contact with the chemist who was his partner in the horse doping case, but the denial hadn't convinced me.

I had not asked to talk to the chemist when I located him at 3M. Maybe now was the time. But how could I do it? What would be my excuse for calling? And what would I say? How about, "Hi, Dr. Lymanski, did you give Vito Luciano a package of strychnine?" No, somehow that didn't seem to be a viable opening line.

I needed to know more about Dr. Philip Lymanski before I called. So I did what any grizzled veteran reporter would do. I Googled him.

There were more than two dozen hits, going all the way back to newspaper reports of the horse doping charge and dismissal of same. I started with those and worked my way forward through a string of postings from scientific publications. These included both articles about his work and articles written by him. I got the impression he was widely known in the field of chemistry for his research and his writing.

The most recent posting was only a week old. It was from a biweekly chemical journal with national circulation. I actually let out a whoop when I read it.

Dr. Lymanski was scheduled to receive an award for a recent research discovery at an upcoming conference at the University of Minnesota. This award was to be presented at a dinner on October 1, just eight days in the future. The article also gave a brief description of Dr. Lymanski's procedure and the results. Although I got an "A" in chemistry way back in my freshman year of college, I didn't understand a word.

No matter. This was the perfect opening. I would call the honored chemist for a story about his award, and somehow work my way into a question about his current relationship with Vito Luciano. I would call him now.

I found the phone number in my file. I punched it in and was transferred to Dr. Lymanski's extension. It was answered by the same woman as before and I asked to speak to Dr. Lymanski.

"I'm sorry," she said. "Dr. Lymanski is not available."

"Will he be available later today?" I said.

"No, sir. Dr. Lymanski is attending a conference in Michigan."

Good grief, did this man have a conference every weekend? "When will he be back in his office?"

"I expect him on Monday. May I take a message?"

I gave her my name and number and told her why I was calling him.

"In all honesty, I doubt he'll return your call," she said. "He never speaks to the non-scientific press."

"Not even his local paper?"

"Especially his local paper. He's afraid of being misquoted or misinterpreted. He's had some difficulty in the past."

"Does this go back to the incident at the race track?"

"I think I've said enough," she said. "I'll give him your message but I doubt you'll hear from him."

"If I don't, I'll call back," I said.

"Good luck, Mr. Mitchell. Have a nice day."

*   *   *

I WAS ALMOST OUT THE DOOR of my apartment Saturday morning when the phone rang and I was told that Augie Augustine had called in sick. This time the caller was Eddie Gambrell, who took over as city editor on Saturday. Eddie did not sound as sympathetic toward the ailing police reporter as Don O'Rourke, but I kept my thoughts about Augie to myself and went to the police station.

"You're turning into a regular here," the desk sergeant said as I walked in.

"Augie seems to have a chronic problem," I said.

"Augie's problem comes in a bottle. The paper should send him up to Hazelden for some rehab."

"The paper can't send him unless he's willing to go."

"Pretty soon he's going to be sick on more than just weekends if he doesn't get some help. Then maybe the paper will find a way to persuade him."

"I'm familiar with the process," I said. "I'm an alcoholic."

"Then you know what I'm talking about," the sergeant said. "Augie's fucking up his career."

I expressed my agreement and went to check the overnight reports. The best one involved a man who called police because a woman locked him out of his own apartment, but punched an officer shortly after the two-man squad arrived. The report said the caller became "visibly upset" while the officers were discussing how to resolve the situation.

"He clenched his fists and charged at us," the reporting officer wrote. "We grabbed him as he threw a punch." The punch hit one officer in the face. The same officer's motorcycle boots were ruined in the ensuing scuffle as both officers wrestled the man to the floor where he continued to struggle and kick. As I've said before, you can't make this stuff up.

I wrote that story and half a dozen additional shorts, e-mailed them to the city desk and sat back to think about what I would say on Monday. I absolutely had to talk to Dr. Philip Lymanski, no matter how he felt about the non-scientific press. My problem was twofold: how to persuade him to do the interview and how to slip in a question about Vito Luciano.

*   *   *

DON O'ROURKE AGREED that I should talk to Dr. Philip Lymanski when I broached the subject Monday morning. Seeing no need to remind Don of the connection between Dr. Lymanski and Vito Luciano, I pitched the interview solely as a story about a local chemist's winning of a prestigious award.

However, Don's memory for names and events was infallible. "Isn't Lymanski the chemist mixed up in a horse doping charge a few years ago?" he said.

"He is," I said. "The charge was dropped."

"Wasn't Vito Luciano the other guy charged?"

"He was."

"Is there any chance your interest in Lymanski goes beyond the scientific award story at hand?"

"Vito told me there hasn't been any contact between them since then. I might try to verify that, but I'll wait until the end of the interview."

"Don't get us into any more trouble," Don said. "Louie Luciano was raving about a libel suit while he was cussing you out last Friday."

As Dr. Lymanski's secretary had predicted, he did not call me that morning. I waited until 2:30 p.m. to call his office again. The secretary said she had given him my message, but it was in a pile with many others.

"May I speak to him now?" I asked.

"He's on another line," she said. "And he hates to be interrupted."

"I'm willing to hold."

"Okay, but I'll cut you off if he hasn't picked up in ten minutes."

Just after the nine-minute mark a male voice said, "Dr. Lymanski."

"Hello, doctor," I said. "This is Warren Mitchell from the *Daily Dispatch*. We'd like to do a story about the prestigious award you're receiving Saturday."

"Why the sudden interest in me?"

"You're receiving a very newsworthy honor."

There was a moment of silence before he said, "I've seen your byline. Don't you do mainly crime stories?"

"I'm an investigative reporter. I do a wide variety of stories."

"How'd you get picked to call me about this one?"

"I guess I'm the only one here who ever took chemistry in college."

"So you're familiar with chemical terms?"

"More than most reporters," I said. This wasn't a lie. Everything is relative and I was reasonably certain that nobody else in the newsroom knew more about chemistry than I did.

"How'd you find out about the award?"

I told him I'd read about it in the scientific journal.

"You read that paper?"

"I check a lot of publications for news about prominent local people."

Another silence. Then he said, "Do you want to do this on the phone?"

"I'd rather talk to you in person if possible." I hoped I wasn't stretching my luck.

Yet another silence. "Be at my office at 7:30 tomorrow morning. I'll give you half an hour before I start my work day."

I almost whooped again. "Would it be all right to bring a photographer?" I asked and held my breath.

"Be sure you're both on time," Dr. Lymanski said. "Now good afternoon to you."

I really did whoop as soon as the phone was out of my hand.

Corinne Ramey jumped four inches off her chair. "Did you finally score with that stonewall cop?" she asked when she came back down.

"No, but I have a date with a nationally-known chemist," I said.

"I hope the chemistry is good."

"It's not that kind of date. The chemist is a man."

"Now days you never know," Corinne said.

Chapter Twenty-Six

Manipulation

HOW THE HELL ARE YOU going to move from asking this bird about his chemistry award to finding out about his contact with cousin Vito?" Al asked as we pulled into the 3M Company parking lot at 7:15 Tuesday morning.

"I'm going to use his dislike of the non-scientific press to make the connection," I said. "By alluding to what he considers poor treatment by the press in the horse doping case, I might be able to slip Vito's name into the interview. It's called manipulation."

"Well, good luck with that. I might get a shot of him manipulating you right out the door on the end of his foot."

"He didn't sound like a violent man," I said.

Nor did he look like a violent man when he greeted us at the reception desk at 7:30 on the dot. Dr. Philip Lymanski was short of stature, sparse of hair and broad of belly—definitely not the physically abusive type. He wore a dark-gray pin-striped suit, a white button-down-collar shirt and a plain pale-blue tie. If you looked up the word "bland" in an illustrated dictionary, Dr. Lymanski's photo would be there.

He led us down a long hall to his office, which was devoid of anything personal. The décor on the walls consisted entirely of framed diplomas and award documents. No photos of family or works of art. The carpet was beige, his desktop was devoid of clutter, and the chairs he invited us to sit on were only a shade darker beige than the rug. More shades of bland.

"So, you scan the scientific press for story ideas," Dr. Lymanski said after he settled himself behind his desk, which held little more than a blotter and a calendar. It could have just been delivered from the factory.

"We look everywhere for news," I said with what was meant to be a disarming smile. "You never know where you might find something local, like the story about your award." Dr. Lymanski nodded but did not return the smile.

I started the interview by asking him to tell me about the research that led to the award, hoping he would get rolling and I wouldn't have to ask any questions that would reveal the true state of my knowledge of chemistry. Luckily he was a free-wheeling talker once he got started, and I wasn't forced to prompt him. His discovery had something to do with particles several sizes smaller than atoms and required a symbolic explanation on the chalk board. I copied the equations and reactions, and wondered if I'd be able to decipher my notes when I began to write the story.

When Dr. Lymanski wound down, I said, "This is a fascinating story and you seem suitably proud of your research and this award. I'm surprised the local media weren't notified by the institute sponsoring the award."

"I asked them not to send out any local publicity," he said. "I don't like dealing with the Twin Cities press."

"Have you had a bad experience with the Twin Cities press?" I asked with what I hoped was an air of innocence.

"Several years ago I was falsely accused of a crime and the papers and TV played it up as though I was a major gangster. The case was blown a thousand miles out of proportion. I'm sure every asshole reporter, pardon my French, who covered the case was in a state of depression for weeks after all the charges were dropped."

"That must have been before I started at the *Daily Dispatch*. Anyway, I don't remember your name being connected with a court case. What did it involve?"

"Nothing that has anything to do with my current work," he said. "And as I told you, the charges were dropped because we were innocent."

"We? Someone else was involved with you?"

"A friend."

"Another 3M scientist?"

"No, just a friend."

"Is he still a friend?"

"It doesn't matter. Our occasional get-togethers have nothing to do with my work or this story, so let's not discuss old dead issues. At any rate, Mr. Mitchell, I believe our time is up. Nice meeting you—and you, too, Mr. Jeffrey. I'll be looking forward to the story and hoping you got my good side with the camera."

"Should be in tomorrow or the next day," I said. "And don't worry about the photos. Al always gets the best side of his subjects."

As we left the building, Al said, "You're as slippery as a greased pig skating on an icy sidewalk."

"The best laid schemes o' mice and men don't always gang a-gley," I said. "And sometimes we asshole reporters catch asshole citizens like Vito Luciano in a lie."

"Our reluctant researcher certainly had some lousy chemistry with the press."

"You might say he had a bad reaction."

"That seems elementary. But where does all this leave us with Vito?"

"It leaves us needing to challenge him on his lie about having no recent contact with his partner in alleged chemical crime. I need to ask him exactly where he was and what he was doing the day his cousin swallowed the strychnine."

"You don't think your pal at the Falcon Heights PD has done that?"

"If she has she hasn't shared it."

"So you're going after Vito when we get back to the office."

"That's my first phone call of the day."

"Lucky you. I'd rather have a root canal than talk to Vito again."

"Don't say that. I might be needing some dental work after I call him a liar."

* * *

OZZIE BERGMAN, THE BARTENDER, answered the phone at King Vinnie's Steakhouse. He said Vito was in his office but wasn't taking any calls. "Don't bother to leave a message," Ozzie said. "He ain't returnin' any calls neither."

"Either," I said, automatically correcting Ozzie's grammatical faux pas.

"Huh?" he said.

"Nothing. Just a knee-jerk reaction. I'll ask Vito my questions in person later on. Will he be around all day?"

"He's generally here till closing, but he don't hang around half the night like Vinnie did."

I started to say "doesn't" but caught myself and instead said, "See you this afternoon."

"Cheers," Ozzie said. "Maybe he'll buy you a drink."

"Maybe he won't," I said after hanging up. "Not after I ask him what I'm going to ask him."

"You're talking to yourself again," Corinne Ramey said. "You must have been calling the Falcon Heights PD."

"No, but that's next. Better get ready to cover your ears when you see me put the phone down."

"Better yet," she said. "I'm going out to interview an old coot who drove into a house on the East Side."

"We're doing interviews with old coots hitting houses now?"

"It was the fire chief's house. And he crushed the stuffed bear that was standing on its hind legs in the chief's den."

"Good grief. Does the chief hunt bear?"

"How are you spelling that?"

"Get out of here," I said, picking up the phone. Corinne jumped up and double-timed it to the elevator.

To my surprise, KGB was available to take my call. Not surprisingly, she made very little information available.

"Are you following any new leads?" I asked.

"We are still questioning Mr. Grimes," she said. "We set up a lineup for his viewing and he exonerated Mr. Louis Luciano, who some people were quite certain perpetrated the crime."

"Hey, I just asked some questions and wrote a story based on the answers. You were the ones who went out and arrested him."

"You're right. Hopefully we have learned from our mistake and we won't arrest anyone on purely circumstantial evidence again. Will you do the same with your reporting?"

Ouch! "I always try to be careful," I said. "In this case I followed up a lead from another family member who convinced me that Louie was the killer."

"Would that be the victim's cousin Vito?" KGB asked.

"The one and only. What do you think of him as a suspect?"

"We aren't discussing any further suspects at this time. We'll admit that Vito did have a strong motive."

"And the opportunity. Do you know where he was at the time of the murder?"

"We're not revealing any information about further persons of interest at this time."

"So Vito is a person of interest?"

"We can't respond to that at this time. By the way, we hear that Louie Luciano is looking for you. Have nice day, Mr. Mitchell."

The phone went dead and my computer monitor came alive with its chirpy "You've got mail" message.

I opened the message. "We need to talk," it said. It was signed "Willow."

I opened REPLY, typed, "No, we don't," and clicked SEND.

* * *

BY MID-AFTERNOON I had finished the story about Dr. Lymanski's research discovery and the upcoming award ceremony, along with a couple of minor pieces that required only a phone call each. Don O'Rourke left for the day at three o'clock, and I checked out at 3:05 after telling Fred Donlin, the night city editor, that I was going out on an interview and wouldn't be back until the next day. I was still trying to decide how to approach Vito Luciano as I parked in the lot at King Vinnie's Steakhouse.

I was greeted at the entrance to the dining room by Max Triviano, the manager, which never would have happened with Vinnie in charge. Vinnie's number one priority as owner of the restaurant was schmoozing his customers. His philosophy was that the office work would still be there to be dealt with after the paying guests were gone and the doors were locked, whether it be after hours or early morning. In fact, most of the bookwork had been left to Max, who was better as a back-office bean counter than as a front-door glad hander.

When I asked to see Vito, Max waved toward the hallway in the back and said, "You can knock but I don't guarantee he'll answer. Vito's nothing like Vinnie, may he rest in peace."

"Don't I know it," I said.

I walked back and rapped on the office door. Hearing no response, I rapped louder. This time a voice inside said, "Who's it?"

Glenn Ickler

"Mitch from the *Daily Dispatch*," I said.

"What the hell do you want?"

"To talk to you. I just interviewed and wrote a story about a good buddy of yours."

"I ain't got any good buddies."

"How about we discuss it without the door between us?" I said.

"Oh, for Chris' sake come in," said Vito.

I did. He was tilted back in a beat-up leather swivel chair behind a desk that was the exact opposite of Dr. Philip Lymanski's sterile workspace. Sheets of paper, magazines, file folders, newspapers, and ledger books were heaped in sloppy piles all across the surface. It was a close call, but I made the grudging concession that Vito's desk was even more of a jungle than my own.

I picked a stack of old newspapers off a chair in front of the desk, dropped the papers on the floor, and sat down.

"So, what phony baloney is claimin' to be a good buddy of mine?" Vito said.

"Dr. Philip Lymanski," I said. "And he seems to be the real thing."

Vito sat up straight and put his arms on the desk. "What the hell were you talkin' to him about?"

"He's famous in the world of chemistry. He's getting a big deal award at the 'U' this weekend. I thought you'd be there to clap when he was introduced. I'm hoping you'll make a comment for my story." No reason to tell him the story was finished and probably already set in a page of the morning paper.

"Why would I be there?" Vito said. "I told you I ain't seen Lymanski since the, uh, the incident."

"Lymanski says otherwise. He says you two get together occasionally."

"You asked him that?"

"In a roundabout way."

"You're a sneaky son of a bitch, did you know that?"

"I've been called worse things than that," I said.

"You are worse than that," he said. "You're a snoopy pain in the ass who never gives a guy a minute's peace. Now that Louie's off the hook I suppose you're back to hopin' you can prove I killed Vinnie. You probably asked Phil if he mixed up the poison for me to put on Vinnie's goddamn fool piece of garbage on a stick."

"What if I told you that I did and he said yes."

"I'd know you were a lyin' little creep in addition to bein' all them other things I just said."

"*Those* other things," I said.

"What did you say?"

"I corrected your grammar without thinking. Sorry about that."

"Oh, my god, you come in here accusin' me of murderin' my cousin and you're worried about my fuckin' grammar?"

"It's a habit with me. Knee-jerk response you could call it. Sometimes I just can't control it."

"Well, I can't control the urge to throw out of this office without takin' the time to open the door, so you'd better get your ass out of here before I come around this desk and grab you by your suspicious little throat."

I stood up. "Where were you and who were you with the day that Vinnie died?"

"Get the hell out of my sight." Vito started around the desk and I accepted the invitation to vanish. I closed the door behind me to slow Vito down in case he was following and walked full speed back into the dining room.

Louie Luciano was standing at the bar.

Chapter Twenty-Seven

Diplomacy

THE SLAMMING OFFICE DOOR had drawn Louie's attention. He was turning to look at me, and I came to an abrupt halt to take stock of my situation. Behind me, at the end of the hall in which I was standing, was the restaurant's back door. Ahead of me was Louie, who was smiling and rubbing his right hand with his left like a jeweler polishing a stone. The right hand was clenched in a fist that looked as big as a cantaloupe to me.

There were two options. One, I could turn and run out the back door or, two, I could try to bluff my way past Louie. A sensible person would have chosen option one, but sensible people don't work as newspaper reporters. I walked slowly forward.

"Nice to see you," I said when I was about a dozen feet away from Louie.

"Even nicer to see you," Louie said. His smile widened. "Would you like your head smashed to pieces right here or do you want to take it outside?"

"I'd prefer to stay in here where there are witnesses." I pointed to three bar patrons and Ozzie the bartender, all of whom were watching with morbid interest.

"You think these birds are gonna help you?" Louie said.

"I think they'll testify against you at your assault-and-battery trial after you beat up a reporter who offers no resistance."

"What do you mean no resistance? Are you just gonna let me bash your head in without fighting back?"

"I come in peace and offer you an apology for judging you falsely. Also I am by nature a pacifist who does not engage in fisticuffs." I gave him my most Ghandian look of peaceful serenity.

The smile turned to a look of puzzlement. "So you're just gonna take a one-two punch to the kisser without any kind of fight?"

"That's right, Louie. I am in the wrong and I deserve to be punched in the kisser. And I will not swing at you in return." This was, of course, pure hogwash. If he came at me I'd break his nose, but I'd rather talk my way out of the conflict.

Louie's fist unfolded. "That wouldn't be no fun."

I started to say "*any* fun," but caught myself in time to say, "*Any* . . . future investigations on my part will assume that you had no part in your father's tragic death." All I needed was to have him explode over a grammar correction.

"Damn right I didn't, you goddamn slimy weasel," he said. "You should have listened to me in the first place instead of getting me sent to jail."

I had just been demoted from a snoopy pain the ass to a goddamn slimy weasel, but I didn't mind as long as the threat of damage to my head was gone. "You're right, I should have, but I'm a suspicious person by nature. I guess it's just in my genes."

"Well, you better get your jeans outta here before I change my mind and give 'em a kick with a number thirteen extra-wide shoe."

Again I accepted the invitation to vanish, walking with dignity past Louie and subduing the urge to run like a rabbit to the front door. "I'm still gonna sue the goddamn paper for slander," Louie said as the door swung shut behind me.

"*Libel*," I said to the air around me as I walked to my car. "You sue newspapers for libel, not slander."

* * *

"So HOW WAS YOUR DAY?" Martha Todd asked when I arrived home.

"I was called a snoopy pain in the ass, a lying little creep and a goddamn slimy weasel, all within minutes of each other."

192

"I didn't know weasels were slimy."

"That kind of surprised me, too. I've always thought of weasels as skinny and hairy and dry. Not that I've thought about weasels all that much."

"Well, if it's any consolation, I was called an overbearing bitch today by a lawyer representing a slumlord our client is suing."

"We have been the recipients of multiple unseemly slurs," I said. "We should console each other."

"I agree. Where do propose that our consolation activities take place?"

"What better place than the bedroom?"

"There is no better place," Martha said. Supper was late again that night.

*   *   *

NEXT MORNING I PARKED my car in the ramp as usual, walked around the corner to the *Daily Dispatch* entrance as usual and ran head-on into Willow. I tried to dodge past her, but she grabbed me around the waist and pressed her body snug against mine. The top of her head was brushing the underside of my nose. Her shampoo had imparted the smell of lilacs to her straight blond hair.

"We really do have to talk," she said.

"Not in this position," I said. She was wearing a flower-patterned, ankle-length, V-necked muumuu, and obviously no bra. I wasn't sure about any other undergarments, but I was guessing there were none.

"Promise not to run away if I let go of your bod?" she said.

"Scout's honor."

She slid her hands up to my shoulders and stepped back about six inches. I tried to twist away, but she dug her fingers into my shoulders and slammed her warm, soft breasts and belly tight against me. "You lied," she said.

"I was never a Boy Scout."

"I was. In fact, I let an Eagle Scout break my cherry."

"Way too much information," I said. "Now let go of me and I swear on a stack of journalistic style books that I won't run away."

"I'll yell rape if you run," she said as she backed off and removed her fingers from the dents they'd created in my shoulders. I suggested that we walk a couple of blocks to a park with benches. She agreed, latched tightly onto my right hand and towed me along behind her. With each step, the muumuu stretched so tightly against her backside that I was able to confirm my suspicion that she was sans panties as well as sans bra. Of course this observation was made purely as a matter of investigative reporting.

We sat side by side on a bench with Willow's right thigh pressed against my left, transmitting heat through her thin muumuu and my summer-weight pants. I asked why she was so desperate to talk to me.

"Because you're my only hope at getting to Al," Willow said. "He's got that awful restraining order out against me and I can't get him to respond to an e-mail, even when I show him what he's missing."

"He's very happily married. He's not missing anything."

"He's the love of my life. I could show him some things in bed that his wife never heard of."

"Don't be too sure of that. Carol's a tiger in the sack." Oh, god, was this me talking about my best friend's wife?

"How do you know what she's like in the sack?" Willow said. "Have you been in the sack with her?"

"Good god, no. Al's my best friend. I wouldn't touch his wife."

"Even if she came on to you?"

"She never would. You're talking nonsense. And you're wasting your time if you keep chasing Al. He wants nothing to do with you."

"You could talk to him. Tell him how much I want him. How bad I need him. Tell him that I get wet down there just thinking about him. Tell him he wouldn't have to leave his wife. Tell him that we could just have a really, really wonderful thing going on the side."

"I would never suggest that to him, and he would never do it," I said.

"He might," Willow said. "If you told him I'm ready to kill myself if I don't have him deep inside me soon."

"That's pure bullshit. Any way, if I told him he'd probably say hurray."

"He wouldn't say that. He's too kind and loving and sensitive. I can see that in his photos. He'd come to me with open arms if he thought it would save my life."

"Forget it. I'm not going to tell him any of this foolishness and you're not going to kill yourself. Go find some other man to pester—somebody single who can give you all the screwing you want."

"There's nobody like Al," she said. "It's not just the screwing. I want his tenderness and caring."

"You're right, there is nobody like him," I said. "And you're not going to ever get near him." I stood up and walked away without looking back. Willow did not follow.

I rode up the elevator to the newsroom with Corinne Ramey, who looked flushed and a bit disheveled. "We're both late," she said. "I overslept; what's your reason?"

"I'm going to have to make one up," I said. "My real reason is so bizarre nobody would believe it." I was tempted to ask her who she'd overslept with but I decided to let it go. I'd already received more than a full day's quota of reports on female sexuality.

As we passed the receptionist's desk, Rhonda Riley called my name. "I've got a message for you from a woman who didn't know your extension," she said. She handed me a yellow slip of paper, which I carried to my desk. Written on the paper was "Call Zoom-I-Yah at city hall, ext. 404."

I translated Zoom-I-Yah to mean Zhoumaya. Wondering what my landlady wanted to talk about during working hours, I called the main City Hall number and followed the directions to reach extension 404.

Chapter Twenty-Eight

City Hall Surprise

AFTER FIVE RINGS, Zhoumaya's voice mail kicked in, telling me she was away from her desk just now, etc. I left a message with my extension number, put down the phone and turned to find Al sitting on the corner of my desk.

"You're late," he said, handing me a cup of coffee. "I had to heat it up again in the microwave."

"I was detained by a crazy lady who says you're the love of her life, poor thing," I said. "Willow literally grabbed me outside the front door and wouldn't let go until I listened to her whine about how devastated she is by your failure to answer her e-mails. She says she'll kill herself if you don't accept her invitation for a rendezvous in bed."

"Tell her I'll send flowers to her funeral," Al said.

"You tell her. I've already killed too much time with her."

"Well, I'm dead certain I'll never open any of her e-mails."

"You'll just let them pass away?"

"Better yet, I'll kill them. And speaking of killing, how'd you make out with cousin Vito yesterday?"

"He called me a lot of uncomplimentary names when I told him we talked to his chemist buddy," I said. "He didn't deny what Lymanski said about still getting together but he threw me out when I asked him where he was when Vinnie ate the poison pill on a stick."

"You really think it's Vito?" Al said.

"Even more so after yesterday's performance. Who had more to gain from having Vinnie dead?"

"Is your pal at the Falcon Heights PD getting anything more from the guy who delivered the naughty stick?"

"My Falcon Heights PD pal was her usual self yesterday. The old 'we can't answer that at this time' routine."

"Well, I have to go shoot a feature with John Boxwood," Al said. "See you at lunch if you're around."

I waved goodbye and centered my thoughts on Vito Luciano. I'd just taken the last sip of coffee when my phone rang. It was Zhoumaya.

"What's up?" I said.

"I don't know if this is in your territory, but something hush-hush is going on in the Public Health Department," she said. "The department head, the mayor and the city attorney are in a huddle and rumors are flying. What might be of interest to you is that I heard Vinnie Luciano's name mentioned by two women talking in the ladies room."

"That does interest me. Did you hear what they were saying about Vinnie?"

"No, they clammed up real quick when they saw me come out of the stall. I'll keep my big ears open and let you know if I find out what's going on."

"Please do that. Meanwhile I'll call somebody I know in the city attorney's office. Thanks for the tip."

My contact in the city attorney's office was Marilee Kohl, a law school classmate and friend of Martha Todd. I knew Marilee because she and her husband had shared several late-night dinners with us during the women's grind through law school. Marilee had been working for the city attorney since passing her bar exam, and she had tipped me to a couple of newsworthy city legal actions that the paper might have missed without forewarning.

I looked up Marilee's extension and made a call. Naturally I got a voicemail recording saying she was away from her desk, etc. Why should she be at her desk when nobody else I call ever was? I left a message and went back to wondering how I could trap Vito Luciano. Don O'Rourke interrupted my musings with an assignment that took me out of the office, away from my desk and my phone. The nerve of the man.

When I returned at about 11:30, I found a voice mail message from Marilee. This time she was at her desk when I called, and I told her about my tip from an anonymous friend in City Hall.

"Whoever your anonymous friend is, he's got good ears," Marilee said. "I can't talk about it right now, but there is something going on with a health inspector, which might explain Vinnie Luciano's name being mentioned."

"Was Vinnie in trouble with the Health Department?" I asked.

"I'm sorry. I can't say any more about it now without risking my job. There's nothing you can write about yet, but I'll let you know the minute something can be made public. Gotta go. Bye."

Don O'Rourke was intrigued when I told him about my two calls. He suggested I go wander around City Hall with my eyes and ears open. "Then have lunch at Callahan's," he said.

Callahan's restaurant was only a couple of blocks from the City Hall and Courthouse, so many city officials, lawyers, and judges hung out there at noon. City Attorney Myles Walters was a regular customer.

Off I went to City Hall. I rode the elevator up to the Public Health Department's office floor and stepped out. The first person I saw in the hall was Vito Luciano.

"Jesus," Vito said. "Ain't there no place a guy can get away from you?"

"*Any* place," I said. Yet another stupid knee-jerk response.

Vito clenched his fists. "What did you say?"

"Nothing. Nothing important." I gave him my most disarming smile. "What brings you here?"

"If you don't know, I sure as hell ain't gonna tell you." Vito turned away and went through the door marked Public Health Department, slamming the door so hard that the glass panel rattled.

While I was debating my next move, the elevator beside the one I had just vacated opened and another unexpected visitor stepped out. He looked as surprised to see me as I was to see him.

"What are you doing here?" I asked.

"I might ask you the same," said Detective Lieutenant Curtis Brown, the police department's chief homicide investigator.

I pointed to the Public Health Department door. "I heard something was going on in there. Do you know what it is?"

"I do but I can't tell you," Brownie said. "Have a good day, Mitch." And through the Public Health Department door he went. I tried to follow, but Brownie put up a hand to stop me and shut the door inches from my nose. Before the door closed I saw two uniformed police officers inside.

The chief of homicide? In the Public Health Department? Had some restaurant's food killed somebody? And was that restaurant King Vinnie's Steakhouse? Why else would Vito be in there?

I was still staring at the door when a voice from behind me caused me to spin around. "Hi, Mitch. Trish Valentine reporting live."

Sure enough, it was Trish and her cameraman. "Do you know what's going on?" I asked.

"All I know is that my source called and said that somebody from public health might be going to jail," she said.

I pulled out my cell phone and called the desk. "Get me a photographer here at the Public Health Department right now."

Chapter Twenty-Nine

Waiting Game

S IX MINUTES AFTER MY CALL Alan Jeffrey popped out of the elevator, breathing hard and holding his camera at the ready. "What's happening?" he asked.

"Somebody in there is about to be arrested," I said, pointing at the Public Health Department door. "We don't know who or why, but Curtis Brown is in there."

"Brownie? Homicide? What the hell?" He wiped a drop of sweat off the end of his nose with the back of his left hand.

"My thoughts exactly," I said.

The second elevator opened and a Channel Five news crew came out to join us.

"Guess you don't get a scoop, Trish," I said.

"Trish Valentine reporting live," she said. "Tied for first with breaking news."

"Who are they arresting?" asked Valerie Karnes, the long-legged, dark-haired Channel Five reporter.

"Nobody knows," Trish said. "But we're ready for them, who-ever it is."

We were, indeed, ready. And we stayed ready through the lunch hour and on into the afternoon. Don O'Rourke called my cell phone every ten minutes to ask what was going on. The two TV reporters took turns standing in front of the office door every twelve minutes, reporting live that breaking news was about to happen. A third TV crew arrived and began reporting live. Soon after them came a reporter and photographer from the

Minneapolis paper. We now had a media circus without a ringmaster or a feature act.

At two minutes past two the office door opened and Andrew Brigham, assistant Ramsey County attorney, stepped out and closed the door behind him. His eyes opened wide and his jaw dropped when he saw the mob. He took a deep breath and swallowed. "Um, you'll have to clear the way folks," he said more as a wish than a command. "Please, everybody back off and let us get to the elevators."

"What's happening?" we all yelled in unison.

"It's complicated," Brigham said.

"So tell us," I said.

"Not here." He looked at his wristwatch. "The county attorney's office at, um, three o'clock. We'll explain everything then. Now please clear a path to the elevator."

Like a spent wave of seawater flowing back off a beach, we retreated en masse to the far side of the elevator. Brigham punched the down button and went back and opened the office door. A parade emerged, led by Curtis Brown, City Attorney Myles Walters and the mayor. They were followed by the two uniformed officers holding the arms of a short, sallow, gray-haired man whose hands were cuffed behind his back. Next was Vito Luciano, who was trying to make himself invisible behind the trio. The two top Public Health Department officials came next, and two dark-suited men who looked like lawyers brought up the rear.

We were all shouting questions and taking pictures as the cordon waited for an elevator. Brigham kept holding up his hand and shouting, "Not now. Three o'clock. Not now."

The elevator arrived and everybody except the two lawyers got on. We kept shouting questions and they kept saying, "No comment," until the other elevator arrived and opened a way for them to escape. When they were in, I slid past Trish and squeezed through the closing elevator doors.

"Who is that in handcuffs?" I asked.

"No comment," said one suit.

"The county attorney will tell you," said the other.

"What's the charge against him?"

"No comment," said one.

"The county attorney will tell you," said the other.

"Are you representing the man they arrested?"

"No comment," said one.

"Actually, we are—temporarily," said the other. "But he has the right to select his own representative and I don't think it will be us."

"Why not you?" I asked.

"No comment," said one.

"His ass is in deeper trouble than we can dig it out of," said the other. The elevator stopped, the doors opened and the two lawyers scooted away at double time.

*   *   *

"THIS IS COMPLICATED, so please bear with me," Andrew Brigham said to the media mob in the county attorney's office. Standing a step behind Brigham in a line at his left were the county attorney, the city attorney and the chief of homicide.

"Quite a high-powered lineup," I said to Trish Valentine, who was standing in front of me.

"It's complicated," she said.

Brigham read his statement from a sheet of paper: "The man you saw brought out of the Public Health Department office in handcuffs is Sheldon Kularski, age sixty-two, who has worked as a restaurant inspector for the City of St. Paul for twenty-seven years. Mr. Kularski will be charged with extortion, specifically demanding money from restaurant owners in exchange either for overlooking violations of the health code, or for threatening to report violations that did not, in fact, exist.

"The charge is based on evidence presented by Vito Luciano, the owner of King Vinnie's Steakhouse, located on West Seventh Street in this city. This evidence was gathered and documented by the late Vincent Luciano, the previous owner of King Vinnie's Steakhouse, who died before he was able to present the evidence to authorities."

Brigham looked up from what he was reading and said, "This is where the complications begin, so listen close."

"Listen *closely*," I whispered in Trish Valentine's ear. She jabbed me two inches below the bellybutton with her elbow.

Returning to the written statement, Brigham continued: "Vincent Luciano informed Mr. Kularski of his intent to present the evidence, which includes demanding substantial amounts of money from King Vinnie's Steakhouse and a number of other St. Paul restaurants. Five days after notifying Mr. Kularski of his intentions, Vincent Luciano was poisoned while presenting a new novelty food item at the Minnesota State Fair. Vito Luciano then took charge of the restaurant, found the material in the office safe and submitted it to the Department of Public Health. Today's action is the result of an internal investigation conducted by department officials in conjunction with the St. Paul Police Department.

"At Vito Luciano's suggestion, the homicide division has investigated Mr. Kularski's whereabouts at the time of Vincent Luciano's untimely death. Mr. Kularski has denied having any participation in the poisoning. He also has denied being at the State Fairgrounds at that time, but a witness who knows Mr. Kularski personally has stated that she saw Mr. Kularski at the fairgrounds on that morning. Therefore, our office is considering the possibility of filing a murder charge against Mr. Kularski in addition to the aforementioned charge of extortion." Brigham looked up and took a breath. "Now I'll take your questions."

He looked at Trish, whose hand was waving, and pointed to her.

"How certain is the witness that the man she saw in the crowd at the fair was Mr. Kularski?"

"The witness is completely certain," Brigham said. "She took special notice because Mr. Kularski was holding hands with another man."

"Do you know who the other man is?" I asked before Brigham could look away.

"We have identified him," Brigham said.

"Is he a suspect, too?" asked Valerie Karnes.

"He is a person of interest. He has not been arrested."

"When will you decide whether to charge Mr. Kularski with murder?" asked someone behind me.

"That depends on the results of Detective Lieutenant Brown's investigation."

"Have Falcon Heights police been working with Detective Brown?" I asked.

Brownie stepped forward. "There has been some exchange of information and we are looking forward to a more cooperative effort in the near future," he said.

"In other words, 'no,'" I whispered. Trish jabbed me again, a little lower. "Keep it above the belt," I said.

The questions soon became irrelevant or unanswerable and Brigham called a halt. I turned looking for Al and heard Trish giving her wrap-up: "This is Trish Valentine, reporting live from St. Paul City Hall."

"Still think cousin Vito's the big bad killer?" Al said as we walked back to the *Daily Dispatch*.

"Can't win'em all," I said.

"By my count you haven't won any. First Louie is released and now Vito turns out to be Mr. Clean."

"Okay, so I'm down and dirty with two strikes against me, but KGB and company in Falcon Heights are also close to striking out looking for the real killer."

"Maybe so, but you've been caught off base twice with the Luciano family."

"Who'd have thought Vito would pitch in for the good guys? And I also remember Louie saying something about bribes to inspectors when we first met him. I wonder if he knew that Vinnie was on Kularski's tail."

Don O'Rourke had left for the day, so I gave Fred Donlin, the night city editor, a rundown on the events in City Hall and went straight to the phone on my desk. "Homicidebrown," was the one-word answer to my call.

"Dailydispatchmitchell," I said. "I've got a few more questions for you, such as how long have you been involved in the Vinnie Luciano murder investigation without me knowing it?"

"Couldn't talk about it," Brownie said. "Couldn't risk having the word get out and spooking Kularski. Didn't want him following his stolen money to the Dominican Republic or some such place before we could collar him."

"How solid is the witness who placed Kularski at the fair?"

"Rock solid. The witness works in the health office and volunteered the information while we were interviewing her about the suspected bribes. She gave Kularski a second and third look when she saw him holding hands with a guy because she didn't know he was gay."

"How would Kularski have known about Vinnie's dog-and-pony show at the state fair?"

"There was a listing of fair events in your great Sunday newspaper three days before Vinnie was killed. It included a blurb about Vinnie introducing a new food on a stick. Even gave the time and place."

"Oh, god, I forgot about that. So are you going to have Grubby Grimes, the stick delivery man, look at Kularski?"

"*Alleged* stick delivery man if you please," Brownie said. "We'll do the same thing Falcon Heights did with Louie Luciano. We'll do a lineup with Kularski and three other guys in a dark room and have all four recite what Grimes says the guy who hired him said in the parking lot."

"Speaking of Falcon Heights, you dodged the question about working with them. What's really happening?"

"I did not dodge the question," Brownie said. "I merely gave a diplomatic answer. Off the record, they weren't all that interested in joining our investigation at first but they're ready to climb on board now. Their problem now is that we've got the guy locked up and they'll have to come to our house to talk to him."

"Have fun working with detective Barnes."

"There's no cop I can't work with, Mitch."

"That's what I thought until I ran into KGB."

"I don't anticipate any problems, Mitch. Have a good day."

My story was nearly finished when my phone rang. I was surprised at the caller's greeting. "Hello, Mr. Mitchell, it's Detective Barnes at the Falcon Heights PD."

"Hello, detective," I said. "To what do I owe this pleasure?"

"We're seeing TV reports on the arrest of a restaurant inspector who might be charged with the Vincent Luciano murder. We're assuming you were at the press conference. In fact, we think we saw you behind the little blond TV reporter."

"That's me—right next to Trish Valentine reporting live."

"Oh, yes, that's her name—Trish. Anyway, we're calling because we're wondering if we could have that lunch you've been asking about."

I almost dropped the phone. "Why the sudden change of heart?" I asked.

"We were aware of the investigation but we're assuming you know more about the evidence than you can print in the paper," KGB said. "And we're also looking for some insight into Detective Brown of the St. Paul PD, the man we'll be working with."

"Sounds pretty one-sided," I said. "What's in this conversation for me?"

"We might be able to give you something of interest." Her tone was more coy flirtation than cop information.

"Such as?"

"Meet us and see."

I wanted to tell the royal "we" to take her lunch and shove it where the sun don't, excuse me, *doesn't* shine. However, professional curiosity and testosterone stimulation won out over my desire for personal vindication. We agreed to meet in a restaurant in Rosedale at 12:30 the next day.

Chapter Thirty

A New Look

HEALTH INSPECTOR SHELDON KULARSKI was arraigned at 8:30 Thursday morning with the usual crowd of reporters, photographers, and busybodies looking on. He was charged with extortion, acceptance of bribes, and obstruction of justice. No mention of murder or manslaughter. Apparently Brownie's investigation wasn't far enough along for that.

The group of law enforcement officials attending did not include anyone from the Falcon Heights Police Department. I expected to see either Chief Tubb or Detective Barnes but neither appeared.

The person whose appearance did surprise me was the lawyer who stood up with Kularski as he entered his not guilty pleas. It was Linda L. Lansing, known throughout the Twin Cities as the premier defender of the guilty.

"What do you think about Linda Lansing appearing for the defense?" Al asked as we hiked back to the office.

"I'm wondering if she'll still be there when the charge is murder," I said.

"Does she ever defend anybody who is really innocent?"

"She defended you when you were accused of killing that umpire." Al had been accused of murdering an umpire with whom he'd had an argument the previous day, and Triple-L had come to the rescue.

"So it's not a sure thing that he's guilty if she takes the case."

"Nothing in life is a sure thing except death and taxes."

"And cockroaches," Al said. "I read somewhere that there will always be cockroaches even if humans exterminate themselves."

"You're buggy," I said. "Cockroaches would starve without humans."

Back at my desk, I discovered an e-mail from Willow on my desktop computer. I was surprised that she hadn't contacted me earlier. It was easy enough to do; my e-mail address appeared in italics at the end of every bylined story.

My mouse started guiding the cursor toward the delete button but my curiosity got the better of me. I opened the message and read: "I really, really enjoyed our little meeting yesterday morning. Please tell my darling sweet Al how much I worship him and miss our sweet little conversations. Please show him the attachment so he can see what he's missing and tell him to get in touch (in more ways than one)."

Also out of curiosity, I peeked at the attachment. It was a full-length, full-front photo of Willow, dressed as she was the moment she was born. Her unclad body at its current age looked, well, willowy. Too bad her brain was behaving as if she'd fallen out of a tree and landed on her crown. I closed the attachment and deleted the message. No sense bothering Al.

*　　*　　*

DETECTIVE K.G. BARNES WAS already seated and the menus were on the table when I arrived at the restaurant at 12:30. She was wearing a filmy white blouse with the two top buttons unbuttoned and a navy blue skirt that ended above the middle of her thighs. I'd always seen her wearing a dark blue uniform shirt and matching slacks, and I had never imagined her body and legs to be so enticingly proportioned.

The new, sexy KGB rose with a wide smile, grasped my proffered hand with both of hers and held on for several beats longer than necessary. Her hands were strong, but smoother and softer than I expected a cop's hands would be.

"We read your story this morning," KGB said. "It went well beyond the TV reports. You obviously have a good relationship with Detective Brown."

"We've developed a mutual trust over the years," I said. "It helps us both."

"Were you anticipating a similar trusting relationship with us?"

I wasn't sure if "us" meant her or the Falcon Heights PD in general. "I didn't expect to form an instant bond but I was hoping for more access to background information."

KGB cocked her head in a flirtatious way. "So all those lunch meetings you kept proposing were strictly for business?"

"Absolutely," I said. "I was hoping to break through the wall you and your chief were building around the investigation." I picked up the menu and opened it, wondering where this conversation was going.

She followed my lead on the menu. "You're sure that you weren't trying to break through anything else?"

"I'm not sure what you mean." I skimmed the sandwich selections while she replied.

"What we mean is that we're a woman and you're an attractive man. We thought you might be wishing for something more than police department information."

"What I'm wishing for right now is that you would drop the royal 'we' and talk like a regular human being."

"Is that all you want me to drop?" Again the tone was a come-on.

"That'll do for now," I said.

"Maybe something else later?"

Before I could respond, our server, who'd said her name was Maria, interrupted us to take our orders. I asked for a cheese and bacon burger, and KGB opted for the portabella mushroom burger. We both ordered lemonade.

I needed to change the tone of the conversation so I asked how much contact she'd had with Detective Curtis Brown. It turned out that her chief had all but ignored Brownie when he reported that he was investigating a new suspect in the Luciano murder case. This exchange led us into a much less sexually charged conversation, with KGB looking for additional information about the activities of the new suspect and the personality of Detective Brown. I gave her little that she didn't already know about either the evidence or the man she'd be working with.

KGB grabbed the check when Maria delivered it. "My treat," she said.

"My thanks," I said.

"Any other treats you're interested in?" She unbuttoned the third button on her blouse and leaned toward me across the table. I was treated to an expanse of creamy cleavage because her bra was cut extremely low. "You never did answer my question about what else you'd like us, I mean *me*, to drop," she said.

I was tempted to say, "Your panties." I was ninety-nine percent sure that's what she was hoping I would say. Instead, I wriggled out of the trap by saying we should discuss treats and drops sometime in the future when we weren't involved in a professional manner.

"We . . . uh, *I* suppose you're right," KGB said. "But I was serious when I said I think you're an attractive man."

"And you're an attractive woman when you let your official guard down and drop the royal 'we,'" I said. "May I ask you kind of a personal question?"

"You may ask it. I don't promise to answer it."

"What do your initials, K and G, stand for?"

She thought for a moment before responding. "You promise not to print them?"

"Swear it on a stack of style books."

Again she hesitated. "The middle initial G is for Gretchen," she said at last. "And the goddamn K is for Kitty. Would you believe my parents named me Kitty? I've been fighting that image all my life."

"Thanks, that explains a lot," I said. "And I promise that you'll never see Kitty in print."

We walked out together and she gave my hand another long, warm squeeze before we went our separate ways.

"You can expect more cooperation and a lot less 'we,'" were her parting words. She left me wondering what had inspired this unexpected turnaround.

* * *

DETECTIVE LIEUTENANT CURTIS BROWN had nothing new to offer when I called him after lunch. He hadn't run the lineup with Kularski because they had only one other man, a guy who had slugged his wife and couldn't make bail, in the city jail.

Brownie invited me to come and stand in the lineup but I respectfully declined. I had done that once when I was subbing for Augie Augustine at the police station and the clowns locked me in a cell and disappeared for ten minutes afterward. I was starting to sweat when they finally unlocked the cell door. "Just trying to make it look real to the prisoners," was the excuse given. Never again.

"I'll come and watch," I said.

"Like hell you will. His lawyer would chew me up and spit me out in little pieces if I let a reporter watch."

"You're right. Triple-L is as ferocious as a tiger."

"Doesn't your sweetie work for her?"

"She does, but that won't help me any. Triple-L is also like a clam."

A Killing Fair

*   *   *

MARTHA AND I WATCHED BOTH the dinner time news and ten o'clock news and we were amazed at how the TV reporters went after Sheldon Kularski. At five o'clock we saw Trish Valentine standing beside the stage at Heritage Square, talking about how Grubby Grimes had delivered the poison after allegedly being hired by Kularski. At ten o'clock we switched channels and saw tape of Valerie Karnes standing almost in Trish's footprints and making the same claim. The anchors on both broadcasts all but declared Kularski guilty, citing the vaguest of comments by City Attorney Myles Walters.

"They've probably got it right but I think they're jumping the gun on convicting him," I said. "I don't think I heard the word 'alleged' used much on either channel."

"They're also poisoning the jury pool," Martha said.

"Spoken like a true lawyer."

"What do you want from a person who is a true lawyer?"

"Turn off the tube and I'll show you what I want from one particular true lawyer."

She did and I did. She already knew that what I wanted had nothing to do with her being a true lawyer. True to form, she started taking off her clothes while leading me into the bedroom. I had no objection.

Chapter Thirty-One

Lining Up

The first thing I did Friday morning was delete an unopened e-mail from Willow. I had no remaining curiosity about either the message or the attachment.

The second thing I did Friday morning was call Brownie, who put me on hold for almost five minutes before he made himself available. I asked about the possibility of a lineup with Sheldon Kularski.

"Looks possible," Brownie said. "We kept a couple of drunk drivers in the tank overnight so we'd have some scumbags to put in with Kularski and the wife beater. I'm trying to set up the lineup before they go to court and the judge sends them home on their own recognizance."

"What this city needs is a crime wave so the cops have enough bodies to put in a lineup," I said.

"What this city needs is a newspaper reporter who doesn't keep us from getting our work done. I gotta go, Mitch. Have a good day."

Don O'Rourke gave me enough work to keep me out of the office and off the phone until almost noon. I was back at my desk, checking my messages and thinking about heading for the lunchroom, when my phone rang.

"It's Brown," said the caller. "They're taking Kularski into court at 1:30 to arraign him on a charge of murder one. That Grubby Grimes character said Kularski's voice sounds like the guy who hired him to deliver the death on a stick."

"We'll be there," I said. I was referring to Al and me, not using the royal we.

* * *

ON OUR WAY to the courthouse, I told Al about my weird luncheon with the new, sexy KGB. "I can't explain the switch from cold fish to red hot mama," I said.

"I can," Al said. "Instead of you needing her for information, she now needs you. The new suspect is being held by the St. Paul PD and Brownie is probably stonewalling KGB. Next she'll be snuggling up and whispering sweet questions into your ear."

"So it's not my boyish charm? The shoe is on the other foot and she's still a heel?"

"She's trying to shine up to you now. But I bet she'll give you the boot once she gets what she wants, which involves verbal intercourse, not the good kind."

The usual media mob was milling about the courtroom when Sheldon Kularski was brought in wearing an orange jumpsuit, handcuffs, and ankle shackles. He looked pale and frail as he stood facing the judge. His hands and knees were shaking so violently I could hear the handcuffs and chains rattle.

Linda L. Lansing, who was nearly a foot taller than her client, rose and stood beside him as the clerk recited the charge. Standing side-by-side among the observers were detectives Curtis Brown and K.G. Barnes. Neither of them looked my way, and I noticed that they did not look at each other. Al's assessment of KGB's motivation for the sexy turn-on appeared to be on target.

Kularski's response of "not guilty" was barely audible. Triple-L asked that he be released on bail and the judge ordered him held without bail. The officers holding Kularski's arms hustled him away as fast as a man can be moved with his ankles shackled together. The whole thing took less than five minutes.

Al and I were at the courthouse door when Linda L. Lansing stopped me with a tap on my shoulder. "Call me at my office before you write anything," she whispered close to my ear. "We need to talk."

"What was that about?" Al asked.

"Either she wants to schedule a secret love tryst with me, which could never happen, or she wants to talk about a case before a trial, which she never does."

"Sounds like plenty of nothing."

"Nothing's plenty for me," I said. "This is one call I'm definitely going to make."

I called Triple-L and Associates immediately after grabbing a cup of coffee and returning to my desk. I was put through to Triple-L immediately by her secretary, which was another thing that never happened.

"Thanks for calling so quickly," said Triple-L. "I've been holding off all my other calls until I got yours."

"I'm deeply honored," I said. "To what do I owe this deep honor?"

"You should be deeply honored. You know damn well that I never talk to reporters before a trial."

"I do."

"And you know damn well that I never talk to reporters about a case off the record at any time whatsoever—before, after or during a trial."

"I do." This was starting to sound like a wedding.

"Well, I'm about to break both rules."

Wow. First KGB turns friendly and now LLL is breaking rules. "May I ask why you're doing this?" I asked.

"Because it will benefit my client," she said. "It can also save you and your paper some eventual embarrassment but I really don't care about that."

"Your lack of concern for me and my paper overwhelms me."

"It should."

"I'm ready to take notes."

"You won't need any notes. This is strictly between you and me and I suppose your editor."

"Okay, no notes. But I have a photographic memory."

"If you write one word of this I'll never trust you or speak to you again. Plus I'll put the Lansing curse on your head."

"What's that?"

"May the fleas of a thousand camels inhabit your pubic hair."

"In that case, Scout's honor I won't write anything," I said.

"When were you a Scout?" said Triple-L.

"Actually, never. How about I swear on a stack style books?"

"Good enough. Here's what I want you to know. The television news reports have been having a field day with my client over the extortion charge and the possibility of a murder charge. Now that he's actually been charged with murder, they'll be having a real circus. I'm hoping that the St. Paul paper will be more circumspect with what it prints, which means I'm hoping you will be extremely careful about what you write and will cast a similar influence over what others write."

"We never go over the top like TV," I said.

"I know that," she said. "Here's my reason for suggesting extra caution on this story. As you know, I have represented hundreds of clients as defendants in criminal trials. Most of them have been guilty, but a few have actually been innocent. My current client, Sheldon Kularski, is guilty as hell of extortion, and the prosecution has him by the nuts thanks to Vinnie Luciano's work.

"Having said that, I want you to know that this man had nothing to do with Vinnie's murder. I have talked to dozens of killers in my work, and I've developed an extremely accurate bullshit detector. Having used that detector in my talks with Sheldon Kularski, I am convinced he is genuinely innocent of murder. I know you have to write as much as you can dig up about this case, Mitch, but I'm asking your paper to use restraint and stick to the known facts so that he's not convicted in the press before he goes to trial."

"What about Grubby Grimes identifying your client's voice as that of the man who hired him to deliver the poison?" I said.

"At this point, that little shit will say anything to get a reduced sentence," Triple-L said. "No jury in the world would convict a man of murder on the basis of the Grubby guy's testimony, and there's no evidence that connects Mr. Kularski to the poison. He was simply one of many people who happened to be walking around the fairgrounds that day. He stood out in one woman's eyes because he was holding hands with another guy, but I have a witness who will provide Mr. Kularski with a valid and believable alibi. So again I'm saying that you'll benefit both my client and your newspaper by sticking to the facts as they're made public and not letting the commentary go wild."

"If you're right, the cops should still be looking for the real killer," I said.

"They should be," she said. "But if cops think they can see an easy conviction they sit back and wait for the trial."

"So you're basically telling me that I should be looking for the real killer. Al and I should be looking."

"You guys have done that more than once. Have a nice day, Mitch."

Chapter Thirty-Two

Starting Over

B Y THE TIME I FINISHED briefing Don O'Rourke and writing my careful, strictly factual story there wasn't much day left. I was looking ahead at a three-day weekend, with Saturday, Sunday, and Monday off, needing to start all over on the hunt for Vinnie Luciano's murder. I had no idea where to begin the search.

My two chief suspects, Vito Luciano and Louie Luciano, had both been eliminated. Vinnie's restaurant competitors, Oscar Peterson at Northern Exposure and Luigi Bunatori at House of Italy, seemed like very poor prospects. Who was left to investigate? Vinnie's wife? Vinnie's other two children? They just didn't seem to fit the profile of a killer.

I had to respect Linda L. Lansing's judgment of her client, which almost certainly meant the real killer was still out there somewhere. But nothing made sense. There was nowhere to go to pursue the story.

"We need to start from scratch and refigure this whole story," I said to Al. "I don't want to wait until next Tuesday to do it, but Martha expects me to help with finishing our move to the new apartment this weekend."

"I'm with you," Al said. "Bring your laptop along when you and Martha come for dinner tonight and we'll get started right after dessert. Maybe we can unravel this can of worms."

So after consuming a hefty plateful of cheese and veggie lasagna and a large slice of Carol's apple pie, I joined Al in his home office to review the events, starting with the pictorial history on Al's laptop. Every photo he had shot from the presentation at Heritage Square to the murder arraignment of Sheldon Kularski was on file. He always saved everything he'd shot until the story had been completed. After the killer was caught and convicted, Al would cull his photos, saving those that had been published and others that he liked.

We flipped through the Heritage Square pix, looking for familiar faces in the audience and onstage. We saw the fake Fairchild deliver the strychnine-loaded square meal on a stick. We studied the background, looking for anyone who might be reacting to the delivery. We found nothing.

We arrived at the shots of Vinnie taking his first bite of his last meal. The series that followed included close-ups of Vinnie and overall shots of almost the entire stage, including the cluster of square dancers standing behind Vinnie and Scott Hall. "My mother felt sorry for those guys having to watch Vinnie die," I said, pointing to the square dancers.

"That must have been tough, but there's one dancer who isn't hanging around to watch," Al said. He zoomed in on the group and pointed to one man in square dance attire whose back was toward the camera. The next overall shot showed the same man jumping off the back of the stage.

"Go back a few shots," I said. "See if we can see the face of the guy who can't bear to watch."

Al reversed direction and stopped several shots farther back. Vinnie was taking that first bite and the square dancers were visible. "Zoom in," I said.

The man we were looking for was still facing Vinnie in that shot. "Zoom in some more," I said. "Maybe we can see his face."

The man's features became less distinct as the image grew larger, but his expression came through clear enough. It was a look of open-mouthed, wide-eyed horror at what he was seeing.

"Makes sense that he'd be horrified," Al said.

"Except that Vinnie is just taking the first bite," I said. "Vinnie doesn't realize he's in trouble but it looks to me like the man behind him does. The guy looks vaguely familiar. Move ahead a few shots."

Four shots later, as Vinnie was staring at the stick with his mouth open, probably saying the food didn't taste right, the dancer in the background appeared again. His expression was changing from the horrified look to something else. Fright, maybe?

"Who is that guy?" I asked.

"We don't know any of the square dancers do we?" Al said.

"I think we might know that one. It looks a lot like Erik what's his name, the president of the Oles and Lenas."

"Our host after the play," Al said. He looked closer at the photo. "I think you're right. Isn't his last name Erickson?"

"Yes, his name is Erickson. Why does he look like he's seen a ghost, I wonder."

"He can't know the stick is poisoned."

"No, he can't," I said. "Or can he?" There was a beat of silence before Al responded.

"Holy shit, you're not thinking what I'm thinking?" Al said.

"I think I am. Hang on while I look up what the Sunday paper blurb actually said about that program. I've never taken the time to go back and read it."

"Neither have I."

I had copied everything written about the case, including the announcement that Brownie had talked about, into my laptop Vinnie Luciano file. It took several minutes of searching but I finally found it.

I clicked to open it and with our heads almost touching we read: "Everything will be on the square Wednesday when a new treat is added to the Minnesota State Fair menu of foods on a stick. The square-shaped goodie, cooked up by Vinnie Luciano of King Vinnie's Steakhouse, will be introduced at a 10:00 a.m. ceremony on the Heritage Square stage. First to sample the new square concoction will be St. Paul's nationally-known square dance caller, Scott Hall."

Our heads turned in unison until we were staring at each other with our noses an inch apart.

"Christ on a crutch," Al said. "The wrong guy ate the poison."

"Scott Hall was supposed to be the one to die."

"We and the cops have been chasing the wrong suspects for killing the wrong victim all this time."

"And now our suspect is right there in the photo, looking horrified because he knows the wrong man is eating the poison."

"Erik Erickson, square dancer," Al said.

"Erik Erickson, pharmacist," I said.

"Bingo!" we said in unison.

"Do we call Brownie?" Al said.

"Let's think about what we can do on our own before we call Brownie," I said. "Maybe there's a way to bring Scott Hall's would-be killer to the halls of justice without any TV cameras around."

"A square deal all around," said Al.

"Right. Now let's not cut corners as we think this out."

"Well, as for having the means for murder, he wouldn't have had to promenade very far to get the poison."

"But why would the president of a square dance club want to kill the club's caller?"

"He didn't like the guy's singing calls?"

"Be serious," I said. "We're trying to figure out what would motivate a normally law-abiding man to wheel around and become a killer."

The door behind us opened and Martha stuck her head in. "How's it going?" she asked. "Finding anything?"

"Tell Triple-L she's right about her client not being a killer," I said. "We've just found the star of the show."

Carol appeared beside Martha and we invited them into the room. I quickly ran through what we'd done and told them about Erik Erickson looking horrified before the horror show started.

"He's got to be the one who supplied the poison, but why would he do it?" Al said.

Martha looked at me and said, "Wasn't it Erik's wife, Joyce, we saw having a very late dinner with Scott Hall in Minneapolis?"

"That's right," I said. "And the night we had drinks with Erik and Joyce she told you that what we saw wasn't what it looked like."

"Maybe Erik had a different view," Al said.

"The way I see it, we should do something," I said. "The question is: what?"

Chapter Thirty-Three

The Setup

We decided to sleep on it. Even that was a flop. After a night of tossing and turning while various scenarios ran through my head, I met Al for breakfast at a coffeehouse near his home. His eyes looked as red-rimmed and baggy as mine felt.

We drank coffee and swapped ideas. Al had printed a series of pix showing Erik looking on before Vinnie's first bite, reacting to the first bite and beating a hasty retreat. Our plan was to show these pix to Brownie and set up an arrest scene that would be photographed and witnessed only by Al and me. Warren Mitchell and Alan Jeffrey reporting live.

We decided to schedule an interview with Erik on the pretense of talking about the financial problems at his theater and slide into questions about his reaction at Heritage Square as Vinnie began eating the poisoned food. I would have my trusty mini-recorder running and try to get him to talk about why he tried to kill Scott Hall. When I had what I needed, I would yell for help and the cops would rush in, one step ahead of Al with his camera.

"We have to call Erik today and set up the interview for Tuesday when we're back to work," I said. "Then we can show your pix to Brownie first-thing Tuesday morning and set up the sting."

"The sooner the better," Al said. "Remember, a stitch in time saves nine."

"How do stitches apply to snagging Erickson?"

"The quicker we sew him up the less stitches we're likely to get."

"*Fewer*," I said. "The correct word is *fewer* stitches."

"We're being picky about our grammar while we're bagging a killer?"

"I can't help myself. It's a knee-jerk reaction."

"Well, stop being a jerk or I'll give you a knee where your reaction will be tears and loud wailing."

"No kneed for that. Let's get started with Mr. Erickson." I took out my cell phone.

Erik had given me his card printed with the home and pharmacy numbers. He had written his cell phone number on the back with a ballpoint pen. I called the pharmacy first and was told that Mr. Erickson does not come in on Saturdays.

Next I tried his home, and Joyce answered. I greeted her and asked for Erik.

"He's at his damn old theater," she said. "Where he always is on Saturday."

"This early, even when the theater is dark?" I asked. The next production at the Parkside Players Theatre wasn't scheduled to open until Thursday of the next week.

"He practically lives there. If it wasn't for square dancing he'd never leave the goddamn place."

"Can I get him there on his cell?"

"Damned if I know. I've never tried."

"Thanks, Joyce. I'll give it a shot."

"Make the shot bourbon and he'll be your friend forever," Joyce said. "Have a good day." She set her phone down harder than necessary.

"Sounds like a wife who's tired of playing second fiddle to a theater," I said.

"A woman scorned is a woman who answers the call of her square dance caller," Al said.

"I think you called that one right." I punched in Erik's cell phone number and the call went to voice mail. I asked him to call me as soon as possible to discuss a potential story about the theater.

"Whatever he's doing at the theater this early on Saturday he's too busy to answer the phone," I said.

"Maybe Joyce isn't the only Erickson getting a little on the side."

*   *   *

AL HAD GONE HOME to mow his lawn, and I was stuffing a bag filled with who knows what kind of stuff into the already overstuffed trunk of my Civic when Erik called. "Why not come down right now?" he said when I asked about setting up an interview at the theater. "I'm here alone and ready to talk."

I couldn't tell him it was because I also wanted to set up an arrest, so I said, "I can't get a photographer to go with me right now. I'm not actually working today so I'm not in the office."

"Do you always call people about stories on your day off?"

"A reporter never rests. I guess I've gone from alcoholic to workaholic."

"I know how that goes. My wife is always bitching that I spend too much time in the theater when I'm not doing my day job."

"Wives can be a problem."

"Ain't that the god's truth? Listen, I'm working at the pharmacy from seven until four Tuesday, but I can meet you and your photographer at the theater around 4:30 or so," he said.

"Sounds good," I said. "See you then."

"I'll look forward to it."

I snapped off the phone. "So will I," I said as I went back to stuffing the bag of stuff into the trunk.

*   *   *

THE PROBLEM WITH MOVING a short distance is that you think it's foolish to spend money on a mover so you do everything yourself. During the last two weeks, Martha and I had hauled dozens of carloads of clothing, small appliances, light furniture, and general junk from the Grand Avenue apartment to our new home on Lexington Avenue. Then on Saturday afternoon we rented a small truck to carry the big stuff—refrigerator, stove, bed, and a couple of dressers. Al, Kevin, and Kristin helped us load and unload the truck, and Carol fed us supper.

The timing couldn't have been tighter. We had to be out of the Grand Avenue apartment by Sunday night because the landlord was inspecting the place for damage and cleanliness Monday morning so the new renter could take possession later that day. Martha and I were up at dawn Sunday, and spent the day huffing and puffing like the Little Engine That Could removing all traces of our inhabitance of the Grand Avenue apartment.

"You could eat off the floors if we had anything to eat," Martha said at a few minutes after five o'clock.

"I scraped some chunks of dried cat food off the kitchen floor near where the refrigerator used to sit," I said. "They're in the trash barrel if you want a quick snack."

"I'll wait and eat fresh food with Sherlock," she said.

We were as tired as marathon runners on an uphill course by the time we dragged ourselves into our cars and drove to Lexington Avenue. All we were thinking about was having a pizza delivered, attacking it like vultures ripping apart a road kill and tumbling into bed. When we got to our new home, Zhoumaya Jones was sitting in her wheelchair on the porch. "Your cat is gone," she said.

"What do you mean?" I asked.

"I mean your cat is gone," Zhoumaya said. "I went to your apartment to deliver a welcome gift, and he shot out past me the second I opened the door. He barely touched the stairs on the way down, and he took off like a Vikings running back when he hit the bottom. I'm really sorry, but there's no way I could chase him."

We had taken Sherlock Holmes to the apartment on Saturday morning to keep him out from under our feet while we lugged furniture and appliances to the truck. When we'd gone back to clean, we'd left him in the new place with more than a day's supply of food and water and a brand new container of kitty litter. Apparently it didn't feel like home to him.

"Which way did he go?" Martha said.

Zhoumaya pointed north. "That way."

"That's the right direction if he's trying to go home," I said. "How long ago did he leave?"

Zhoumaya checked her watch. "Almost an hour."

I turned to Martha. "Shall we drive back at crawl speed and see if we can spot him on the sidewalk?"

"It's worth a try," Martha said. "You drive and I'll spot."

"I'm really, really sorry," Zhoumaya said.

"Not your fault," I said. Actually, it was her fault but this was a good time to be gracious. After all, she'd been delivering a welcome gift, not merely going in to do the snoopy landlord thing. At least that's what she'd said she was doing.

We crept along, retracing the route we'd just taken, drawing some angry scowls, a few horn honks and at least one extended middle finger from other drivers. We saw two cats, neither of which was Sherlock.

When we reached our recently abandoned apartment, we turned around and went slowly back, frustrating another set of drivers. Again no Sherlock. By the time we returned to our new home, the sun was about to disappear. In a few minutes it would be too dark to hunt for a mostly black cat.

We dragged ourselves out of the car and up the steps and into the apartment. On the counter in the kitchen was a large basket of fresh fruit, wrapped in translucent red plastic and tied with a huge red bow. I picked up the attached card and read it out loud: "Welcome, dear friends, to your new home. May you find peace and happiness here. Your friend always, Zhoumaya."

"Not a very good start on the peace and happiness," Martha said.

"Couldn't be much worse," I said. "I'll walk the route back to Grand Avenue tomorrow. It's only a couple of miles each way. For now, we might as well get the pizza and go to bed."

"I'll pass on the pizza. I'm going straight to bed."

I also passed on the pizza. My appetite was gone, but I ate an apple from Zhoumaya's gift basket to partially fill the void I knew was there before heading for bed. By the time I crawled in beside Martha, she was as responsive as a stone.

Even though I was exhausted, I lay awake for a long time wondering where my feline companion of almost ten years was spending the night. When I finally fell asleep, I dreamed of dozens of black-and-white cats zigzagging through speeding cars, trucks, and buses on an extremely busy street.

Chapter Thirty-Four

The Walking Man

USUALLY I WAVE GOODBYE from my side of the bed when Martha leaves for work on my day off. This day was different. I was up before Martha and was out the door to look for Sherlock Holmes while she was still standing naked brushing her teeth after her shower. I only paused long enough to pat Martha's lovely bare ass on the way to the door, and she mumbled something around her toothbrush that sounded like, "Good luck."

I walked all the way back to the apartment on Grand Avenue, checking every driveway and alley along the way. I encountered six dogs, three cats, half a dozen squirrels and one small rabbit, but didn't find Sherlock. I made a mental note to keep my distance from two of the less friendly dogs on the way back.

I checked the parking lot and the back steps of the Grand Avenue apartment building while calling Sherlock's name, not that he had ever answered to it. Nothing. I went in and knocked on the door of what had been my apartment for twelve years. The door was opened by Israel J. Eisenstein, also known as Izzy, who stepped back with a look of surprise. Izzy, a seventy-five-year-old retired accountant, lived at the other end of the hall and served as the building owner's onsite manager.

"I'm looking for my cat," I said. "He took off and I thought he might have come back here."

"I only just started inspecting the apartment," Izzy said. "I didn't see your cat anywhere around when I took my morning constitutional." Izzy measures five feet, four inches in both height and breadth, and his morning constitutional consists of taking a bag of trash to the barrel beside the back door.

"Please grab him if you see him. I'll give you my cell number so you can call." I pulled an old grocery list out of my back pocket and scribbled the number on it with a pencil I'd left beside the kitchen phone.

"I'll keep an eye out," Izzy said as he pretended to pluck out his right eyeball. "The apartment looks great so far, by the way. Compliment Martha for me."

"Hey, I did a lot of the cleanup work," I said.

"So tell me, who bossed the job? A messy schmuck like you would not have left this place so spotless without a push from somebody."

He had me there because he'd seen how I lived before Martha moved in with me. "Okay, I'll compliment Martha," I said.

I had coffee and a bagel for breakfast at a nearby restaurant before hiking back. There I passed the word that a hungry black-and-white cat might come scrounging for food around the back door. I walked on the opposite side of the street on my return trip and had similar results: five dogs, two cats and three squirrels. No rabbits this time.

I considered making lost kitty posters and tacking them to power poles, but decided it would be a waste of time and paper. I thought my best bet would be to keep checking around my old neighborhood. Sherlock had to be heading that way.

After the lunch hour, I called Detective Curtis Brown's private number and got his voice mail. It said that Detective Brown was away from his office and would return on Thursday.

Thursday? Damn! There went our plan for catching Vinnie's killer without sharing the arrest with all the other media hawks. I wouldn't even suggest our idea to anyone but Brownie. I wasn't sure that even Brownie would agree, and I knew that anyone else in homicide would send the troops charging out to collar Erik Erickson as soon as they saw Al's pix. The chief would announce the arrest to the world, and there would be no exclusive for the *Daily Dispatch*.

I called Al at home and told him the bad news. After a long conversation in which we weighed all the advantages and disadvantages of a police backup, we decided to keep our date with Erik and record the conversation without assistance from the cops. After the meeting with Erik, we'd take the pix and a copy of the tape to whoever was subbing for Brownie and let the police do their thing.

"What else is happening?" Al asked. "The move go okay yesterday?"

"It was okay until we lost Sherlock," I said. I described the cat's disappearance and our futile search.

"You should put up some posters. You know, missing cat, call the number on his collar, that kind of thing."

"I thought of that but it's probably a waste of time and paper."

"Okay, paper costs money but how valuable is your time today?"

I decided Al was right; to hell with paper and time. I made a batch of lost kitty posters and tacked them to poles as I hiked the circuit to the Grand Avenue apartment and back again. Still no Sherlock. I stopped counting dogs, cats, and squirrels. There were no rabbits.

I also called the *Daily Dispatch* and put a missing kitty notice in the paper. It was not a waste of money because as an employee I got the ad for free.

When Martha came home, we walked the circuit again, one on each side of the street both ways. By the end of this trip my feet were growing blisters as big as golf balls. Or maybe they were hailstones. They felt awful damn big anyway.

For the first time in many years, I missed my Monday night Alcoholics Anonymous meeting on a week when I was at home. I was just too pooped and pain-ridden to go. I resolved to make time for getting back into the running routine that I'd dropped because there wasn't time for running.

*   *   *

I LIMPED INTO THE OFFICE on sore and aching feet Tuesday morning.

"Moving that tough on you?" asked Don Boxwood, who had turned down an invitation to help.

"It's a long story," I said. "See me at lunch if you want the gruesome details."

Someone else really did want the gruesome details. That someone was my faithful AA buddy, Jayne Halvorson. She had already left a message on my voice mail. "What happened to you last night?" it said. I called and told her.

"You should have come to the meeting," she said. "We all could have gone cat hunting afterward."

"I couldn't have walked another step," I said. "Besides, you'd never see Sherlock in the dark."

"Well, just keep checking around the old apartment. Cats are known for returning to their old homes."

"This one turned up there as a homeless stray in the first place. I'm expecting him to go back but I'm worried about what might happen to him on the way."

"Have you taught him to look both ways before crossing a street?" she asked.

"The only thing he ever looks both ways for are his food dish and our bed. I'm counting on him surviving with at least one of his nine lives."

My luck stayed bad. Don O'Rourke sent me on assignment that required walking at least a half a mile with a woman who was walking coast-to-coast for peace. She was determined to log eight hours of actual walking time per day so she was stopping only briefly for interviews. If you wanted more than a canned three-minute spiel, you had to walk with her. Just what my poor feet needed.

Al and I weren't sure how much to tell Don about our scheduled interview with Erik Erickson. We decided not to break the news about either our discovery of a switch in intended poison victims or our suspicion that Erik was the poison provider. I told Don we were doing a story about Erik's theater being in trouble, which was true. We just didn't delve into the nature of the trouble on the program.

"Did you get another message from Willow this morning?" Al asked when we met for lunch.

"I deleted it without delay," I said. "I assume you got one, too."

"I did. And I deleted it deliberately."

"The woman could be delightful if she wasn't so deranged."

"Her determination depresses me."

"Likewise. My patience is depleted. So what have you been doing all morning when you weren't deleting e-mails? I could have used you on my interview with the interminable walker."

Al took a long drink of coffee. "I had a shot at City Hall and another one at the old Federal Courthouse. I had a weird feeling—almost like I was being followed—while I was walking to them both."

"Did you check to see if you really were being followed?"

"Sort of. I looked around but I didn't see anybody."

* * *

AT 4:02 P.M. THAT AFTERNOON, two cars—one headed east and one headed west and turning south—came together at the

235

intersection of Kellogg Boulevard and Robert Street. They met each other with considerable force because one was trying to beat a yellow light and the other was jumping the green. The cars were demolished and several of their occupants were injured. Police cars and ambulances swarmed to the scene.

At 4:04 that afternoon, Al came to my desk armed with all his portable photo equipment. "I've been all over town today and now they want me shoot a crash at Kellogg and Robert," he said. "You go ahead to the theater and I'll meet you there."

"Still feel like you're being followed?" I asked.

"Yeah, now that you mention it I do," he said. "I've had that crazy feeling all day but I haven't seen any bad guys behind me."

"Well, I'll go over to the theater to talk to the bad guy we know is ahead of you. To paraphrase old Will Shakespeare: 'The play's the thing wherein I'll catch the killer of the king.'"

"The king?"

"King Vinnie, ruler of King Vinnie's Steakhouse."

"Don't catch him before I get to the theater. I don't want to miss the curtain call."

Normally I would have walked to the Parkside Players Theatre, but my feet were complaining so vehemently about their sorry treatment of late that I chose to drive. This wouldn't save much pain going to the theater because I had to hobble in the opposite direction to get my car from the parking ramp. However, it meant I wouldn't have to walk back after the interview. I could drive directly to the police station.

There were no open parking places in front of the building so I circled the block. By some divine intervention, I arrived at the back of the building just as a car was pulling out. I zipped into the spot behind a BMW with a bumper sticker that said, "I'd rather be square dancing." Now whose car might that be? I limped into the building through a rear door that led into the lobby and turned on my pocket tape recorder.

The lighting in the theater was akin to a cave full of bats, and I didn't see anybody when I walked in. I yelled, "Anybody home?"

"Over here," came the reply. "Stage right. Backstage right, actually. I'm adjusting some things."

Erik Erickson was standing in the shadows in an area normally blocked from the viewing audience by a black teaser. I walked down the center aisle, stepped onto the low platform that served as a stage and took a couple of steps toward Erik.

"Stop right there," he said.

It was barked like an order so I stopped. Was he on to me?

"I'm fooling with lights and teasers and you might get caught in something," he said. "What did you want to talk about?"

"A few weeks back you told me the theater had financial problems because of declining attendance. I was thinking that a story just before your next show goes up might bring back some people who haven't been coming."

"It also might drive more people away," Erik said.

"Not if it's worded right," I said. "I'm pretty good at spinning stories if I do say so myself."

"Really? I noticed you had a little trouble with the one you spun about Vinnie Luciano's son being the one who poisoned him."

How unkind of him to notice a minuscule mistake like that. "That wasn't my finest moment."

"And you seemed pretty sure that Vinnie's cousin was the killer, too, as I recall."

This was too much to absorb without a counter punch. "What if I was wrong because everybody was looking for suspects where there weren't any?"

"What do you mean by that?"

"I mean, what if Vinnie wasn't the intended target? What if somebody else was supposed to eat the poison?"

"That's crazy," Erik said. "Who else could it have been?"

"Well, according to the advance story in our paper, a square dance caller named Scott Hall was supposed to have been the one who sampled the square meal at Heritage Square that morning."

"Really?"

"Really. Now suppose that for some reason somebody who had access to strychnine wanted to kill Scott Hall. Suppose that person was the one who hired that goon to steal Fairchild's costume and deliver the poison."

"Who'd want to kill Scott, for god's sake? He's a great caller."

"Somebody might have had an issue with him. Something personal perhaps." I was thinking it was time for Al to show up. We were getting close to got'cha time and I wasn't sure I could stop Erik if he decided to take off running before I had something incriminating on my tape.

"Any idea who that somebody might be?" Erik asked.

"Actually, I do," I said. "Al has some photos of a square dancer on the Heritage Square stage looking guilty as hell just as Vinnie is taking a bite."

"Really?"

"Really. Want to see them?" I held up three prints that I'd pulled from my inside sport coat pocket.

Erik was standing against the stage right wall with his left hand behind his back. I could see motion in his shoulder and arm but I couldn't see what the hand was doing. A metallic clanking noise above my head told me what it was. He had loosened a line that held a heavy steel pipe hanging high above the stage. That pipe, to which several hundred pounds of stage lights were attached, was falling toward the spot where I was standing.

I dove forward, launching myself headfirst farther onto the stage, but I didn't go far enough. The rigging missed my head and torso, but it crashed onto my right ankle, pinning it to the stage. Where the hell was Al when I needed him?

I was lying on my right side, with my head toward Erik. As I struggled to pull my leg free, he walked toward me and picked up the photos that had gone flying when I hit the deck. He looked at them and smiled. "Interesting," he said.

"We thought so," I said. "The police have a copy. They're on their way here, even as we speak."

"Then I should probably be going elsewhere, shouldn't I," he said.

"Help me up before you go?" The ankle, which had been numb, was beginning to feel like someone had jabbed a red-hot knife into it.

"I kind of like you where you are. In fact, I think you're going to still be there after acquiring a fatal head wound from your fall. I'm sure the police will be happy to pick you up when they get here." He turned and went backstage.

"Tell me, why'd you want to kill Scott Hall?" I yelled.

"You were right when you said it might be something personal. The son of a bitch was banging my wife." He bent down with his back to me and picked up something.

"How'd you find out?" At least my tape was rolling, recording the story even if I couldn't move.

"I came home half an hour early from the theater one night and saw a car pulling away from in front of the house. It had license plates I recognized. They said 'Do-Si-Do' on them." What Erik had picked up was a wooden belaying pin heavy enough to use as a deadly club. He came back and stood over me with the club in his right hand while he continued to tell his story.

"I knew it was Scott's car and that Scott has a reputation as a skirt chaser, so I hired a private detective to shadow my wife. Sure enough, our high-level club caller was calling some basic horizontal figures at my house while I was working at the theater at night. And when there was too much time between available nights, they were dosi doing it in a motel during the day.

"What the private eye also found out was that Joyce and Scott were draining money out of the theater—she's the treasurer—and they were planning to take over as anonymous buyers when I was forced to give it up."

"No wonder you were pissed," I said. I paused in my struggle to get loose because the ankle was hurting too much. Where the hell was Al?

"Pissed isn't the word for it," Erik said. "When I read in the paper that Scott was going to be the taste tester at the fair, I had a really bright idea. At first I was going to knock out Fairchild and deliver the stick myself, but then I thought of Grubby. If he did it, I could be onstage when Scott bit the dust, or in this case the stick. The perfect alibi."

"How did you know a scumbag like Grubby?"

"He works in this building as a janitor. He has a thing for theater so he'd stop in and chat. Told me all about doing time for assault, how he almost killed a guy with his bare hands. Seemed like the perfect messenger to deliver the goods to Mr. Scott Casanova Hall and send him to that great dance hall in the sky."

"The perfect crime that went awry," I said.

"Who'd have thought the asshole would pass the stick to Vinnie? I really feel bad about that. I liked Vinnie."

"Did you also plan to send your wife away to resume dancing with her caller?"

"Oh, yeah. That little slut was next on my list. In about six months she was going to have a terrible accident. But I can't stay here running lines with you, pleasant as it is. So if you'll be kind enough to turn your head a bit I'll give it a whack so it looks like you bumped it when you fell. After that I'll be calling 911 and telling them there's been a terrible accident here in the theater—a reporter was standing in the wrong place when a loose line let go. I hope you've enjoyed your time under the stage lights, Mr. Reporter."

Like a striking snake, his hand darted out and his fingers grasped my hair. He yanked my head up and twisted it sideways so the back was exposed to the club he was raising over his head. "I read somewhere that right behind the ear is the best spot to hit," he said.

"What's going on in here?" a male voice yelled from the entrance to the theater.

Erik released his grip on my hair, letting my head slam onto the floor. "Exit stage right," he said, and in a flash he was gone out the back. Thank God for Al.

Chapter Thirty-Five

Where's Al

BUT IT WASN'T AL. The man who'd hollered ran down the aisle and onto the stage. As he looked down at me, I realized that I'd never seen that chubby-cheeked, red-bearded face before.

"What the hell happened?" the man said. "I heard a crash all the way upstairs in the bar."

"Lights fell on me," I said. "I'm pinned. Please call 911."

"You're lucky you weren't killed. What a freak accident." He pulled a cell phone out of his pants pocket and punched in the three magic numbers.

"You don't know how lucky," I said. "It wasn't an accident."

"Jesus, you mean somebody dropped them on purpose?"

"That's exactly what I mean."

A 911 dispatcher answered the call and the man explained the situation. When his conversation with the dispatcher ended, he squatted beside me. "They're on the way. While we're waiting, let me see if I can lift this thing enough for you to pull your leg out."

He was a short, stocky man with thick arms, big shoulders and a beer gut. He wrapped his hands around the steel pipe and grunted. The only noticeable change was his face turning red.

"This son of a bitch is heavy," he said.

"Guess we'll have to wait for the rescue squad. My name is Mitch. I'm a reporter here to do a story. Thanks for showing up when you did."

"I'm Ernie. I'm the bartender in the restaurant upstairs. Lucky for you there were no drunks making a racket so I could hear the crash down here."

"As I said, you don't know how lucky. The bastard was about to finish the job with a whack on the head."

"Jesus, do you know who he was?"

I was about to reply when another male voice yelled, "Hello," from the back of the theater. This time it was Al. "What the hell happened?" he said.

I sat up and braced myself on my elbows to answer him. "You won't believe what happened."

Al was starting down the aisle toward us when a figure appeared behind him. As the figure came closer, I saw it was a woman dressed in black. The figure was carrying something in her right hand. The figure was Willow and the something was a knife with a blade long enough to disembowel a cow.

Willow's shriek was loud enough and shrill enough to wake the ghost of Hamlet's father or any other spirit residing in the Parkside Players Theatre. "If I can't have you, nobody can," she screamed as she leaped toward Al with the knife raised at arm's length above her head. Al spun to face her at the sound, saw the knife and swung the camera bag that hung from his neck forward and upward just as Willow brought the knife down.

The knife sank deep into the heavy canvas camera bag. Willow tugged at the handle to pull the blade out of the bag, but the blade didn't move. Before she could give the knife a second pull, Al slugged her in the face with his right fist. Willow staggered backward with blood running from her nose. The knife remained impaled in the camera bag.

Willow screamed again. "Why didn't you read my e-mails? I showed you what I was going to do."

"What the hell?" Ernie said.

"Help him," I said. "He's my photographer."

Ernie rose from beside me and started running toward Willow. Al also started running toward Willow, who had turned and was dashing up the aisle toward the exit. As she reached the open doorway, she collided with a man in a blue-and-white EMT uniform, bounced off him and disappeared.

"What the hell?" said the EMT.

"That's what we all say," Al said. "Welcome to the Parkside Players madhouse production."

Two EMTs, whose nametags said "Jack" and "Jill," squatted beside me. Jack said, "Looks like it's gonna take some muscle to get this thing off of you."

A light bulb blinked on in my brain. "Actually, if you pull on the ropes that run through those pullies, you can lift it without busting a gut," I said, pointing at the line that Erik had released. I asked myself why I hadn't thought of this simple solution while Ernie was grunting and straining his gut. I chalked this mental vacuum up to shock.

Jack grabbed the line and raised the rigging enough for Jill to pull me out while delivering the news that my ankle appeared to be broken. In addition to the searing pain in the ankle, my head was throbbing from banging down onto the floor. I thought about what would have happened to my head if Ernie hadn't interrupted the action and decided not to complain about this little bump.

The EMTs stabilized my ankle with inflatable braces, loaded me onto a gurney and wheeled me out to the ambulance. Meanwhile Al was on his cell phone, calling the police to report the attacks by Erik and Willow, and the city desk to report my injury.

As Jill was poised to close the ambulance doors, I tossed my car keys out to Al and told him where it was parked.

"I'll drive it home and you can get it after Martha picks you up at the hospital," Al said.

Oh, god, Martha! I would have to call Martha and tell her I'd been wounded by still another killer on the run. "Martha might just leave me there," I said. "She keeps telling me to be more careful."

"You can tell her you were stage struck."

The ambulance doors closed with a clang that started bongo drums pounding in my aching head.

*   *   *

I HAD JUST BEEN WHEELED out of x-ray and was counting the ceiling tiles in a little room somewhere in the bowels of Regions Hospital when a trio of cops, two in uniforms and one in a baggy brown suit, appeared. Wearing the suit was Mike Reilly, a stocky, crew-cut homicide detective who hated reporters and photographers. In my case at least, the feeling was mutual. We had crossed verbal swords at more than one crime scene during my tenure at the *Daily Dispatch*.

"What kind of a mess did you make this time?" Reilly said, bending over me until the tip of his wide, flat nose was approximately three inches from mine. His breath was a combination of today's cigarette smoke and yesterday's garlic. I wondered if he'd ever heard of mouthwash.

"Erik Erickson killed Vinnie Luciano," I said. "I've got a confession on tape."

"It looks like you've also got a busted leg. So who's this Erickson character? Where is he now? And where's the tape?"

"Erickson owns Parkside Players Theatre. He took off and I've got the tape."

"Let's have it." He straightened up and held a hand palm up over my face.

"Not till I've copied it," I said.

"Bull shit. If you've got evidence I want it now."

"I could make you get a warrant. If you play nice I'll speed things up by giving you a copy as soon as I can make one."

Reilly's face turned the color of a red delicious apple but he pulled his hand away. "So tell me what happened at the theater. How did you get this so-called confession and the broken leg?"

I told my story while Reilly took notes. I had reached the point where Erik was grabbing my hair when a doctor interrupted the narrative to tell me that my ankle was broken in two places. "We'll take you down and put on a walking cast as soon as these officers are finished," he said.

"This story's just gettin' good," Reilly said. "It might be awhile."

"Just press the call button for the nurse when you're ready," the doctor said.

"Lucky me; I've just been on stage and now I'll be in the cast," I said. The doctor chuckled politely but Reilly did not even smile.

The doctor stopped in the doorway on his way out. "Oh, I almost forgot," he said. "Your wife is in the waiting room ready to take you home when you're ready."

Martha must have claimed to be my spouse in order to get in. "Does she look friendly?" I asked.

"She looks beautiful," he said. "Is that enough?"

I wasn't sure. Martha always looked beautiful, no matter what her mood. I silently hoped for forgiveness and went back to answering Reilly's questions. He finally ended the session when I promised to deliver the tape of Erik's confession by 8:00 a.m. the next day.

It seemed like hours before Martha was able to join me. A kind nurse led her to the room where the walking cast was being applied and she stood patiently, and silently, beside me while the work was being done. When the man wrapping the cast stood back and pronounced it complete, Martha threw her arms around me and gave me a long, long kiss. I assumed that I was forgiven for my not-so-careful behavior.

"Let's go get my car," I said when I came up for air. "Al took it to his place. I can take him downtown to pick up his car."

Glenn Ickler

Martha pointed at my heavily encumbered right foot and ankle. "How are you going to drive? We'll take my car to Al's house, let him drive your car to our place and then I'll take him downtown to get his."

When I climbed the steps to the Jeffreys' front door wearing my walking cast, I had a problem keeping my balance. Once inside, Carol greeted me with a running hug that almost tipped me over. When I regained my balance, Al greeted me with an open laptop computer and an order: "Sit down and look at this shit." He put the laptop down on the kitchen table and I pulled out a chair and sat.

The excrement in question was an e-mail from Willow that said she planned to send both him and herself to heaven, where they would be joined forever in a loving embrace. The attachment was a photo of the knife she'd left embedded in Al's camera bag, with a notation that this blade would transport them to heavenly bliss.

"This woman is way nuttier than we thought," I said.

"She's a total psycho," Al said. "I've got the cops hunting for her. I forwarded this e-mail and they came to the house and pulled the knife out of my camera bag. The guy questioning me left just a minute before you got here."

"Do they know where Willow lives?"

"I couldn't help them with that. She never told me where she hung out, but it's probably upside down in a cave along the river bluffs."

"I'm surprised she can come out in the daylight. Anyway, let's hope they pick her up, or down, before she comes after you with another weapon."

"I'm wearing a helmet and a Kevlar vest until that loony's in a padded cell."

"You're saying you have a vested interest in her capture?"

"I'm a-dressing the situation appropriately."

We got my car home with a Japanese three-vehicle shuttle: Martha and I in her Toyota, Al driving my Honda and Carol meeting us at our apartment with her Subaru to take Al home.

Martha helped me up the steps and into the dark apartment. We saw the red flasher blinking on the kitchen phone before Martha turned on the room light. I hobbled to the counter, picked up the receiver and pushed the play button.

"I've got your cat," said a female voice. "I'll call again tomorrow."

Martha was exuberant. "Somebody's found Sherlock."

I was less enthusiastic. "That somebody sounds an awful lot like Willow."

Chapter Thirty-Six

A State of Chassis

W HEN MY LIFE GETS HECTIC, I often think of the last line of Sean O'Casey's classic Irish play JUNO AND PAYCOCK. The drunken Captain Boyle, whose neighbors call him a "paycock" because of his flamboyant strutting manner, closes the show with this observation: "The whole world's in a terrible state of chassis."

"Chassis" is, of course, Captain Boyle's pronunciation of "chaos," which was the state my whole world was in on the Wednesday following my encounter with Erik Erickson on the Parkside Players stage.

The day began with Martha dropping me off at the police station shortly before 8:00 a.m. to deliver a copy of the Erickson tape to Detective Mike Reilly. Instead of thanking me, Reilly gave me a bilingual (English and profane) lecture on the foolhardiness of accosting a murder suspect sans police backup.

Al was planning to pick me up in front of the building when I was finished with Reilly, but before I could make the call I was accosted in the hallway by Detective Lieutenant Curtis Brown.

To say that Brownie was rip-shit would be an understatement. Had I not been wearing a cast on my ankle he probably would have thrown me bodily into his office. As it was, he invited me to join him there in a tone that said I had no choice but to accept. Once we were inside, Brownie slammed the door like a clap of thunder, stomped around his desk and stood behind it glaring at me for a full minute before he said, "I'm not sure I'll ever talk to you again."

"All I can say is, I intended to ask you for backup but you were away on vacation somewhere," I said.

"Vacation hell," he said. "I was in Duluth burying a cousin who died way too young of Lou Gehrig's disease."

"I'm sorry for your loss."

"Of course you are. That's the standard line we all use. Now getting back to the subject at hand, namely your idiotic move on a suspected killer and the suspected killer's subsequent escape to God knows where. Did it ever occur to you that there are other officers in the homicide division of the St. Paul PD?" The color of Brownie's face progressed from bright crimson to deep maroon as he spoke.

"It did," I said. "But I have much less faith in them."

"Faith? You don't think they're capable of arresting a suspect?"

"I was looking for a special setup. I wanted to get a confession without any TV microphones around."

"God damn it!" he yelled, pounding the desk with his fist. "Is getting a fucking scoop all you ever think of?"

"Pretty much. I'm always thinking about bringing a criminal to justice but I'm always looking for a way to do it ahead of everybody else."

"Oh, my god, talk about competitive. If you were an athlete you'd be sneaking around on steroids sure as hell."

"I always stay within the law," I said. "I just push the envelope a little too far sometimes. Like yesterday."

"It'd have served you right if Erickson had bashed your head in," Brownie said. "I'm not sure I'm sorry that he didn't."

"You'd miss me if I was gone."

"Like a flaming tooth ache I'd miss you. All you do is fuck up my work. We should have Erickson standing in front of a judge this morning but instead we're looking all over hell for him."

"Does his wife know where he might go?"

"She has no clue. She's just hoping he doesn't come back to whack her. We've got a twenty-four-hour watch on her."

"What about Scott Hall?"

"What about him?"

"What if Erickson still wants him dead?"

"Jesus, I hadn't thought about that. We'd better put a watch on him."

"See? What would you do without me to help?"

"I'd live with normal blood pressure for one thing. Okay, I'm glad the son of a bitch didn't kill you, but the next time you call my private line looking for news I'm going to remember how many times you've gone out on your own and left us to chase a killer on the run."

"It hasn't been that many."

"Do you want me to run the list?"

Three others came quickly to mind. "Not necessary. I concede that even once is too much."

"I wish it was only once. Now get your ass out of here before I find a way to put it behind bars. An obstruction of justice charge might stick, you know."

"I'm on my way," I said. "Can I ask one quick question?"

"No," Brownie said. "What is it?"

"Who do I talk to about a kidnapped cat?"

"What do you mean a kidnapped cat?"

I explained Sherlock's desertion and described the anonymous phone call that I was certain came from Willow. Brownie had heard all about Willow's attack on Al. He referred me to Detective Aaron Goldberg, who was handling the search for Willow.

"Please don't take that woman on without backup," Brownie said as he pointed me down the hall toward Goldberg's cubicle. "She sounds more dangerous than your play director friend."

"She's a hell of a lot nuttier," I said. "Not to worry: I'll be super careful with Willow." Well, I really thought I would be.

I learned from Goldberg that they'd located Willow's residence—an upstairs apartment in a private home seven blocks from Al's house. The cops had searched the apartment, confiscated Willow's laptop and put a twenty-four watch on the house. At first the house's owner, who occupied the ground floor, objected to the constant presence of two police officers, but when he heard about Willow's knife attack on Al he offered them coffee and doughnuts.

Goldberg and I worked out a plan whereby I would call his office immediately when Willow contacted me. Under no circumstances was I to meet with Willow without police backup. "That means no, never, no way, nada," Goldberg said. "Understand me?"

"I understand," I said.

"Good. I've heard about you from homicide."

"Don't believe everything you hear."

"Normally I don't, but when Brown gets so worked up that his face turns purple, I believe what he's saying."

I tried to imagine Brown turning purple. It was not a pretty picture.

By the time I called the paper to ask Al for a ride, he was out on an assignment. I took a cab to the *Daily Dispatch* and clumped off the elevator with all the grace of a drunken three-legged mule on my walking cast. Work stopped all across the newsroom and a cacophony of voices rose to question me. The general gist of the questioning was, "What damn fool stupid thing did you do this time?"

"Later," I shouted above the din. "I've got a great story to write. You can read all about it when I'm done."

The phone call I was waiting for came just as I was describing Ernie's efforts to hoist the rigging off my ankle. "I've got your cat," Willow said. "And if you want him back you'll do what I tell you."

This was a delicate moment, a time that called for a calm, cool response and smooth diplomacy. So I said, "Listen you crazy, whacked-out skank, if you harm one hair on that cat I'll wring your scrawny neck with my bare hands like a farmer strangling a chicken."

At the next desk, Corinne Ramey looked up and stared at me with eyes so wide I could see white all the way around.

"My, my, the writer certainly has a big vocabulary," Willow said. "If that's your attitude, I'll hang up and you can say goodbye kitty."

This called for additional diplomacy. "How did you get him, you loony creep?"

"The cops are watching Al's house, so I went to your apartment, the one you've apparently moved out of, to persuade you to have Al talk to me. I saw your lost pussy signs, and lo and behold, there he was sitting by the back door of the building, waiting to be let in. He's very friendly. I didn't have a bit of trouble scooping him up, but he did squirm a little when I stuffed him into the saddlebag on my bike."

My blood pressure was slowly returning to normal. "All right, you crazy bitch, what do you want me to do to get him back?"

"You could be more respectful for one thing. But the main thing is to bring your friend Al to meet with me so I can apologize."

"Do you think an apology is going to keep you out of jail?"

"No, but it will make me feel fulfilled," she said. "Then I'll leave St. Paul and you'll never hear from me again."

"Is that a promise or another one of your nut cake tricks?" I said.

"Swear it on a stack of Bibles. You'll get your cat and I'll get my goodbye hug."

The thought of Al having to hug that psychotic maniac was repulsive, but I forged onward. "Do you have a time and place picked out?"

"Como Park, a bench thirty steps west of the conservatory, at 11:30 tonight. And no cops. If I spot a cop, my pussy is out of there and your pussy is dead meat."

"No knives," I said.

"The only knife I own got stuck in Al's camera bag."

"We'll be there."

"Remember, no cops or no cat." The line went dead.

I started to call Goldberg, but stopped after punching the first four numbers. Goldberg would flood the park with cops, and Willow, who was as clever as she was crazy, would surely spot at least one. She would disappear, and so would Sherlock Holmes. I had to discuss the battle plan with Al before making any calls.

*　　*　　*

WE DECIDED TO MEET WILLOW without a police backup. Even if she had another knife, she couldn't attack two of us simultaneously. Al agreed we couldn't risk losing Sherlock to Willow if she smelled a cop anywhere in the park. As defensive insurance, I pulled an aluminum softball bat out of my closet and Al borrowed a can of pepper spray that Carol carried in her purse.

Oh, yes, Carol. And Martha. We had to tell them where we were going. We also told them that Goldberg had instructed us to call him when Willow contacted me. We didn't tell them whether we had or hadn't called Goldberg. Call it a sin of omission.

We arrived in the park half an hour early so we could watch for Willow from behind a flower garden near the designated bench. I had a tough time dragging my cast across several yards of grass-covered lawn, but I would have walked through acres of cactus with my both legs cut off at the knees to bring Sherlock back into my arms. When we reached the flower bed, we hunkered down and waited. The light of a nearly full moon darted in and out behind a moving parade of clouds, giving us the illusion of flowing spotlights interspersed with theatrical blackouts.

Looming over us was the dome of the sprawling Marjorie McNeely Conservatory, where an entire acre of lush fauna that wouldn't survive outdoors in a Minnesota winter was thriving under glass. The conservatory was opened adjacent to the Como Zoo in 1915 and maintains six indoor gardens and three outdoor gardens, including the one we were hunkered behind.

At 11:28, a figure appeared from behind a tree near the conservatory and walked slowly to the bench. It was Willow, wearing the full-length black dress she'd had on when she tried to stab Al. What looked like a gray book bag hung from her left shoulder and she was carrying a dark plastic garbage bag in her right hand. There was something bulky in the garbage bag. That something had to be Sherlock. Could he breathe in there?

With Al leading, we emerged from the flower bed and walked toward the bench. Willow stood facing us as we approached. "Have a nice time snuggled together in the bushes?" she said. "I saw you come in and do your little hide-and-seek stunt."

We stopped walking when she spoke. "Good for you," Al said. "Before we come any closer, do you swear you don't have another knife?"

"On a stack of Bibles, like I told your buddy," Willow said.

We moved forward, and when we were about ten feet from Willow she dropped the garbage bag and reached into the shoulder bag with her now empty hand. The hand emerged holding a small dark object.

"This time I've got a gun," she said.

Chapter Thirty-Seven

Cat Out of the Bag

A SMALL, DARK PISTOL WAS POINTED midway between us. I took a step to the side.

"Stop," Willow said. "Get back where you were. If you spread out I'll just have to shoot quicker."

I took the requested sideways step, but moved half a step closer to Willow in the process. I didn't have any idea how I could jump her, especially dragging a cast, but I was playing all the angles.

"Now what?" Al said.

"Now we carry out my original plan," Willow said. "I told you I was going to leave St. Paul. And so are you. First I shoot you, then I shoot myself and we entwine our spirits together in heaven for an eternity of love. Poor unlucky Mitch here has to stay alive and take his cat home to Mama."

"If you shoot Al there's no guarantee that he'll go to heaven," I said. "He's done some real badass sinning in his life."

"Anyone as creative and sensitive as Al is sure to have a place reserved in heaven," she said. "I'm not worried about that."

"Maybe you should worry about yourself," I said. "I'm not sure murderers are all that welcome in heaven."

"This is for love, not a criminal killing. I've prayed about it for weeks. God tells me over and over he has a special place for lovers."

I saw movement in the plastic bag on the ground beside Willow. "Maybe it's a special hot place," I said.

"Maybe you shouldn't tempt me to include you in the trip to heaven with your smartass remarks."

"Maybe if you kill me it isn't about love any more. The Bibles in that stack you just swore on say, 'Thou shalt not kill,'"

More movement in the bag. A rustling sound and the head of a cat emerged. Willow looked down when she heard the sound and Al and I both made our moves.

I don't know how I did it dragging the cast, but I got to Willow first. Maybe it was the half-step advantage or maybe it was a higher level of adrenaline. Whatever propelled me, I slammed into her and we fell to the ground with me on top. The gun went off and my ears began to ring like church bells but I felt no pain. Then Al was stomping on her hand and kicking the gun away.

Willow tried to sink her teeth into my shoulder and I punched her in the side of her face. Al kicked her in the exposed side of her head and she went limp. I rolled off her and sat up. I saw Sherlock Holmes sitting on his haunches, looking on with what appeared to be feline approval. His captor must not have been feeding him properly.

Willow moaned as we rolled her onto her belly. I took off my belt and wrapped it tightly around her wrists while Al was calling 911. Willow tried to roll over but I pushed her face into the grass and sat down on the small of her back. "You're going somewhere, crazy lady, but it won't be heaven," I said.

As I sat on Willow, the moon broke through a large open space between the clouds, providing enough light for me to see my legs. I was wearing my oldest trousers with the right leg split to fit over the cast. Through the split I could see a dark streak across the white cast, about halfway between my ankle and my knee. I touched it with my hand and felt a jagged gash that ran the width of the cast. "Guess where the bullet went," I said to Al.

He looked where I was pointing. "No shit?" he said. "It was that close?"

"It was."

"We're going to catch holy hell from the cops, especially when they see that."

"The cops I can handle. It's the holy hell from Martha that I'm worried about."

"Oh, god, yes," Al said. "Carol can't afford to divorce me but Martha could break off your engagement."

"I don't want to think about that," I said with my eyes turned up toward the moon.

"It's too late to start thinking now," Al said with his eyes on the road, looking for flashing lights.

"Mmmf," Willow said with her face still flat in the grass.

Sherlock Holmes climbed onto my lap and began licking my face with his sandpaper tongue as we heard a siren wailing in the distance.

* * *

WE DID CATCH HOLY HELL from the cops. Willow was taken to Regions Hospital to have her cheek x-rayed where Al had kicked her. We followed a squad car to the station where we were split up and interrogated in separate rooms. The interrogators in both rooms were not complimentary when we told them that we had decided to meet a mad woman in the dark of the night without backup.

On the way to the station, I phoned Martha on her cell. She and Carol were both waiting up for us at the Jeffreys' house, and I told her we had captured our quarry and retrieved our kidnapped kitty with minimal collateral damage. Martha asked what I meant by minimal collateral damage and I explained that my cast had acquired a crack. I thought it best not to tell her that the crack was left there by a passing bullet. Ever the diplomat, I.

On the way to Al's house, he asked, "By the way, what were all those badass sins you told Willow I committed?"

"Merely words of fiction to dampen her desire to kill you," I said. "I'm sure you're as pure as the driven snow."

"You're right. I've been told more than once that I seem to be driven. Is that a good thing?"

"Depends on where you're being driven to."

When we finally got to the house at something after 2:00 a.m., the women were so excited to see Sherlock Holmes that they forgot to ask about the crack in the cast. They also talked as if they assumed the police had been on the scene from the start, and we saw no reason to clarify the sequence of events. I would have to be extremely careful how I described Willow's capture when I wrote the story a few hours hence.

*   *   *

WE CAUGHT HOLY HELL from the police again in the morning. We were summoned to the station where first Detective Aaron Goldberg and then Detective Lieutenant Curtis Brown chewed our butts up one side and down the other. We heard a lot of "if you ever do anything like that again" and "we'll throw your ass in jail next time" before they told us to get the hell out of their sight.

"The fact that they followed 'don't do it again' with 'we'll throw your ass in jail next time' leads me to believe they doubt our ability to refrain from taking action when we believe it's required," Al said.

"Our record speaks for itself," I said.

"And they don't like what it's saying."

I was getting into Al's car when my cell phone rang. It was Don O'Rourke.

"You still at the police station?" he said.

"Just leaving," I said.

"Don't. You're going be working there for the next three weeks. Augie Augustine has decided it's time to get some help before another lost weekend. He's checked himself into Hazelden."

"I'm here for three weeks?"

"It's a good place for you. Maybe you won't be able to try to get yourself killed for three weeks."

"What about my story from last night?"

"You can write about last night's craziness from there. Oh, and go talk to homicide and get a statement. Your play director/square dancer buddy was picked up this morning in Duluth."

"In Duluth? How'd they find him there?"

"The knucklehead ran a red light with a squad car sitting on the other side of the intersection. You'd think a guy would drive a little more careful when there's an APB out on him."

I almost blurted out "*carefully*," but I remembered it was Don, who could do no wrong grammatically. "Yes, you'd think so," I said.

"What was that all about?" Al asked when the call ended.

"It was Don with the final piece of the pie," I said. "The killer is in custody, the crazy woman is in a padded cell, Sherlock Holmes is safe in our new home, and all's right with the world."

The End